Challenge

Samantha M Thomas

Contents

Chapter 1
Remi

Ten months ago . . .

Sometimes, I doubt my decision to pursue Formula 1. Today is not one of those times. The Formula 1 Academy had one of its few races in Japan today, and I dominated on all fronts. Now, I'm enjoying a drink at some off-the-beaten-path bar, soaking in my win without the usual fanfare.

After most races, the absence of my family and the lack of support for my career hang over my head like a rain cloud, drenching my success with sadness.

But not today.

Today, I want to bask in the win. Revel in the fact that I'm doing everything in my power to work my way up and have a real chance to make history.

I sip the Japanese whiskey, closing my eyes to savor the clean flavor.

"This seat taken?" A deep yet smooth voice pulls me from my analysis of the drink.

Startled, I look up, then up farther to see navy eyes staring at me with curiosity. I take a second to look him over, not sure what his looks will tell me about how much of a pest he'll be, but it's worth a glance. Blond, shaggy waves and a plain white shirt give off surfer vibes. The colorful ink spanning his arms and dipping under his shirt sleeves is wildly attractive, and the way his jeans fit his muscled thighs is a distraction. But he doesn't look like he'd be an asshole if the vibrant smile sandwiched between a pair of dimples is anything to go by.

"Nope, all yours." I gesture to it, hoping he didn't notice me doing the fast perusal of his body.

The bartender walks over to get his order.

"I'll have one of those, thanks." He points to my drink.

"You don't even know what I'm drinking," I comment before cursing myself. Do not engage. This is "me" time, the only time I have to soak in my win before I have to turn my focus back on working my ass off.

"Your face when you took a sip was pure bliss, so I think it's a good bet that it'll be delicious. I'm not picky." He smiles, and his eyes are filled with flirtation.

I'm rendered speechless. It's not that I've never been hit on—being one of the few females in a *very* male dominated field means it happens more than I'd like it to—but this is the first time I feel an inkling of flirtatiousness back.

"Does this method usually work on the ladies?" Snark is my preferred method of communication with the opposite sex. If they can take it with ease, then they're probably worth my time. I cannot deal with a guy who gets butt hurt by some innocent banter.

Not that I've had any prospects for a long while.

"Is it working on you?" His bright eyes and easy smile make it extremely hard to stay firmly solo tonight.

"Hmm, hard to say. Might need to keep trying and see where it goes." I wink at him.

I didn't think it was possible, but his entire face brightens up more. *God, he really is hot as hell.*

"I'm not a stranger to hard work."

Laughter bursts out of me at his unexpected words.

"So, now I'm hard work?" I smile.

"The best things usually are, if I'm honest." The bartender sets down his drink, and the man takes a small sip then a larger one. "God, that is delicious."

His Adam's apple bobs as he swallows the whiskey. I realize I'm staring again, so I pick up my glass and sip to hide the fact that my mouth is hanging open, and to rein in my drooling.

"So, what brings you to Japan?" He turns his body toward me. Our knees bump against each other.

"Work," I clip. No need to get into the whole thing. It always changes a man's perspective of me when he finds out I'm tied to Formula 1. "You?"

"Same, actually. Heading out late tomorrow, though." It's a timeline. He's telling me this is a one-time thing if I'm interested.

Decision time.

Do I continue this game and see where the night goes or bow out now and call it day?

"Same, actually." I stare at him.

Sex would do me some good. It's been far too long since I've had any action, always too busy at work for much of anything else.

But I feel fucking *good* tonight, and sex with an incredibly hot guy would be the cherry on top of the proverbial sundae.

"Do you have a room nearby?" he asks.

"Straight to the point." I chuckle, swirling the remainder of the amber liquid in my glass.

"I like to think of it more like knowing what I want and not wasting time." There's that damn wink again.

If it were any other man, I'd roll my eyes. But on him . . . Fuck, I don't even—

"What's your name?"

"Nate. You?"

"Remi." It's actually Margret, but he doesn't get to know that and the fact that I've refused to go by it since I was five years old. "And my hotel is about a ten-minute drive from here."

"That's a very interesting name. Mine is about a five-minute walk." His eyes sparkle in the dim light. He's waiting me out, letting me make the choice, and I can tell he'd be fine if I said no.

Such a change to the men in my world, who rarely hear no and have a hard time accepting that anyone would go against them.

I down the last of my drink and watch his smile grow. "Ready when you are."

He copies my action, finishing his drink in record time before tossing some cash onto the bar. "You are a surprising woman, Remi."

"Well, everything is a surprise when you don't really know me."

He holds out his hand, helping me off the bar stool and leading me out the door. "Then I think I'm going to enjoy getting to know you better."

"Yikes." I suck in an exaggerated breath. "That was borderline too cheesy."

"You know, I knew it as soon as I said it." He laughs.

"Hey, at least you're aware."

"Painfully so, I'm afraid."

He's really adorable, and I can't have him be adorable on top of being wildly hot. That's a lethal combo.

"So do you travel a lot for work?" If I can deflect for a moment, maybe I can regain my bearings.

"I do, actually. It's one of the biggest perks of the job. Getting to see so many places and explore them when I have time is the dream."

"It really is." I sigh because I wish I could explore more. "I'd like to do more of the exploring part, but I never seem to have time."

"That's a shame. You seem to have set aside some time to explore tonight."

"We shall see how good the exploration truly is, won't we." The corner of my lips tips up into a smirk, and one eyebrow arches.

"Damn, woman, putting up the challenge so soon?" He clutches his heart like I just shot him, which makes me laugh.

"A woman's gotta lay down the law early."

"Challenge accepted then. I think you'll find I'm very, *very* good at exploration."

"So cocky."

"How about you give me a report card at the end?"

I choke out a laugh, slapping my chest to gain control of myself. His unexpected humor and wit just may be as sexy as his ink. Everyone in my world is overly serious, and it's a big downer sometimes.

"Easy, Remi. We're here." His hand on my lower back leads me to the lobby doors of an expensive looking hotel. A Vanstone hotel. Comparable to mine, actually, so his job must be pretty prestigious.

We're not asking those questions tonight, though. We both know the score. There's no need to delve deeper into each other if we're just here to fulfill a carnal desire.

My nerves kick into high gear when we step into the elevator. I can't even remember the last time I liked a guy, let alone attempted a one-night stand, and suddenly, I'm feeling very out of my comfort zone.

He must sense the shift in me because he says, "Hey, we don't have to do anything. I promise. If we get upstairs and all you want to do is have another drink and talk, I'm one hundred percent okay with that." He ducks down a little to catch my eyes.

The earnestness I see there eases every ounce of insecurity I'm feeling.

So, I stop thinking and do something impulsive for once.

The first tentative press of my lips to his sends a lightning bolt through my nervous system. Then all shyness and caution are gone. Our bodies slam together. His hand threads through my hair, the other down my back. All I can do is hang on for dear life as his tongue glides along my lip before nipping it, making me gasp. My back hits the wall as his tongue invades my mouth, our fight for control, for dominance, turning me on more than anything has.

The elevator dings, and we both rip apart, breathing heavily.

"Jesus." He steps back, brushing his hand through his hair as he eyes me with pure want.

"Was that good or bad?" I tilt my head, still panting.

"So fucking good. Get your ass over here." He grabs my hand and yanks me out of the elevator.

I have to almost sprint to keep up with his pace, but before I know it, we're standing in front of his door. He pulls me in front of him, my back to his door, and he descends on me once more. My hips move without my consent, desperate for more. I reach back and try to turn the handle, but somewhere in my hazy brain, I realize I need his key card.

When he magically produces it while still kissing me, I manage to get the door open while we're still connected. He picks me up before I fall backward, tossing his key on the table just inside as I wrap my legs around his torso. He's taller than I realized back at the bar. Much taller than my five-foot-two stature, but it makes crawling up him that much easier.

Weightlessness surrounds me before I hit the bed. It's a shock to my system to no longer be kissing him, but when I look up at him, his navy eyes are hooded with arousal.

"I think you have too many clothes on." I arch an eyebrow.

"I'd say the same for you." His gaze travels from my eyes down every single inch of my body.

Goosebumps rise on my flesh everywhere his gaze passes over, followed by a shiver, as I lie there. I shimmy out of my wide-legged pants—thank God for elastic waistbands—before sitting up and peeling off my tight shirt. With the flick of my wrist, it lands on the floor to join my pants.

"Seems you're behind." I grin as his hand goes to the front of his jeans and squeezes the very sizable erection he can no longer hide.

"That can be fixed." His voice is all gravel. It goes straight to my pussy, and I can't help but rub my legs together, seeking out every little bit of friction possible.

He reaches behind his head, grabs the collar of his T-shirt, and rips it off in one pull. My breath catches in my throat at the array of muscles and tattoos he was hiding. His chest has a few bigger pieces, but the majority of his stomach is ink free, leaving me with a view of his evident but soft abs and that V disappearing under his pants' waistline that has my mouth falling open again. Nothing super showy, but damn, he is *fine*. None of his tattoos are black and white; all of them are busts of color that say more about his personality than any conversation ever could. And then there's the flash of silver through his nipples. *Dear God*, I never thought that I would find nipple piercings attractive, but on him, they just fit.

"Holy hell," I murmur as I watch his hands work on his belt.

"Like what you see?" he asks, breaking my gawking and pulling my eyes back up to his.

I see the twinkle in his eyes that lets me know he knows how hot he is. He's worked for it, so he's not oblivious by any means.

"You already know the answer to that." Instead of words, I open my legs and show off the nice little wet spot that's blooming on my very basic briefs. His eyes zero in on it, and the groan he can't contain lets me know he likes what he sees.

Neither of us have the upper hand, it seems, and I kind of love it.

"You're going to be the death of me, woman."

"And you still have pants on."

The sound of his belt sliding from the belt loops draws my attention once more. In seconds, he's unbuttoned and unzipped them, before hooking his thumbs into them and his boxers and stripping them off.

If I thought the top half of him was hot, I was not prepared for everything below the belt.

Heavily muscled thighs are the first things I see. One has a giant tattoo of a lighthouse on it, with waves crashing around it. It's volatile and beautiful all at once.

Then my gaze catches on his hand moving to his dick, and my eyes nearly pop out of my head. He's not overly long, but he is girthy. Much more so than the small number of partners I've had before him.

"You good?" he asks as his hand works lazy strokes up and down his shaft.

"Yep," I squeak.

"You nervous?" That delicious smirk is back, and there's mischief in his eye.

"I— Nope. I'm good." *Very convincing, Remi.*

"I'll get you nice and ready for me. Don't worry your pretty little head." He kneels on the bed in between my legs, and one finger whispers over the wet spot on my panties. "I think you'll be surprised how well you can take it."

"Jesus, your mouth," I huff out. He laughs, which makes me laugh and releases all the tension in my body.

"I'm serious. We'll go slow, and I won't give you more than you can take." He leans over me and presses a too-soft kiss to my lips.

It throws me for a loop. It makes me want more than this one night.

Nope. No can do.

I feel his fingertips graze my sides before he hooks them in my underwear and drags them down my legs.

"Take your bra off," he murmurs against my lips before going back to kissing them, then moving down my neck as I shift to unhook my bra.

He leans back on his knees and takes all of me in. Not all that long ago, I would have shied away from his attention. But I've worked my ass off over the past year, and my body is in the best shape it's ever been in. I'm proud as hell of it, and if the look on Nate's face is anything to go by, he likes what he sees.

"You are a work of art," he mutters. He begins to make his way back up my body. His hand moves from my foot and up the outside of my leg, across my stomach, along my ribs, and to my arm.

The truth of his words that shines through his eyes is too close to adoration. I steel my heart up, nice and tight, and focus on getting as much pleasure as I can from this night.

That's all we're both offering, and I need to remember that.

Chapter 2
Nate

Oh shit.

That's the only thought repeating in my mind as she removes each article of clothing. She's exactly my type and then some. Her body is incredible. Muscled, strong yet soft, and with no shortage of curves along her ass and thighs. Her breasts are larger now that she's taken off her bra. It must have minimized them, so I didn't notice them at the bar. It's a damn shame, to be honest, because I'm currently drooling over them.

Her dark brown hair is fanned out on the bed, and she looks like a woman picked straight from my dreams.

I really am in trouble with this one.

Tracing the muscles I see, I try to think of a job or a hobby that would lead to this kind of development, this kind of strength. My job isn't just as a physiotherapist, but it is a heavy component of work, and it's hard to shut that part of my brain off sometimes.

Then she shifts her legs. The wetness that glistens between them catches my eye, and all my focus returns to this glorious woman splayed out in front of me.

I open my mouth to say something but shut it promptly when nothing comes to mind. She has my mind blank and my heart pounding, which is a terrible combination.

There are no words that can express what I'm feeling, so I dive right in. My fingers draw up her inner thigh, and her squirm from the touch is my reward. Her body is practically begging me to touch her where she needs it most. She's already so wet as I slide them through her arousal, then drag them up and circle her clit. She arches off the bed, and her knuckles turn white as she grips the comforter.

"Easy," I murmur, mesmerized by her.

Slight circles around her clit get her panting. I have to clench my stomach muscles tight so I don't blow all over her like a fucking teenager. That's never happened to me before. I'm an expert at control, and I feel dangerously close to losing it already.

That just won't do.

Sliding down to lie on the bed between her legs, I spread her open wider.

"What—" Her words are cut short as my tongue takes the place of my fingers, which adjust into a V to frame her pussy.

I slide them up and down, making sure to never hit her entrance as I flick her clit harder. She's moaning now, working me up even more if that's possible. I know she's close. Her muscles are tense, and I can feel her pulsing against my tongue.

I nip her clit hard and shove two fingers inside of her. The second I do, she sucks in a sharp breath, and her pussy starts to pulse as she comes hard. Gritting my teeth, I grind into the mattress as I work her through her first orgasm. Once she's come down from it, her body oh-so-pliable and soft, I work another finger into her.

"Oh God," she moans. Her hips begin to move, and I don't think she even realizes she's doing it.

"Little bit more, then you're taking all of me." My voice comes out more like a growl.

"I don't know if I can," she whines, thrashing her head around as I angle the tip of my pinky into her.

"Oh, you can, Remi." I press just a little more and circle my fingers up to tap her G-spot before I feel like she's good to go. My hand moves quickly, shifting to my hard-as-steel cock and stroking it to feel all her wetness, as I pick up a condom with the other. I tossed a couple on the bed earlier and thank fuck I did.

It takes me seconds to put it on, and then I'm right back on top of the delectable Remi. Her eyes are closed and she's still panting, but I want to see her pretty eyes as I thrust into her for the first time.

Notching at her entrance, I thumb her clit softly as I slowly push in, stretching her. Her eyes pop open, exactly as I was hoping they would.

"I've got you. Breathe," I murmur before leaning down and kissing her.

The slide into her is steady. She's so fucking ready for me that there's no struggle or resistance. She feels fucking phenomenal. I'm barely hanging on by a thread.

But she will come on my cock. I'm not letting her leave until she does, even if that means tying her ass up while we both recover for round two.

Mmm, maybe I should tie her up now.

God no, I'd come in seconds at the sight of her all trussed up for my enjoyment.

My thrusts grow harder and erratic before I realize I've lost control, so I force myself to slow down and focus on not pushing her too hard.

"No! Don't stop!" she groans at my change of pace.

My eyes close slowly as my head tips back.

Jesus, this woman is more than trouble. She's fucking perfect, and I'm not sure how I'll just send her on her way when this is done.

"Nate," she growls, fingers digging into my shoulders. "Get out of your head and fuck me."

Her words do me in.

I pull back all the way and slam into her, jolting her up the bed as her mouth pops open in a silent scream.

Fuck yes. She handles me so damn well.

Normally, I'm a dirty talking fool. But this woman? Well, she's rendered me speechless.

My pace picks up as my thumb continues on her clit. I'm far too close, and I need to feel her clench tight around me. I need to know that she'll leave here and never forget what I did to her body.

It's a compulsion and one I'm not used to.

"Oh shit," she squeals as she tightens hard around me.

One pulse of her muscles around me, and that's it. I'm coming, grunting and yelling, barely in control of my body let alone my mind, as she rides her own orgasm out.

I collapse on top of her without a thought until she shoves at my shoulder.

"Jesus, you are a fucking wall of dead weight," she grunts, trying to push me off of her.

"Sorry." I roll over, pulling out of her.

She winces, and it sends a thrill of dumb male pride through my body. She'll be feeling me for a while, that's for damn sure.

And I fucking love the thought of it.

I rip off the condom, tying and tossing it on the ground, before rolling my head to the side to look at her.

Her eyes are closed, and she has the softest smile on her face.

It's fucking gorgeous, the most beautiful thing I've ever seen—this contentment that shines over her entire demeanor because of me. Because I fucked her so damn well, she's relaxed and happy.

"I can feel you getting cocky over there," she mutters.

I can't help the giant smile on my face. "You would be too if the person you just fucked looked like you do right now."

"It was good. I'll give you that."

"Good? Fucking good?" I growl, rolling over her as she peeks at me with hooded eyes. Her smile only grows, and in that second, I know I'm not done with her. "I'll show you fucking good."

I don't know how it's possible, but round two is even better. It's a showcase of my stamina, and by the end she's a whimpering, wet mess that I want to drown in.

I don't even remember falling asleep, but when I do, it's dreamless and hard.

***

I wake with a jolt. I scan the room as I attempt to get my bearings. Then I remember I brought home Remi last night. There's no sign of her, though. No discarded clothing. Even the used condoms that were on the floor have been picked up. I collapse on the bed, reeling at the loss.

I shouldn't have fallen asleep. I should have stayed awake so I could get her number or find out where she works—literally any point of contact.

Now, I have nothing except a raw dick and incredible memories. Instead of feeling happy, I feel empty, *alone.*

Fuck. I'm so dumb.

From the get-go, Remi didn't feel like my normal hook-up, yet I treated her like one. Now, she's gone without a trace, and I'm left in this pitiful state. It's shameful, really. My best friend, Beck, has been telling me I need to slow down, rein in my . . . loose and free ways, but I've been brushing him off.

I used to work for him—with him, really—when he was on the F1 circuit. Since he retired, I've been wandering. Traveling and getting my rocks off where I can. He called me in to come help out one of their drivers, and that's the only reason I'm in Japan right now.

Somehow, Remi completely flipped me on my head in the span of one night.

My usual MO was completely lost on the woman who is no longer in my hotel room, and I'm shamefully disappointed by that. It's my own fault. I didn't realize it was possible for a woman to affect me like this anymore, yet here we are.

There's no real use in dwelling on it, so I roll out of bed, naked and hard as I walk to the kitchen to get a glass of water.

As I'm chugging a full glass, a note on the little counter beside the sink catches my eye.

Report Card

Orgasms: A+ (Don't get a big head about it.)

Dinner and Conversation: Solid B (Could have been more, but we clearly had other motivations.)

Big Dick Energy: A++ (No explanation needed.)

Knows how to use said big dick: A+ (See Orgasms Grade.)

Sleep: C (The sex stopped me from getting 8 hours, which is really the only complaint.)

Thank you for an incredible night.

I'll probably think of you often.
-Remi

I stare at her words for far too long, but I can't get myself to pull away from them. I should just throw this in the trash and move on like nothing happened.

But I feel like something *did* happen. For the first time in my life, I'm disappointed that a woman walked out on me. It's not because that's usually my move but because I actually *like* her.

What the actual fuck?

I reread her report card, a smile plastered on my face. She's funny, witty. I bet she overthought the fuck out of this note but left it anyway.

That has to be a good sign, right? She'll think about it often . . . That means she's had to have felt the insane connection like I did, right?

Jesus, Nate, you're acting like a fucking sap in love, not someone who just had a fucking amazing one-night stand. Snap out of it.

I try. I really do. But as I prepare to travel with Alejandro to the next racing destination, I keep going back to the note she left, rereading it every so often before going back to packing.

On a final walkthrough, I grab the note and tuck it safely into my suitcase.

A stupid reminder, really, of what could have been, but I can't seem to just let go of her.

Remi is stuck in my brain, and I fear she'll never really be gone.

Chapter 3
Remi

Present Day

My reflection in the mirror is supposed to show a confident, kickass Remi. What it actually shows is a scared-shitless Remi, who feels very ill-prepared for her first day on the job as a Formula 1 driver.

I still think Sydney and Toni made a mistake hiring me on. It's great for optics, but do I really have what it takes to make it?

My phone ringing startles me, but I take a deep breath before answering.

"Remi."

"Are you panicking yet?" Luka Tomic's voice instantly puts me at ease. He's been working with me a lot for the past couple of years at the Formula 1 Academy—pushing me to aim higher, be better. I have a suspicion that he's the one who pulled so hard for me to get this promotion.

"Beyond panicking, I think."

"You know Toni wouldn't put you on the team if she didn't think you could do it. No one at Empress is setting you up to fail."

"You've gotten wise in your dad era." I smile.

He and his wife, Daisy, who also runs Empress with Sydney, just had a baby girl a couple of months ago. He's been around less, but he still makes time to check in on me.

"That just makes me feel old."

"If the shoe fits," I quip before sighing. "How is the munchkin?"

"So fucking good. She's sitting up and babbling, and I swear it's the most precious thing in the world."

At that, I do smile. "Send me a video."

"Will do. And Remi? You're going to kill this. Everyone will love you, and there is nothing to worry about, okay?"

"Okay," I whisper, not quite believing him.

"I've got to go. Evelin is getting fussy." He hangs up before I can say goodbye, but I'm grateful for the pep talk and normalcy.

Today isn't even a true workday. It's my introduction to the team, a tour, and a shit-ton of media coverage. It's daunting nonetheless.

Taking one last look in the mirror, I adjust my light gray blazer rolled up at the sleeves over my purple Legacy shirt and run my sweaty hands on my jeans before heading out.

The drive over is filled with unmotivating words of affirmation and shittier pep talks, but once I park, I'm out of time to convince myself that I fit in here.

Now, I just have to fake it until I make it.

A circle of people with cameras surrounds my car almost immediately. We never had this much hype at the F1 Academy, so I'm not used to the attention at all. I've been able to secure some brand sponsorships, but those are quiet photoshoots or social media videos. Nothing like this grand spectacle.

Then Toni, the team principal, opens my door and ducks in.

"Hey, we're going to run you in and bring you up to my office. Once it calms down a little, we can do the whole big tour."

"Thank you." I sigh, shoulders slumped in relief.

"Everyone is super excited to have you here, and I don't think they all realized how overwhelming they are." She cringes before pulling back. "Alright, everyone, we're going to get Remi up to our offices to do a debrief, and then we'll be walking around so you'll all get the chance to meet her, okay?" she bellows to the crowd.

Groans and agreements sound around us, but people start to back away from my car.

When Toni said they'd run me up to the office, they actually meant "run". There are a handful of people who clear a path, allowing Toni and me to run for the doors. Laughter bubbles out of me as we break through and head to the elevators.

"I didn't think you meant actual run." I huff.

"I didn't, but then you started running, and I had to keep up. Can't let you show me up on the first day. That's really more of a day ten type of thing." She chuckles.

All the tension I was holding drops off. Toni is approachable—I've always known that—but it's still hard to match that up with her being my new boss and the desire to impress her.

We eventually land in front of her office, and when she opens the door, I'm almost tackled by Daisy Tomic, Luka's wife.

"Hi to you too," I grunt.

"I'm so damn excited for you. Was it crazy out there?" she whispers in my ear.

"Very."

"Daisy, let the poor woman breathe." Sydney's voice sounds from behind me.

"Yep, on it." Daisy releases me, letting me take in the room.

I find Sydney Davis and her husband, former world champion, Beck Davis. Then Toni Bailey and her boyfriend, former team principal at Legacy, Felix Karlsson. Daisy is also standing off to the side. As welcomes go, you couldn't really get more heavy hitters in the mix.

"Hi," I squeak and wave before clearing my throat. "Hello. It's wonderful to be here."

"We're very excited to have you. Sorry for all the craziness. They're excited," Sydney says sheepishly, but there's an undercurrent of fierceness there too.

"Have a seat, and we'll go over how today will go, as well as answer any general questions you have. We'll go over the schedule for the next couple of weeks until we get to the car unveiling. And . . ." She looks around. "I think that's it. We'll try not to overwhelm you today since we've got time, but we do want to familiarize you with the building and the way we work our schedule."

"Sounds great to me."

I take the middle seat around the conference table as everyone else filters in around me.

One more deep breath, and I know I can handle this. There's a reason I've never given up. I always felt that I could reach this exact moment in time.

My eyes well with tears at the sheer weight of being the first female driver in Formula 1. It's not only a huge accomplishment, but there's also a pressure that goes with it that I need to manage. Rapidly blinking my eyes staves off the tears for now, and I tuck in for all the information the group is about to hand me.

It's not until a snippet of conversation catches my attention that I realize I had started to stare off into space.

"I'm sorry, can you repeat that?" I ask Beck.

"Absolutely. We've brought on Nathan Murphy to help with all things training related. He's an incredible physical trainer but also has experience in the mental side of this sport, which I think will be extremely helpful for you in particular. His technical title is physiotherapist, but he dabbles in sports psychology on the side."

Nathan . . . Nate?

Just because you think about Nate all the fucking time, it doesn't mean he'll just pop out of thin air. Nate is not Nathan, you delusional hussy.

I just love my inner voice; she's so friendly all the time.

"Sounds perfect. I can't wait to meet him."

"You'll spend the most time with him. He'll travel with you, train with you every day, and be your shoulder to lean on. He used to be with me for years, and I attribute being able to stay an active driver for as long as I did to him," Beck adds. "He'll be in tomorrow to help get you set up and start your training. We thought it'd be best to not throw everything your way today."

"I appreciate that." And I do. However, I also just want to jump in with both feet. I don't really want to go tour the entire grounds and meet a million people. I hate being so front and center even though that's the name of the game. It's easier for me to meet everyone slowly, so I can remember names and details. This is all very overwhelming for me.

We wrap up the rest of the meeting quickly, and then it's time to meet the rest of the team.

"Don't feel like you need to remember everyone. You'll get to know your direct team over the next month," Sydney says, walking with me ahead of the group.

The tour takes well over two hours. Handshakes and conversation flow at every stop, a genuine smile on my face the whole time. As overwhelming as this all is, it's also a literal dream come true. I don't want to waste a single second or forget any of it.

I mentally catalogue how I'm feeling throughout, altering between awestruck and thankful more often than not. When we stop in the area where all the mechanics mostly work, I meet Cruz, who will be my main point of contact for the mechanics. I know instantly we'll be fast friends. He's easygoing, but the respect he garners from his staff is what I aspire to achieve with everyone working with me. Luka frequently told me that's one of the biggest reasons he saw something in me. It was how I treated everyone around me, why they *wanted* to work with me, not just because it was their job to do so.

I never quite understood what he was talking about until I met Cruz.

"At the end of the week, stop by, and we'll give you a progress check on things," he says as I get ready to head out.

"Sounds great. I may stop by sooner. The pit is my happy place." I grin back, waving as Sydney pulls me along.

"Well, that was mildly ridiculous. I'm sorry. I didn't expect this tour to last as long as it did. You still have to do some photoshoots."

I mentally cringe. My least favorite part, but it's all part of the game.

"We have hair and make-up available, as well as all of the new Empress gear to wear. We're not picky, as long as you wear something branded." She leads me to a room I think is close to her office, although I'm super turned around now. When she opens it up, there's a full dressing room with a hair and make-up team waiting for me.

Guess it's showtime.

Four hours, a million pictures, and no less than fifteen posts at different media outlets later, I'm back at my temporary home and crashing before I even wash the make-up off my face.

Chapter 4
Nate

I'm rarely nervous anymore, but ever since the one-night stand in Japan, I've been off-kilter. I won't blame that night on me walking out on Alejandro. No, he did that all on his own.

Fucking prick.

But Beck talked me into coming back. After I fucked around in New Zealand for a couple of months, dreaming of the woman I would never see again, I'm back in Austin, Texas to meet my new ward.

Beck hated when I called them that, so I do it to needle him a little bit every now and then. He's become a little boring in his retirement.

"Hey, Earth to asshole." Speak of the devil.

"What?" I arch an eyebrow at Beck as he rubs his forehead.

"I need you to tone down whatever this is." He waves his hand around in my general direction. "Because we need to keep this one. She has so much fucking potential, but she'll face challenges none of us have ever been through."

Right. I know this. The first woman driver in Formula 1. I don't know how I feel about it, to be honest. It's nice to be a part of history. Being connected to Beck, and all that he and Sydney have accomplished, has afforded me a multitude of opportunities.

But even I can admit I'm intrigued. I know Sydney, and I know Toni. Neither would hire anyone on just for good PR. Which means that this chick, Margret, is the real deal.

And I have to train her.

I've always loved a challenge.

"I'm good and ready to go," I reassure him.

"Good, because here she is."

The second the door opens and her eyes meet mine, the smile drops off my face and my jaw falls open.

No fucking way.

"Remi?" I ask, dumbfounded.

"You're Nathan?" she counters, equally in shock.

"Wait, you know each other?" Sydney looks back and forth between us.

"Know" is a stretch, although I know exactly what brings her to orgasm, so I guess I do know her.

By the blush on her cheeks, her train of thought is much like mine.

Good, I left an impression.

Because I know damn well this woman left one on me. I haven't been able to think about much else. With no way to find her, I've recounted everything we did together multiple times while alone in a hotel room halfway around the world. Nothing helped. I didn't even go out and find another woman to hook up with. I just . . . couldn't do it.

"Ooookay. I feel like I don't want to know. Nate Murphy, this is Remi Bouchard, and you'll be training her this season." Sydney does the official introductions.

"Fuck," Remi—Margret—mutters under her breath.

"Well, we'll give you guys some time to get to know each other," Beck says before leaning down to my ear. "Do not fuck this up. I mean it, Nate. Whatever happened, push it to the side."

Easy for him to say when all I'm picturing is her moaning beneath me, clenching my dick— Nope, you know what? I can't do this here.

"On it, boss," I grit out.

And then Beck and Sydney are gone.

"Have a seat." I gesture to the one across from me when I notice Remi still standing stock-still by the door.

"I—" she starts then snaps her mouth closed before sitting down.

"I was told your name was Margret." Might as well get all of this out of the way so we can really work.

"And I was told yours was Nathan. You know I had a split second where I thought it could be you, but I figured that was ridiculous." Her laugh is hollow.

"So, you've thought about me." It pops out without permission. I'm trying to be a professional, and I'm already failing miserably.

"Okay, we're getting this out of the way. Yes, you were good. Yes, I thought about you . . . more than once. Now we work together, and that's it. Move on. I have shit to do here." Her tone isn't cold, just point blank. This job means a lot to her, as it should, and she's not going to do anything to jeopardize that.

I can respect that, even if it's going to be hard as hell to separate this Remi from the one I dream about every fucking night.

"Message received. I'm not sure how much you know about what I do, but I'm more than a trainer. I make sure you are physically ready for everything, but I also make sure you're mentally ready too. If you need a break, you take it with me. If I see you struggling, I will take action to try to help you work through it. See me as a sort of jack-of-all-trades to help you succeed. I'll be here for whatever support you need while also pushing you to your limits to fulfill your potential." Not once, when I've given this little talk, have I felt the words so hard. I want her to succeed more than I've ever wanted someone to succeed. More than Beck even, and he's my best friend.

"Heard. Where do we start?"

This Remi? Hot as fuck. The determination on her face, mixed with what I have no doubt is capability, is something I didn't realize I was so attracted to.

"We start with journaling." I slide over the Empress branded notebook I made Sydney get for me. "The caveat is that I get access to this." I tap it. "You can write whatever you want in it, but I want you to check in throughout the day and write how you are feeling. It can be short and sweet, or it can be three pages worth of shit. I just need you to do it daily. Talking about things can be hard, so this is my solution until you feel comfortable opening up to me more. Even then, I will want you to write in this. It's a good habit, and sometimes you write until you surprise yourself with what your real problem is. It's a great tool when there's so much pressure on you."

She nods and picks up the book. "So, just feelings about the day?"

"Yes, and whatever else you want to, but I will be checking it periodically. I don't want you to censor yourself because of that, but I need you to be aware of that always. Nothing I read in there will be said anywhere else. This is just for me to help you out the best I can. If I don't know what's happening in your head, I'm not effective."

"Understood."

"Where are you at in your training? I'm not sure what all you've been doing at the academy so fill me in."

We both shift in our seats to get more comfortable as she goes into great detail about what her training looks like. I write it all down, and my head is working overtime to fill in the gaps and where to push her harder.

She collapses back in the chair once she's done talking.

"Good. That's good. I'd like to start in the gym tomorrow." I'm still writing my plan down as I speak.

"That doesn't work for me."

My head jolts up. "If you're serious about this job, we start in the gym tomorrow."

"Listen, asshole, I have to do a brand shoot with Puma in the morning, and I have no clue how long it's going to take. I can't just plan on being here at a certain time, but thanks for asking instead of just assuming I didn't want to start." Her arms cross across her chest, highlighting her perfect tits—tits that I can still taste.

"I apologize." My eyes won't drag up to her face, as hard as I try to force them to.

"Are you just exceptionally horny, or are you a man-whore and this is just what you do?"

That finally pulls my attention. "It's you. I mean, most would say I'm kind of a slut, but I haven't been in a long while even though the reputation precedes me," I mumble out.

Why in the fuck would I tell her all of that? What is wrong with me?

Then she laughs. A full-body, head-thrown-back laugh, with a gorgeous smile on her face, and I know that's why. I'd make a fool of myself ten times over if I got to see that again. I recall her wit, and I know she's the kind of woman who respects truth over sugar-coated shit all day long.

"I can't tell if that was flattery or you're just really struggling to be in this room with me."

"Both," I grumble under my breath before clearing my throat. "It's been a while since I've been on the job, so let's just call it being rusty."

"Whatever makes you sleep better at night." Her smile lights up her whole face.

You do. Or at least, thoughts of you do.

I can't say that, though. That would truly be fucking crazy. She'd fire me then run for the hills. It was one night, but I can't get it out of my head to save my life. And now I get to see her, *be* with her, every single day for months on end.

I'll never survive this.

"So, I'm going to take this home and write my thoughts on the last two days in here. If you want, you can meet me at the photo shoot. I'm not sure how involved in all of that you want to be." She winces, like it would be a hardship for me.

Newsflash, it absolutely won't be.

"Text me the time and place, and I'll be there." I hand her my phone, watching as she puts her number in then texts herself before handing it back.

"Right, well, I'm going to stop by the garage on my way out, but I'll see you tomorrow." She stands up and heads to the door. "And Nate?" I arch an eyebrow at her. "It's good to see you again."

Then she's gone. Poof. Like a mirage. But she was here, and she's my new client.

I slump back in my chair and try to process the last hour.

Remi Bouchard stopped my playboy ways dead in their tracks. I've thought of little else since that night with her. Now she's my ward, and I have to shove that all aside to help her be the best damn driver she can be.

Super easy. No problem.

I am so fucked.

Chapter 5

January 21

The past two days have been . . . overwhelming. I can't think of another word. Meeting everyone, trying to remember names—it was a lot. And I feel shitty that I didn't really get to know anyone. I know that will come in time, but still.

I think I'll get along with Cruz the most. He seems to understand where I'm coming from, and his team is really fucking good. He knows his shit, and I feel like I'll be able to vent or bring concerns to him and it won't just be pushed to the side.

I think I fear being undermined. Not by Toni or Sydney, or anyone in the ownership and management group, but by the day-to-day people I work with. The engineers, mostly.

What if they don't take me seriously? How do I combat that?

This is my only chance. I can't waste it because people refuse to let a woman into this world.

At least Toni will have my back. And hopefully Nate.

I'm ready to work hard as hell, though.

But I'm nervous.

And with that, I think I'll sign off now.

Chapter 6
Nate

Remi works with a photographer to pose, and I have to force myself to take my eyes off of her. She's in Empress purple leggings and a sports bra, nothing else. It's hell on my system, but I have a job to do.

Yeah, asshole, remember she's a job, nothing else.

I roll my eyes at myself before picking up the journal Remi handed me this morning. This is one part of the job I don't particularly like, but sometimes it's easier to be honest with a piece of paper than with a person. And I need honesty from her more than anything. Until she gets comfortable with me, this is the only way I've found that helps me get inside my client's head the fastest.

The second I read about Cruz, I growl. I'll have to keep an eye on them because he's not going to get close to her at all. Then I read farther and see her fears, plain as day. It makes my heart clench in my chest so hard I think I'm having a heart attack.

It takes more time than I'm willing to admit for me to calm down, and then I do something I've never done with a client before.

I write back.

Just a small note, a rebuttal to the fear in the hopes that it helps her see she's not alone.

It's stupid, really, reckless in the worst kind of way because I know how I really feel about the woman. But I won't let her fail. I won't let her sink into the doubt, even from herself.

If I can't be *with* her, then I'll make sure that she succeeds in spades.

I reread her entry a few more times, memorizing her first thoughts and feelings about her promotion, before I look back at her.

Remi's eyes meet mine. An electric shock would probably feel less jolting than her gaze does. She's changed since the last time I looked at her.

She's sporting flowy, long pants and a tan tight tank-top thing. I stop breathing entirely.

No matter how many times I remind myself that she's a job, nothing breaks through the haze that is my attraction to Remi. It's not just her body, although now that I remember what she looked like underneath me, her muscles and build make a whole lot more sense. I'm shocked I didn't recognize it that night. It's her entire demeanor. She's confident in her skin. Not cocky, just assured in who she is.

Her journal casts doubts, but looking at her now? She knows she's something special.

It's sexy as fuck.

I have to adjust my jeans around my hardening dick, to get comfortable again, just thinking about it.

"Okay, one more outfit change, and we're done," the photoshoot director calls out, startling us both.

When she comes out again, dread replaces any horniness I had. Well, it's still there, that's for damn sure, but the dread at seeing her dressed up in a tight short-sleeved crop top and a flowing skirt that looks like it has stars on it has me nearly falling out of my chair.

I want to take her out on a date in that. I want to see it on my floor as we repeat that night from so long ago.

Holy shit, she's more than gorgeous. Her hair is down and curled—something very different to how I've seen it thus far. My fingers twitch, wanting desperately to run through the silky threads and pull her to me.

Shit. Shit. Shit. Mayday, I'm in trouble.

Watching the rest of the photoshoot is akin to torture. I think about the list of things I want to get done today with Remi. I think about the groceries I need to get. I think about how I need to find some permanent housing here since living out of the Vanstone isn't going to work long term. I think of anything I can to keep my mind from wandering to the danger zone—the place that remembers what Remi feels like coming around me, the look on her face as I gave her orgasm after orgasm.

I pull out my phone and text Beck, in an attempt to distract myself, as Remi changes back into her normal clothes.

Me:

> Any leads on an apartment? I can't stay at the Vanstone forever.

Could I look? Sure, but Beck owes me for helping him win the championship, so this is more enjoyable.

Beck:

> You are a pain in my ass. Sending a listing over to you. Look at it, then let me know and I'll secure it.

Me:

> See, you love me.

Beck:

> No. I put up with you because I know you're the best.

Me:

> And because I was your only friend for a long time.

Beck:

> Oh, look, and now you're barely that.

I bark out a laugh. Looking around, I see everyone is starting to break equipment down.

Me:

> Thanks for finding something for me. I'm sure it's great. I'll see you at dinner on Thursday.

"Ready?" Remi's smooth voice hits me out of nowhere.

"Yep. Totally ready." I stumble out of my chair, having to adjust myself again while I gather my things, and follow her out the door.

"Sorry, that was boring. I didn't realize we were doing so many outfits," Remi says as she climbs behind the wheel.

"Totally fine. I never had any of this with Beck because his photoshoots were, like, twenty minutes long. It gave me time to plan and get some things together, so it was good."

"The good ol' double standard." She grins over at me as she pulls into the traffic.

"I guess I didn't realize just how big the discrepancy was." It's the truth. My mind flashes to her journal and how she's worried about people taking her seriously. I knew it would be tough—hell, that's why Empress brought me in to begin with—but I guess I didn't realize exactly what she would be up against.

It's becoming clearer, though.

"So, anyway, what's on the agenda for the rest of the day?"

"Well, the plan is to go back to headquarters and work out. Hard." I smile at her, hoping it felt more like a joke than an innuendo, but judging by the eyeroll, I failed.

"Is this how it's always going to be? You making sexual innuendos because you don't know how else to deal with me?"

"No! God no." I sigh and rub my forehead. "This is just how I usually am, but I seem to be second-guessing everything with you, and it's coming out all wrong. Usually, I'm pretty funny."

"When people say they're pretty funny, it usually means they aren't as funny as they think they are."

"Are you busting my balls already?"

"I mean, someone has to." She shrugs, but I can see the smile she's trying to hide. "Your head would be ginormous if no one knocked you down once in a while."

"That's what I have Beck for," I grumble.

"Nah, he's too easy on you."

"Jesus. Are you like this *all* the time?"

"Only with people I like."

She likes me.

The stupid grin on my face stays until we park at Empress headquarters.

"Don't read into it," Remi says before she climbs out of the car, grabbing her bag. She's halfway to the door before I've even opened my door.

A spitfire, that one.

Her ass sways as she walks into the building, and it's the only thing I can focus on. I give myself a second to gain my bearings because she just threw me off yet again.

My head tilts back against the headrest, and I blow out a breath.

I'm not sure how I'm supposed to survive this entire season with Remi. It hasn't even been a week, and the struggle is real.

When I make my way back to the well-equipped workout room, I stop in my tracks at what I see.

It's not the fact that Remi changed into a sports bra and tiny-as-fuck shorts. No, it's Sawyer fucking Joseph leaning over her that's way too close for my comfort.

Remi's eyes meet mine. All I see is annoyance as she stands up straight.

"Ready to get to work?" she asks as she walks over to me.

Sawyer turns my way after he lingers on her ass for far longer than necessary. *Exactly like you just did.* Well, I'm not being a sleazy asshole about it . . . Hopefully.

"Nate. Interesting to see you back." His word choice isn't lost on me, but Remi doesn't pick up on it.

"Good to see you. Shall we start?" I ignore Sawyer completely, turning to Remi with an arched eyebrow.

"Let's do this." She sighs, grabs her water bottle, and follows me to the corner where the treadmills are.

I give her quick instructions before changing and then joining her.

I warm up with her. One of my biggest strengths as a trainer is being in the thick of it with my clients. When she starts to beat my pace, though, I hesitate to continue for a second.

Competition is a good thing; I am just used to winning.

"Gotta keep up, Coach," Remi calls out over the sounds of our treadmills.

I look over at her, shocked by the audacity to call me out. She's trouble with a capital T, and I'm not entirely sure I'll be able to handle her.

But fuck if I'm not going to try.

"You forget I've been doing this a long time, Ace." I grin back before slamming my hands down on her stop button then mine. "Time for weights."

She stumbles for a second before regaining her balance and glaring at me.

"A simple 'we're done' would have worked wonders."

"Where's the fun in that? This keeps your heartrate up."

It was actually a stupid-as-fuck move. I could have hurt her, tripped her up—most of which could have caused an injury. But my brain isn't really functioning at full capacity right now.

Especially when I see Sawyer watching us from the corner of my eye.

"Bench press," I relay to Remi as I go and set up the rack. We've already gone over her usual weight settings, and I've mentally tracked where I want her to be by the time the season starts. I wasn't lying when I said we were working out hard today.

"I can't lift that." Remi cocks her hip and nods to the weights I'm putting on the bar.

"You can and you will."

"If I hurt myself, I won't be able to do anything," she grumbles before taking her spot.

"I won't let you hurt yourself. Just try it. If it sucks and you really are struggling, I'll adjust it, but trust me . . ."

"Well, it's going to suck," she mopes, but she takes a deep breath and prepares herself.

Five reps later, she racks the bar and spins to look at me, eyes wide in wonder. "Holy shit. I did it!"

I wish I could snap a picture of this look. The one where she surprises herself. Someone so sure of her ability being pushed past what she thinks she's capable of is indeed a sight to behold.

"Told you." I leave the bench press as is because we'll be back, but now it's time to move on to the next group of exercises. "Neck flexion next. I want to start easy on these and add weight as we go. No need to be a hero here, but we do need to strengthen your neck up a lot more than it currently is."

She glares, but she knows I'm right. An F1 Academy car is comparable at a base level, sure, but a true Formula 1 car is going to test her physical limits. She thinks she's been training well, and she has for the car she's been driving, but Formula 1 cars are another animal. I won't have her getting hurt because I didn't train her well enough.

We add weights as we add repetitions, and by the end of the neck rotation, Remi is a sweaty, panting mess of beauty.

It takes me right back to that night. When she looked exactly like this except it was my dick that had made her this way.

I close my eyes and try to refocus myself.

The next two hours are spent much the same. Sawyer watches most of our workout like a fucking creeper, and I try my damnedest not to pop a boner as sweat trails down Remi's chest after every exercise.

Remi kills it, proving she deserves this chance to shine in this field. We make plans for the next day before I drive back to the Vanstone, with my head a wreck and my libido going to war with it. Nothing about the next ten months is going to be easy.

Chapter 7
Remi

Torture.

That's what Nate is doing to me in spades.

Between the workouts that are kicking my ass more than I want to admit and the journaling, it's a lot of change in a very short amount of time. Not to mention, all with a man I would do a hell of a lot to see naked again.

Nope. Can't even think about it.

Lying on my bed at the Vanstone, barely able to move my body with my journal resting on my stomach, is about as far as I got tonight.

The week is catching up with me, and all I want to do is crash hard, but I know I need to journal or it won't get done.

I'll never admit this to Nate, but writing all my thoughts and nonsense into this stupid little journal is really helpful. It's helping me work through my hesitations and doubts with this new team, as well as providing the ability to bitch about things in a safe environment. I know Nate reads it, but I honestly don't care. If I happen to gripe about him in it, I know he won't hold that against me.

Nate.

He's a conundrum. We've both wordlessly decided that we're strictly coworkers at this point. No hints of anything else, but there are times I catch him staring, and my God do I wish we could do more.

His dumb tight T-shirts, that barely contain his biceps and show off his vivid tattoos of the galaxy so beautifully, distract me so damn much. Add in his ass in joggers or basketball shorts, and I'm fucked on a daily basis. Well, not *fucked,* sadly, but any opportunity to hook up with another man while he's just flaunting himself around like that is fucking hopeless.

A boyish smile accompanies his charm, and I can see why he has a reputation on the grid. It seems many women lust after him, or at least the little tidbits I've heard from the mechanics would suggest so. Who can blame them, really? He's gorgeous and kind, and funny when he wants to be. I'm waiting for the other shoe to drop. For him to go after someone else and for me to have to witness it firsthand.

I'm not sure what my reaction would be, but I know I wouldn't handle it well. I don't own him, and he doesn't owe me anything, but I think I would be crushed if I saw him flirting with another woman.

Because you like him more than you want to admit.

Sighing, I pull the journal off my stomach and start writing. It's short and sweet tonight. It's too much effort to put more into it, but it'll do. Every day doesn't need to be multiple pages with my deepest, darkest thoughts.

Clicking the pen and closing the journal, I roll over and fall asleep immediately—with a gorgeous, navy-eyed, dirty-blond man on my mind.

***

A meeting with Toni wasn't what I was expecting first thing on this lovely Friday morning.

I stand outside of her door, bracing myself for a lashing about what I'm doing wrong and what I need to step up on. Instead, when I walk in, Toni's bright smile greets me, and all the stress melts off my shoulders.

"Hi! I feel like I haven't seen you since that first day. How's everything going?" she asks as she gestures to the chair in front of her.

"Oh, umm, good. Busy. Really busy."

"I'm sure. I just wanted to check in and make sure things were okay, or if you have any issues with anything."

"No! Not at all. It's all been really great. Everyone's been really great." Dear God, every ounce of confidence I have is nowhere to be seen right now, and I can't figure out why.

"You okay?" Toni tilts her head.

"I . . ." I sigh. "I'm exhausted." I laugh. "Nate's been working me hard, and when I'm not with him, I'm with engineering and the mechanics making sure everything fits correctly. Then photoshoots," I ramble.

Toni's eyebrows shoot up before she catches herself and brings them back down. "Is it too much? I can have Nate pull back if you feel like he's overworking you." She tries desperately to keep a straight face as she says that, but a little smile tips the corners of her mouth, making my cheeks flame.

"No. Really, it's great. It's just more structured than I'm used to. I'm used to doing this all on my own, so it's just getting used to having the support, honestly."

"Okay, I'll trust you, but you can always come to me if it's too much. I also wanted to ask you about the gala that's coming up."

"Gala," I repeat, trying to rack my brain for a clue about this gala.

"The gala for Daisy and Luka's foundation. Their first one. So Empress, as a family, is showing up in spades. All the drivers and leadership will be there."

"Oh, of course. I'd love to come. Send me the details."

"Will do. I also think it would be prudent to bring a date. It's less pressure if you come with someone. Men are less likely to hover and try to hit on you." She cringes. "I hate that I even have to say that, but men are assholes for the most part and very, *very* predictable."

"I get it. I really do. That's a great idea, though, and I'll see who I can bring."

My immediate thought is Nate, but I know that's a terrible idea. I have a hard enough time separating our jobs from what happened in Japan last year as it is, let alone seeing him in a fucking tuxedo.

Nope. I won't survive it.

"Wonderful. I'd like to keep a weekly meeting unless we have other things planned. It'll be harder during race weekends, but I think it's important that we keep an open dialogue about how you're feeling and my expectations for the season. Nothing formal, just a quick sit-down."

"I love it. Send me a calendar invite, and I'll be there. If it isn't in my calendar, I will completely forget about it." One of my downfalls, I regret.

"Perfect. I know the beginning of the season is hectic, but everyone has been really impressed by you. Keep it up."

"Will do, thanks." I stand up and take that as my cue to leave.

I let my feet carry me down the hall; the pictures on the walls and the faces of those I'm passing are no more than a blur. I have to figure out who the hell I could take to this gala. Everyone I know is married, or Nate, or they technically work with or for me, and I don't want the power imbalance to be a thing.

"Woah, where's the fire?"

Sawyer grabs my shoulders tighter than I would have expected, jolting me out of my thoughts.

"So sorry, just a lot on my mind." I give him a quick, tight smile, but it doesn't reach my eyes.

"I'm glad I ran into you. Literally." He chuckles. "I was thinking it would be smart for us to go to the gala together. No pressure, but if we go together, it's easy publicity and no one will think twice about it."

He sounds genuine. Perhaps for the first time since I've met him. It's really not a bad idea either. We go as colleagues in support of a good cause—nothing more, nothing less.

"You know what? I think that's a great idea. A united Empress front." Impulsive? Maybe, but if it's one less thing I have to figure out right now, I'll take it.

"Something like that. We'll get together as it gets closer and go over the details."

This version of Sawyer? He's cool, easygoing, and kind of sweet. The last time I saw him, he was being an asshole who wouldn't just leave me alone to workout. It might have been a Nate thing, but who the hell knows.

Before I reply, he's walking off to the engineer's offices, leaving me standing there with whiplash from his behavior.

I don't get time to dwell on any of it, though. My phone dings with a new message.

Nate:

> Get your ass to the gym. I've got something new for us to do today.

Me:

Lovely. Can't wait.

Nate:

> You're excited and curious. Don't lie.

I'll never admit that to him, but he already knows me better than I'll give him credit for. I am curious. I find myself moving before I realize I'm doing it, heading down the stairs to the gym, eager to see what he has in store.

"Good morning." Nate smirks as I barrel into the large space. He's dressed in joggers and an Empress hoodie covering up his colorful arms. *Lame.*

"Hi."

"Do you have a jacket here?"

"Umm, yeah, in my office." I'm not even sure why drivers have offices here. It's not a traditional office, but more of a small living room where we can get away from the hustle and bustle of the rest of the building.

"Great, we'll stop there on our way out."

"We're not working out today?"

"We are, just differently. Have you been out around Austin yet?"

"Umm, no. I don't have a ton of free time currently." I arch an eyebrow at him.

"Wonderful. Let's go." His overly large smile doesn't give away a hint of what we're doing.

I follow blindly, grabbing my jacket before we head to my car. "Where to, *Nathan?*" I smile to myself as he settles in.

"Never call me Nathan again." He rolls his eyes. "And I'll plug it into GPS."

"Why don't you like being called Nathan?"

"I just don't," he snaps.

I leave the subject alone . . . for now, but it only piques my interest more.

Twenty minutes of silence later, we pull up to the Barton Creek Greenbelt.

"A hike?" I ask, excited about the change of pace.

"It's good to switch things up once in a while. Nature does wonderful things for the body and the mind."

A breeze of cool air hits my face as I open the car door and washes over me like a soothing breath—one I didn't know I needed after the hard week.

I'm no stranger to hard work, but this first week at Empress has been a whole new level of hard.

Somehow, Nate saw I needed something like this before I did, and I couldn't be more grateful. I bounce on my toes, feeling the smile taking over my face.

"So, we like hiking." Nate steps up behind me.

"Love it. Honestly, I'm game for anything outside. Thank you." I spin and wrap my arms around his neck. The closeness is intoxicating. His scent transports me back to Japan, when all I could smell was him wrapped around me as he showed me things I've never known about myself.

A deep breath doesn't help anything—in fact, it makes it worse—before I realize where we are. He's my trainer. I'm his client.

Shit.

"Sorry," I mumble as I pull away and take three huge steps back.

He just stares at me, eyes shifting between mine, before he shakes his head and steps back even farther. His hand runs through his hair like he's trying to get a grasp on himself.

It only makes me want him more. Seeing that he's struggling as much as I am has my head too caught up in the what-ifs of it all. Realistically, there's no real situation where things don't go sour between us. Being tied up personally and professionally isn't something I even want to attempt. Hell, it's not like I have a wonderful example of a great partnership to begin with. Lord knows my parents can barely tolerate each other, only sticking it out for appearances.

Everything I despise about the idea of marriage is everything my parents are.

Nate clears his throat. "Ready? It's thirteen and a half miles to the end, then we turn around and come back. Think you can handle it?" Gone is the look of want. Gone is the flare of heat in his eyes. A playful challenge replaces it all, and

I kind of hate it.

But this is how it must be.

Chapter 8
Nate

Pull yourself together.

The phrase becomes my cadence as I hike with the woman plaguing my every thought. When she hugged me, it was sensory overload. I was seconds away from kissing her, hauling her away back to the car, and saying "fuck it". Fuck the job, fuck Formula 1, fuck professionalism. I just wanted to fuck *her.*

And then the daze I was in snapped as she stepped back. I could see the visible change on her face, her disconnecting from us. It hurt far more than I'll ever admit.

Instead, I focus on how happy Remi was to get outside and go for a hike. It wasn't simply the change of pace; she was genuinely excited about it. Now, my mind is working overtime to create more workouts outside. More hikes, more fresh air incorporated into her everyday grind, just to make her happy. So that smile on her face right now stays permanently.

"So . . . what do you do for fun?" Remi's voice pulls me out of my head.

"Umm, great question. Travel, read, try new physical activities or sports," I rattle off a list.

"What do you read?" She pants as this particular incline gets harder.

"Everything. Fiction, non-fiction. A lot of non-fiction, honestly. It helps me stay sharp for the job, and I enjoy reading about different takes or philosophies on mental health, motivation, things like that."

"Huh," she murmurs.

"What?"

"Nothing. I just didn't peg you as a big reader, let alone on those topics. It makes sense, though. You know your shit."

I preen at her compliment.

"Why thank you."

"Don't get a big head about it."

"Too late." I couldn't wipe the smile off of my face if I tried.

She rolls her eyes. "Anyway, what's your favorite sport?"

"Mainstream? Rugby. No offense to Formula 1—you all are badass—but rugby is still my top. Lesser known? Probably rock climbing."

"I will attempt to not take offense to that." She looks over at me before smiling. "You are quite the conundrum, Nate Murphy."

"Oh yeah?"

"I mean, it's not like I really know you—"

"Oh, you know me," I interrupt before I realize what I'm saying. "Shit. Sorry."

Remi doesn't reply for a second, and I slow down to look at her.

"It's weird, right? I mean, we . . . hooked up, and it was . . . really fucking good, but now we just have to act like I don't know what your dick looks like. Or that you have that thigh tattoo." Her whole face flashes red in a nanosecond.

"So the thigh tattoo does it for you," I say instead of addressing the huge elephant in the room. More like a glacier. It's in every action I do around her. Hell, I still have that damn report card in my backpack.

"Be serious."

"Hey, you're the one who brought it up." My hands go up in defense.

"I just mean, it's weird to pretend Japan didn't happen. But we have to." She sighs.

"We have to," I whisper, repeating the words like a vow, because she's right. She doesn't need more trouble than she'll already have this season. The uphill battle of being the only woman on the grid is far enough of a challenge without having to deal with me or the rumors that could arise just from us being together.

I clear my throat and change the subject. "So, what do you do for fun?"

"With my copious amounts of spare time?" she chuffs as we continue our hike.

"You still need something outside of this job."

"Then that is something I need to work on."

"You don't do anything outside of this?" I ask, shocked that she doesn't have even a mundane hobby.

"Nope. I eat, sleep, breathe, Formula 1, and have for as long as I can remember."

"That's . . . sad." I realize the truth in my words. It is sad. She may be in her late twenties, but that's not a reason to only focus on your career. There's more to life than this. And Lord knows it won't last forever. What are you left with when this is all over?

I make another mental note to work on her life outside of this sport, set her up for longevity and happiness even without driving.

If I can't be with her as a partner, then I'm going to damn well make sure she has an incredible life regardless.

Woah, Nate, slow the fuck down. This is extreme even for you.

For some reason, it doesn't feel extreme, though, and that's a real problem.

Is this how Beck felt with Sydney? I gave him so much shit for his obsession with her. I can understand it a bit more now, I suppose. It takes over without effort, without conscious decision. This need to help Remi in any way I can is now my priority. Yeah, Beck's actions make a lot more sense now.

"I don't know if it's sad. Pathetic, probably. I just haven't had time to think outside of my ambitions. Becoming the first woman in Formula 1 was always a long shot, but I wanted to put every ounce of effort into it. Hoping on a prayer that all the years spent on nothing else would actually pay off. It's wild to do that for a sport that will spit you out in a minute without a second look if you don't produce." She sighs.

"Toni won't do that, though."

"Maybe. Maybe not. Money makes the world go around here, and if I can't make the team money, I'm of no use."

I mull over her words. She's not technically wrong, but I know Sydney, Beck, Toni, and Daisy would never reduce their team to that. It's the only reason I came back when Beck called me. They want to run their team differently, away from all the cutthroat bullshit. I just hope it actually pans out for them. Remi isn't wrong: money is the only thing that matters in this world, and it's hard to break with that even with the best of intentions.

"Well, let's make sure that doesn't happen then," I say with confidence. If it's the last thing I do in this job, I'll do everything I can to help Remi succeed.

"Let's do it." She lights up with a blinding smile and nods to the trail, refocusing my attention.

Safer topics are a must right now before I cross lines we can't. "So, testing next week—you feel ready?"

She shrugs. "Yes and no. I think I'm ready overall, but I'm not sure how to navigate everything outside of the actual racing. There's a gala, and Toni wants me to do a bunch of media shit. It feels like an act I'm not cut out for."

"Totally get that. It's a lot, especially when you didn't grow up in this sport. Going to all the fancy events and interviews is just part of the gig, but I think it's probably going to be a lot different for you in general. As the first woman in the sport, you're bound to get a lot more attention. Now, it's about balancing it all so you aren't overwhelmed. If we need to talk to Toni about cutting back on engagements, I'll be there to help with that as well."

Her shoulders slump in relief. "Thank you. I am worried that the expectations will be different for me, and I'm not sure how to navigate it and when to say no. Hell, if I can even say no. We didn't get this kind of attention in the academy."

"You can always say no."

"Can I?" she asks as we reach the end of the trail.

"Your job isn't dependent on all the outside shit. Sure, the team wants all the good press, but there are only certain events you *have* to go to. What your job is dependent on is how well you drive."

We pause at the river. The sun glints off the rolling water, so bright it's difficult to look at for long.

"Thank you for this," she says as she turns her face to the sun and fills her lungs with air.

"I'm glad you enjoyed it," I say honestly. As much as she clearly needed the fresh air, I think I needed it just as much.

With Beck, this job was easy. We are best friends, and being with him every hour of every day wasn't a hardship. I knew him as well as I knew myself, and it was easy to figure out his moods or what he needed to do more of in training. When I came back last season for Alejandro, our personalities clashed. I couldn't be around him all the time, and he made it clear he didn't want to be around me either. It's part of why I left and was *very* hesitant to take this job with Remi.

But things with Remi are so fucking easy. Too easy, really. And not just because we slept together and have insane sexual chemistry. We just work well together. I can push her without fear of retaliation. Learning what works for her, what motivates her, gets me excited and I'm actually looking forward to this season with her.

I just have to remind myself that it's strictly professional. I won't ever be the person who jeopardizes her career.

"Shall we?" she asks.

"We shall." The walk back feels shorter, and by the time we get to her car, I'm not ready to call it a day even though we've been hiking for hours.

"Thank you again for the hike. It was nice to get a break from the usual."

"Definitely. We'll try to add more into your routine as we can. I have dinner and breakfast being sent to your room when you get back, so you don't have to worry about your meal plan. Then tomorrow, we'll be doing weights early. You have a meeting with Toni and Jason after that, and then I'll touch base and see how you are feeling. I might have something else on the agenda, but it depends on how the day goes," I ramble out the schedule she already knows because I'm trying desperately to keep myself in check.

"I have a feeling I'll crash immediately tonight, so good call. I probably just wouldn't eat today otherwise." She chuckles.

I eye her with horror. "You can't just not eat. Do you know how many calories you are burning every single day while you are training?" I scold.

"I know."

"I'll start sending you food whenever there isn't something else going on," I mumble, pulling out my phone and making a note to start on a meal plan, and see if I can get the company I used with Beck to start making her meals.

"I'm not a child, Nate. I can handle food. It's just one day when I'm overly tired," she says so matter-of-factly.

"Nope. I did this with Beck so it's not a big deal. I'm not risking you not fueling up enough. You have a tight schedule and can't afford to fall behind."

"Nate."

"I can figure it out when we start to travel heavy. It's been a while, but it has to be like riding a bike. Catering can handle most of it—"

"Nate."

"I'll have a meeting with them this week."

"Nate!" she yells.

"What?" I turn to her, more annoyance than I intend in my tone.

"I'm not a child. I don't need you to micromanage every single aspect of my life."

"I'm not. I'm just trying to help, making things streamlined for you."

"Then let me have input."

I see the pleading in her eyes. It stops me in my tracks.

I open my mouth and then pause. "I apologize. I was mostly thinking out loud, but let's set aside time to menu plan this week. I'd like food to be something you don't have to spend a lot of time thinking about regularly."

"And what if I go out on a date? Do I need to bring an allotted meal out with me?" She smirks over at me, but it instantly drops when she sees my face.

"Do you plan on going out on a lot of dates?" My voice takes on a dangerous quality. It's low and unyielding.

She eyes me as we stop at a light. I don't even register the mischievous look on her face.

"My, my, someone is positively green with jealousy."

"Don't even start with that shit. We need to make a rule that I don't hear about your love life . . . ever. I—" I breath in deep. "I can't handle that, Rem."

Her eyes soften. "Nate. I was giving you a hard time. I don't have a spare second to even think about dating right now."

"Right. Of course." I wring my hands together.

Neither of us says another word for the rest of the drive. I can't tell if I'm more embarrassed for showing my hand yet again, or if it was so lost on me because I can't see past the haze of anger at the thought of her on a date. Either way, I need to do some soul searching and find a way to set my feelings completely aside so that I can provide the best for Remi.

Her career is the only thing that matters.

Chapter 9
Remi

Things have been going, dare I say, well? Nate and I still have this undercurrent of sexual tension that I don't think will be going away, but we are more focused on getting into a routine and making sure I'm physically up to speed.

But the gala is coming up in four days, and I'm very much not ready. I'm not sure going with Sawyer is actually a good idea, but I'm locked into it now. I didn't realize I would need to navigate social events and plus-ones when I took this job, but it's something I need to figure out immediately, so I don't implode from the stress and overthinking.

"Remi! How's it going?" Toni finds me in my office looking at specs for my car.

"Good. How are you?" I get up and hug her before she sits next to me on the couch.

"Great. I wanted to touch base with you on the gala. You ready? Luka and Daisy are excited. All you need to do is show up and be ready to listen to a bunch of old men talk about their money. Pretentious, but a necessary evil, I'm afraid." She gives me a crooked smile.

Toni comes from a similar world to mine. We were both thrust into our current positions without actually growing up in this business. Sure, we've busted our asses and proved we're good enough to be here, but the money and luxury that surround everything in Formula 1 aren't something either of us are really comfortable with.

"Oh, good. I was just thinking about that. I finally got my dress, and Sawyer asked to go together as a show of unity for the team. Keep it simple. Lord knows I don't need the media only focusing on my love life, however false it is."

"I one hundred percent understand that." She smiles knowingly at me. I forgot what she and Felix went through last season with all the media attention surrounding their relationship. It was nearly a big scandal with them being team principals for competing teams.

"Are you ready for the livery unveiling?" I ask her.

"I am, but I'm more excited to just get the season underway, honestly. Ready to get into the action, see where we are in the field, and kick some ass."

"I'm glad you have that confidence." I chuckle, a little unease leaking into my words.

"Hey, you'll do great. Sure, it'll be an adjustment, but once you get a couple of races in, I know you'll be wiping the floor with everyone."

"Thank you."

"How are things going with Nate?"

"Good," I squeak.

"You sure about that?" She arches an eyebrow.

"It's been good. He's been helping me with what to expect jumping into Formula 1 compared to the academy. I guess I just didn't expect him to be in all aspects of my life."

"Like what?"

"Food, mental stuff, and micromanaging most of my days."

"Beck always raved about Nate and how he was the key to his success, but I suppose I didn't realize just how much he was intertwined into his life. He wasn't that way with Alejandro, that's for sure," Toni says.

"I think it'll be good. Built in support, which I'll probably need more than I even realize. It just takes some time to get used to having him around every single day." *To say the least.* It's more that I have to get used to seeing him every day when I know what he feels like, how he kisses, and just how badly I want him.

The struggle is very real.

"Well, I just came from a meeting with Luka, and we were discussing the new changes to the academy and how many more races they'll be at this year. I think it'll be nice for you, in particular to see friends from there more often than you would have in other years."

"That's great!" It truly is. I remember when Luka took the job working with the academy and how he wanted to implement all of these changes so that we could be seen more, on a larger scale. TV rights and more races were all his top priority, and I think that none of us really thought he would get it done so quickly. Though, knowing what I know about Luka now, no one should underestimate him.

"Well, I just wanted to check in with you. My door is always open, and by that, I mean my phone. Call me or text me anytime. My goal is to make sure you are getting the support you need, so don't be afraid to speak up, okay?"

"I will. Thanks, Toni."

She nods on her way out.

I feel more confident in this transition than I have all week, thanks to her visit. But she's left me with even more to think about. An impromptu yoga session in the gym sounds perfect. The movement and meditation will help clear my head and prepare me to meet Nate in an hour.

Once I'm in the gym, I lose myself in an easy flow. Nothing strenuous, just something to get lost in.

"Well, it must be my lucky day," a voice I was hoping not to hear today says from behind me while I'm doing downward dog. Because of-fucking-course it's while I'm bent in half with my ass in the air. How cliché of Sawyer.

"Sawyer," I say as I straighten to standing.

"How are things going? I feel like we haven't had a chance to really talk, interact, you know."

"Things are going well, thank you for asking. I suppose we'll be able to talk more at the gala."

"That's good to hear. I know we have some social media crap to do tomorrow, but I saw you on my way to engineering and thought I'd stop by without the cameras in our faces. I don't think we'll get as much time at the gala as you think we will."

Huh. That's semi thoughtful of him.

"I appreciate that. How are you feeling so far? Think it's going to be a good season?"

"Canned answer? Absolutely. We're going to build on last year, and I'm feeling very confident with our team."

"Non-canned answer?" I ask.

"I actually am feeling good. I think you're a good addition, and the team is super motivated. I'm excited to get in the car and see what we're dealing with on the actual track. But overall? I'm beyond ready to start the season."

I nod at his assessment, which is decidedly different than what I thought he was going to say. He feels more . . . human today. Less cocky asshole. I'm afraid to hope that this is the real him instead of the cocky act he's been putting on most days. It seems too good to be true.

"I actually am glad I caught you. I was planning on picking you up before the gala, around five. Get there before the big rush of media and sneak in. Maybe help with any last-minute things they need." His head tilts in question.

"That's super thoughtful, and I love the idea. I'm actually staying at the Vanstone, so I'll be ready in the lobby at five."

"Sounds great. I can't wait to see what a dressed-up Remi looks like." He smiles.

I see the appeal. His bright, wide smile with all the cocky charm probably gets all the ladies swooning, but I only see a potential ally.

"Friends only. That's my rule, Sawyer," I scold gently.

"I know, but you can't blame me for being interested in what you look like all glammed up. It's all workout clothes and polos here."

"As long as our boundaries are clear, I'm looking forward to it." I smile. I'm not looking forward to going with him necessarily, but I am excited to see Luka and Daisy's foundation get some attention.

Sawyer gives me that easy smile of his, but I still feel nothing.

He's too clean cut. No tattoos, no dimples, no sloppy hair.

Shit, not the time to think about Nate.

"Sawyer."

Speaking of Nate. I turn to face the object of all my dirty thoughts.

"Nate, how's it going, man?" Sawyer says cheerfully, and I cringe. Nate isn't buying it, and Sawyer just makes it all the worse as he continues not picking up on any cues. "Just talking to Remi about going to the gala together. Empress united and all that shit."

The faceoff between the two of them is as close to a dick measuring contest as I've ever seen. I roll my eyes at the blatant display.

"Well, great chat. I'll see you later, Sawyer. I've got a meeting with Nate now."

The cocky grin is back on Sawyer's face. He's not even trying to hide the fact that he's needling Nate. "I'll be seeing you later, Remi."

"Jesus." I sigh, rubbing the bridge of my nose.

"What the fuck was that?" Nate demands.

"Okay, first . . ."I point at him. "You don't get to come in here and act all possessive. Second, we're going as friends and racing teammates. Nothing more, nothing less. It's good optics for Empress, and he promised it was just so we both didn't get hounded by the media."

"And you believed him?" He sounds appalled.

"For the most part. You know, I am a twenty-nine-year-old adult who can make decisions for herself. Even if he wants more, I don't, therefore he won't be getting anything other than companionship from the night out of me." I use my firm, annoyed voice.

Nate's jaw clenches enough for me to see the muscle in his cheek. Gone is the happy-go-lucky man he usually is. In his place, there is someone darker, more dominant. And dammit, it's hot as fuck.

"I don't like it."

"You don't have to. You don't make all my decisions for me." I smile with a tilt of my head.

His hand scrapes through his already messy hair as he sighs. "I'm sorry. Just be careful with him. He doesn't have a good reputation."

"I'm well aware. I need you to trust that I'm capable of not falling for some pretty-boy bullshit." The double meaning isn't completely lost on me. Nate, after all, had a reputation for having many good times while traveling with Beck.

"I do trust you. I'm just a jealous prick," he admits.

His honesty surprises me as much as it makes my heart beat faster. I won't lie;

I wish I was going with Nate, but I also know there are too many obstacles in the way of that being reality. It would never just be friends for us.

"Well, now that we've cleared that up, you ready to go over things?" I ask, gesturing to the conference room across from the gym.

Chapter 10

February 2

What a fucking week. Somehow, I'm going to this damn gala with Sawyer of all people. I'm not sure how I really feel about it, but I also know I won't be pressured into anything I don't want to do. This is just friendship, possibly getting to know each other better, since we'll have to spend time together throughout the season. I'm thinking of it more like a friendship interview . . . at an event with all the bigwigs of the Formula 1 world.

That sounds so fucking stupid.

It's good for Empress, though. I know that. It's strategic for us to show up together. The two drivers getting along and forming a united front means we're an even bigger threat to other teams. If we aren't fighting each other, we're working together to win races. That's the biggest motivation for me: to scare the other teams with how well we work together.

I'm nervous for the big livery unveiling next week. It means I'm only a week out from testing, seeing everyone in Bahrain for their first big practice. It's where we all size each other up, and I pray to every single god I can think of that I don't make a fool out of myself. The pressure is unreal. I knew it would be a lot when I signed my contract, but now that it's really here? Now that I have to shut up and prove my worth? It's scary as well. I get one chance. It starts in two weeks. I need to show the other teams that I'm not just a pretty headline. I'm not just here to be a pretty face. I'm here to kick some ass and pave the way for other women.

I'm here to change the fucking world.

And I'm scared shitless I'll fuck it all up and ruin it for every girl after me.

I don't want little girls to lose hope because I can't get my shit together. I don't want little girls to give up on dreams because I couldn't succeed.

It's hard to sleep, knowing what's at stake.

I know that's dramatic as fuck, but it truly feels do-or-die for me.

One chance for every single little girl who has an interest in the sport. One chance to plant an idea in their head. One chance to show them they are capable of anything. No pressure and completely doable.

Now, time for a pep talk after all the dramatics.

You will kick ass at this gala. People will love you, and you will look hot as fuck while not looking slutty. You will be poised and intelligent. Then you will smile and do interviews at the livery unveiling like you've been doing it your whole life. Nothing to stress about at all.

Then you will kick everyone's ass on the track. Beat everyone's time and scare the shit out of them all.

Because you are a THREAT. You will WIN. And you will look damn good doing it.

Chapter 11
Nate

I wasn't supposed to be here.

I told Beck I wouldn't be coming because I wasn't considered management or a driver, but I guess Luka, or more likely Daisy, extended the invite.

Now, I wish I never came.

The one-shoulder, royal-purple gown with the high slit in the flowy skirt that Remi walks in wearing is sure to be my downfall. It's not showy at all. If anything, she's fairly conservative in this crowd, and yet every single head turns to watch her walk into the ballroom.

"Holy shit, she cleans up well," some asshole standing next to me at the bar says.

I swear I growl at him.

She's surrounded almost immediately, but the one thing that draws my eye is her smile. It's not her carefree smile nor her happy smile. No, this one is the PR one. The smile that tells me she's nervous and unsure but has to put on a happy face even if she doesn't want to.

She glances up at Sawyer, with his overly confident grin, and nods before stepping forward into the throng of people.

It should have been me. I should have manned up and brought her here. If she is able to platonically come with Sawyer, then I should have been able to do the same.

I would stand by her the same as Sawyer and watch her own the crowd. Hell, I'd be thrilled to do so. I'd support her in any way I could. Except it would never be the same for us.

I couldn't do it platonically.

God knows I'd be sneaking off with her multiple times just to taste her lips.

Smear some lipstick on my cheek for good measure to mark me as hers.

I shake my head, refocusing on why I actually came.

"That sure doesn't look like how you used to stare at me." Beck's voice sounds from behind me.

"Well, you aren't nearly as hot in a ballgown. Sorry, man," I return in jest.

"You want to tell me how you know each other yet?" he asks, dismissing my words.

"Nope. Sure don't." I won't betray Remi's trust like that. If she wants to tell her bosses that we've slept together, I'll stand by her side and take the fallout as it comes. But I won't be the one who spills all those details.

"I'll warn you once and then let you be." I roll my eyes at his fatherly talk. "Do not fuck with her. Do not jeopardize this opportunity for her. Do not, and I mean this with my whole chest, sleep with her for a quick fuck. I don't really know what's been going on for the last year with you, but I won't let you bring her down. She's worked too hard to get here, and I—hell, all of us—won't let anything get in the way of her success, and that includes my best friend."

I stare at him for an extended moment. A million things run through my head, but one sticks out.

"Do you really think I'm that bad of a guy?"

"No, Nate." He sighs. "I think you're a great guy. A little misguided sometimes, but I wouldn't have begged you to come in and work with her if I thought you were a bad guy."

"Just bad for dating then." I scoff.

"If you actually dated, I'd say no. But that's not what you've historically done." His words are picked carefully as he eyes me.

Maybe this is why being around Remi is so hard for me. I want her, desperately, but I have no experience dating. Sex is easy. I know for a damn fact that I'm good at it—the report card on my nightstand proves that—but a relationship? I wouldn't even know where to begin.

Remi isn't a woman to get your rocks off with. Everything I've learned about her knows that with my very being. I also know that she won't date, not while so much for her depends on this year.

The universe seems to be against us, but maybe it's for the best.

I turn to look at her talking to Empress's largest sponsors, smiling. They are practically eating out of the palm of her hand. "I won't ever hurt her. I . . . I can't. I'd rather fall asleep in a tub with a toaster in it than hurt her."

"That's fairly dramatic, even for you," Beck says, watching me hard.

Turning to face him again, I take a deep breath. "All I want to do is help her thrive. I'm dedicated to making that happen, and the last thing I want to do is ever hurt her in any way."

"Whatever happened between you two . . . I feel like I'm going to regret saying this, but . . . don't give up on it so quickly. You're different, in a good way. More grounded, serious in a way you've never been before. If she has a part in that, maybe don't be so quick to push things to the side. But only if she's not just a hook-up to you."

"Beck . . ."

"I'm just saying." He holds his hands up.

"It's not that simple, and you know it. What happened between us doesn't matter. This season? Her one shot to be a trailblazer? That's what matters."

His eyebrows rise almost to his hairline as he tilts his head.

"Just think about what I said. And my door's always open if you ever need to talk about any of it. Now, I've got to go find Sydney and make sure she isn't overworking herself."

The way he's constantly looking after Sydney, watching her every move to make sure her rheumatoid arthritis isn't flaring or if she's hurting, is wild to watch. He does it in such a way that's not overbearing. Hell, I doubt Sydney even knows how attentive that man is. Nonetheless, it's strange to look at it now—their relationship dynamic—and how I can imagine being exactly the same with Remi.

I get it now. I always thought he was crazy for pining after Sydney for so damn long, but maybe you just have to meet the woman who knocks you on your ass and makes you rethink everything you thought you knew about your life.

Holy shit, I've lost the fucking plot.

Purple fabric falls into my eyeline and disrupts the spiral I was just in. I look up to see Remi walking toward me, a small secretive smile on her face.

"I didn't realize you were coming tonight," she says, stepping up to me. With heels, she's taller but still barely grazes my chin.

"I wasn't supposed to, but Daisy and Luka invited me so how could I say no?" I shrug, taking a sip of my tequila on the rocks while shoving my other hand in my pocket.

"You definitely can't. You look good in a tux, although I'm a little sad the artwork is all covered." Her eyes twinkle.

"We may have to make a bet since you like the tats so much."

"Oh?"

"Sure, why not. The first race you win, I'll get a new tattoo. You get to pick what it is," I say without thinking. I have a ton of tattoos. I sure as hell wouldn't offer if I wasn't serious, but even Beck winning the whole damn championship didn't afford him the honor of picking one of the tattoos.

"Oh, hell yes. Shake on it." She holds her hand, and I take it in mine. She may be tiny, but she's strong as hell. We share a firm handshake with an intertwined promise that neither of us will break.

"You're trying to figure out if you can win the first race, aren't you?" I smirk.

"Abso-fucking-lutley." She laughs.

"Well, it was lovely to see you, but I won't hog your time. I know you have to schmooze everyone." I realize I'm still holding her hand, so I pull her in closer just so I can murmur in her ear, "You look good enough to eat in that dress, and I'm not sure I'll be able to handle being this close to you for the rest of the night." Dropping her hand and stepping back, I let her see the vulnerability of that statement on my face.

Her eyes shift between mine, mouth opening a couple of times like a fish's when out of water, before we're interrupted by all of the Empress leadership.

Beck catches my eye, eyebrow arched high in question, but I shake my head and walk off to our table. I need a breather before I do something really stupid, like drag Remi to an empty room and ravage her through that slit in her fucking dress.

I'm forced to do a shocking amount of glad handing all night as I watch Remi from the sideline. She's a natural. All her fears and concerns that she writes about in her journal are unfounded. I know it's hard to see that internally, but she's already winning people over. Hell, she's winning over the FIA president, which is notoriously hard to accomplish. Sawyer is never far, but he keeps his hands to himself. His promise to keep things platonic is actually panning out. Maybe he's grown as much as I have in the past year, but only time will really tell on that one. I'll be sure to keep an eye on him either way.

Before I know it, the night is wrapping up. Sydney looks ready to drop, so I know she and Beck will be gone shortly. Daisy is looking at her phone with longing as Luka joins her at their table. One can only assume they're missing their baby and will be going home soon as well. The rest of the place is almost cleared out except for Remi and Sawyer, who are talking animatedly. I sit my happy ass down and wait them out. There's no way I'm leaving before making sure Remi gets out of here safely. Maybe I will follow them and make sure she also gets home okay. It's definitely not creepy and borderline stalking. I just don't trust Sawyer, is all.

Absolutely has nothing to do with Remi and how I haven't stopped thinking about Japan since I woke up alone.

Remi's laugh rings out clear from across the room. She grabs her small handbag and stands up, Sawyer following her actions dutifully. They make it to the doors, leaving the ballroom, before I stand up and follow at a distance.

By the time I catch up to them, they're waiting for valet. I check in and tell the desk that I'd rather go pick up my own car to save them the trouble. They hesitantly give me my keys but say nothing. I bet they've never had a patron who did not want them to get their valeted car.

But I'm on the clock, and if I want to make sure Remi gets back home safely, this is the fastest option.

Maybe Beck is right. I am being dramatic as fuck with all things involving Remi.

It doesn't matter now. I'm already committed.

By the time I pull around the corner, Sawyer is just getting into the front seat. I follow them for ten minutes before the area starts to look familiar.

The Vanstone.

Of course she's staying there. I figured she would have gotten her own place, but if she didn't have time or if Sydney wanted her to not stress about where to live right away, this makes sense. Hell, it's the same reason I'm staying here.

Although now, knowing that Remi is in the same building as me every single night makes me want to check out that listing that Beck sent over ASAP.

I just know I would find a way to her room and cross every single line of professionalism.

It would probably only take me a couple of days, if I'm truly honest with myself.

Sawyer doesn't even get out of the car to escort her in. He stays long enough for her to shut the door and then drives away like he's on the fucking track.

What a prick.

Once Remi is through the front doors, I relax a bit. I know she's safe inside. It takes me all of five minutes to park my car and head inside too. My head is on a swivel, looking for the woman I can't stop thinking about. By the time I hit the elevators, she's nowhere to be found.

It's just as well. If I did see her, I don't think I could be responsible for my actions right now. My willpower has dwindled to nothing watching her in that dress all night.

A shower to clear my head doesn't help. Jacking off to images of her with that thigh-high slit doesn't help. The only thing left is to sleep it off and hope that when morning comes, I'll be back to professional Nate.

Chapter 12
Remi

It's been a hectic couple of weeks. We had the gala then the livery unveiling, which boasted a gorgeous new purple body with a carbon front wing. It's sexy and feminine, exactly what Empress tries to embody, and I'm lucky enough to get to drive in it every week.

But as I currently stand in front of my new car at testing in Bahrain, I feel like I'm going to throw up.

This is the first big step. My first time in this car for others to see. *To judge.* I just hope I don't fumble it and have every single person in this sport questioning if hiring me was the right choice.

"Stop overthinking." Nate's voice barely registers.

"It's kind of what I'm known for."

"You are known for taking the entire racing world by storm and working your way up from the academy straight to Formula 1. No one else has ever done that."

"Hmm, are you sure it's not my neurotic tendencies mixed with sheer stubbornness?" I ask as I finally turn around to face him.

"Only the people you are closest to get to see that special side of you." He smiles and winks at me.

His words have the desired effect, and a small smile tips up my lips. "Special like annoying? Or special like 'look into a better psychiatrist because whatever they're doing isn't working'?"

"Special like you are going to get into that car, pull out onto the track, and show them who you are. Because you, Remi Bouchard, are a fucking ace."

His dimpled smile almost makes me believe his words. It does, however, give me enough confidence to get my ass in gear.

I nod, my eyes locked on him, as I take a big deep breath before turning to my gear.

Once I'm hooked up to my water supply and have my helmet on, Cruz taps it twice, gives me a huge smile, and walks off to get the mechanics ready. Nate is next, grabbing the sides of my helmet like he's holding my jaw about to kiss me.

"You can do this. Once you're in that car, you'll stop thinking about everything outside of you and the track."

I nod again and suck in a deep breath. He steps away, and I climb into the cockpit.

"Radio check: 1, 2," I test.

"Loud and clear, Remi. You ready?" Jason Blackburn, my lead engineer, asks.

"As I'll ever be."

The mechanic who directs me out of the bay slowly walks out into the pit to check for traffic. I can't remember his name yet, but I make a note to talk to him after this practice run. When he gives me the go-ahead, I speed up and get ready to hit the track for the first time ever in a Formula 1 car.

My pulse pounding in my ears blocks out the roar of the engine. There's one car ahead of me, but they hit the entry point onto the track before I even need to slow down.

Directions in my headset tell me when to go for my practice start, and like flipping a switch, I let the muscle memory take over.

Sure, I've done simulations and practiced at our home base, but this is different. Being on the track for the first time in the new car feels like magic.

The G-force hits me first. It's like a wall pressing down on my entire body. I focus on my breathing as I take the first turn, slowing down and hugging the corner tight, before accelerating out of it and flying past someone on my right side.

That's the weird thing about these practices. It's more of a race against yourself, as well as a way to judge how the other teams' cars are going to fare against yours. That's not to say there isn't some gameplay involved. Sometimes, we hold back our true speed to give the other teams a false sense of security.

Today, though? My instruction is to feel things out however I want. If that's going full speed and really testing the car, so be it. And right now, I want to squash every single doubt on this track.

I'm not to be messed with. I'm not a spectacle; I came here to compete.

On the first main straightaway, I crank up my pace. A smile cracks my face at the freedom, at the adrenaline coursing through my system. It almost feels like flying, except it's bumpier and way rougher on the body.

"Pace looks great, Remi. Keep it up. We'll bring you back in after this flying lap."

"Sounds good."

I know from simulation that Turn 11 goes uphill into Turn 12, so I need to really focus. It switches directions quickly, and I have to be ready to shift side to side in order to navigate it properly. Every millisecond counts, and if I'm off my line even a little bit, it'll show in my time.

Thankfully, I seem to hit every maneuver exactly how I want to.

"Great job. Oil pressure looks good so far, but keep up what you're doing," Jason says in my headset.

"Copy."

As I hit Turn 13 and into the next sector's straightaway, my confidence grows like a physical being in the cockpit with me. I'm more certain with every minor adjustment. The metaphorical pressure lessens on my shoulders as the physical pressure takes over like a blanket. *This*, I know. *This*, I can handle. All the doubts I've had since I got to Austin seem to get smaller and smaller in the rearview. No longer are they the center of my attention. Driving a Formula 1 car is.

It feels fucking phenomenal.

Normally, drivers putz around the track for a few laps before taking their flying lap, but I had so much nervous energy I asked Jason what he thought about just going for it right out of the gate. It'll give us a quick baseline, and we can adjust from there. He was on board in a second. As I swerve through the last two turns, the most difficult ones, Toni's voice comes over comms.

"Damn, girl, you are absolutely killing it. Just bring her home."

"Copy that."

A few moments later, I'm pulling back into the garage to a crew with the biggest smiles on their faces. As I unhook myself and hand my steering wheel to Cruz, I finally let what just happened sink in.

Nate is the first to greet me when I rip off my helmet.

"Holy fucking shit, Remi. You have the whole grid running scared right now."

"Yeah?" I chuckle.

"You beat the fastest time here from last season."

"No." I scoff.

Nate shakes his head in awe. "Go chat with Jason and Toni."

For a second, I instinctually lean in for a hug, but then I realize where we are, who he is, and just how many cameras are on us. A bucket of ice-cold water would probably feel less jolting.

"I'll be back," I tell him and rush around him to the back room.

Toni and Jason are waiting for me with the largest smiles I've ever seen on their faces. Hell, I'm not sure I've ever actually seen Jason smile before.

"Fucking stellar first lap," he says.

"You should have heard the radio chatter. Everyone out there didn't know what to do with you!" Toni says, practically bouncing in her seat.

"Thank you. I'm glad it went well. How are things looking with the oil pressure and power reserves? Do I need to try and conserve more before those final turns?" I cut right to the chase. I may be feeling on top of the world, but this was the first lap. There's always room for improvement, and it starts now.

"Cruz will get the oil pressure tested now, and we'll wait to hear from him. The power reserves looked okay. For today, it worked, but if this was a race, you'd be struggling toward the end."

I nod. "Okay. I'll check that out more before the next lap."

"Hey." Toni waits until I look at her. "I admire your need to do better, be better, but don't dismiss how badass that was, okay? There's always more work to do, but make sure you take in that lap and really feel how it felt. Don't brush it aside as anything less than extraordinary."

I swallow past the lump in my throat, trying to keep my tough exterior in place before I well up with tears and make a fool out of myself. It was one lap;

I have a million more to do. While it was a good lap, it doesn't actually mean anything in the grand scheme of things. It's not a race; I don't get points for winning or having the fastest lap. None of it matters. So I need to stay strong and continue at this pace.

Fifteen minutes later, I'm back on the track. This time, I'm taking things slower. I won't do my flying lap until we check out how a few functions in the car are faring. This is the easiest way for the team to determine what still needs to be adjusted and what is looking good. The mechanics have the hardest job, I'm convinced. They have to find flaws on the fly and correct them just as fast. If God forbid I crash, they have to practically rebuild cars overnight. It's a thankless job, really. When I was at the academy, some of my best friends were my mechanics. We formed a bond, and I tried to recognize them whenever I could.

Three leisurely laps later, I get the go-ahead to do another flying lap.

Unlike my first lap, I feel strong from the get-go, less unsure about everything. I'm comfortable in the car. The feel of the steering wheel in my grip is the closest thing to home right now.

Composed.

Strong.

Motivated.

It's a burst of emotion that has me thinking I can actually pull this season off. A sense of rightness that this is where I'm supposed to be.

When I pull back into the garage after another fast lap, I see nothing except Nate. Pride beams on his face.

Knowing I put that look on his face makes me feel ten feet tall.

Maybe I can pull off something incredible this season in more than one way.

Maybe I will find a way to put myself into a position to go after Nate once the season is over.

If he waits that long for me.

Chapter 13
Nate

What an insane couple of weeks. Testing went phenomenal, and we were back in Austin within a couple of days. We've been training Remi to the max ever since.

She continues to impress me at every turn, no matter what I throw her way.

Now, we're a couple of days away from heading to Australia for the first race of the season, but Remi said she had a surprise for me. I'm very, *very* skeptical of her surprises. I feel like I know her well at this point, but who knows, this surprise could be anything from a spa day to a dirty as fuck workout she wants to try.

"Spare me more misery and tell me what the surprise is, you menace," I say with my hand over my heart and a pained look on my face as I enter her office.

Her chuckle has me contorting my facial muscles to stop smiling.

"Are you allergic to any animals?" She arches an eyebrow.

"Cryptic as fuck, woman, and no."

"Perfect. Let's go." She jumps off the couch.

"Absolutely not. I'm not letting you drive me anywhere until you tell me where we're going. You're too excited, which means I should be weary."

"Weary of little ol' me?" Her head tilts.

"Yes." I nod vigorously.

Her laughter makes me almost cave, but the back-and-forth with her is too much fun to let up on.

"I wanted to incorporate some charity work throughout the year, so I found an animal shelter that's really struggling. I figured I'd bring some attention to them, make some social media posts about it, and hopefully drive some traffic their way while we go help out." She shrugs, but I can see how important this is to her. "It's not flashy, but I didn't want to go places that already have a ton of funding."

"I think it's a great idea, Remi," I breathe out.

"Yeah?"

"Absolutely. Let's go."

Twenty minutes later, a chorus of dogs barking greets us as we walk through the doors of a slightly run-down building.

Remi takes the lead, introducing us both to the woman at the front counter. We find out her name is Dee and she runs the place.

"What we could really use help with today is running some of the dogs and then feeding them after," Dee says as we walk back.

"Sounds great. We'll get a workout in today as well." I smile.

The barking only gets louder as we enter the large room filled with kennels. I'm hit by the sheer number of dogs just in this room alone. I know they have other animals here as well.

"Okay, I'm going to give you both a section, and then straight through the back door is the outdoor area. They can be unleashed there, but only take one at a time because some aren't friendly with other animals. This whole section is great with people, though." She guides us to a stretch of ten cages, and my heart clenches in my chest.

"All right, my cute little babies, who's first?" Remi kneels down in front of the closest kennel and holds her hand out to the gate. The mostly black and white dog immediately licks Remi's hand, tail going a mile a minute.

I peek at the name tag. *Murphy.* Fitting.

Remi unhooks the gate, grabbing the leash off the side, and attaches it to his collar.

"Well, hello, Mr. Murphy. You have a wonderful name." I have to practically yell over the other dogs. He tilts his head up to me, like he's really listening. I show him my hand, and he immediately puts his wet nose to my palm.

"Aww, he likes you. What do you say, Murphy, you ready to go play?" At Remi's words, Murphy jumps and spins in place, making us both laugh.

Once we're outside, we let him off the leash. He sniffs around a little before I coax him into racing me. We sprint around the little area, Murphy heartily beating me every single time, before I make Remi do a round.

We repeat this nine more times with the other dogs, but my mind keeps going back to Murphy. I stop by and check on him while Remi takes pictures and makes some videos.

"I've never seen him warm up to someone so fast," one of the workers, Tally, calls from behind me.

"Really? He immediately put his head in my hand when we brought him out earlier."

"We call him Mr. Antisocial." She cocks a brow and can't hide her smile.

Murphy licks my hand when I stop petting him through the gate, so I scratch the top of his head. "Well, I've never been much of an animal person, so maybe you just have to meet the right match." I shrug.

"Ever think about adopting a dog?" she asks.

I scoff. "I travel so much it wouldn't be a good fit."

"Just something to think about," Tally says as she walks away.

Remi takes her place, watching me with a too-keen eye. "I'm almost done, just need to do a video from the front entrance. You have fun?" She's trying hard not to smile, but it's there in the thinning of her lips, the slight crinkle at the side of her eyes.

"More than I anticipated. I'll meet you out front in a second." I wait until she heads toward the door before kneeling down in front of Murphy. "I'll be back, okay? I have to go travel for work, but when I get back to town, we'll hang out again." Murphy licks my hand like he really heard me. "You're the bestest boy," I whisper before dragging myself out of the room.

Remi is only a few feet away from me in the hallway. My cheeks heat at the possibility of her having heard me talk to Murphy like he's a person.

Clearing my throat, I attempt to distract her. "Do you need me to take some video? I can film while you walk and talk."

She whips around so fast she could have given herself whiplash. "Yeah, that'd actually be really helpful."

"I think you'll find I'm quite helpful." The natural flirtiness I always feel around her comes out without permission.

"Is that so? Does your type of 'helpful' include kicking my ass in the gym every day?"

"Absolutely." I grin at her as we walk through the main doors to see Dee in the same spot we found her in hours ago.

"How'd everything go?" she asks.

"Wonderful," Remi says at the same time I say, "So good!"

"That's great to hear. We are so grateful to you for coming out this morning. We're always looking for volunteers or people to adopt." She looks directly at me as she says it.

"Oh, I'm sure we'll be back." Remi interrupts my inner turmoil at leaving Murphy here.

"Of that, I have no doubts. Thanks again, you two," Dee says as we head out front.

We take a quick video. Remi is way more natural in front of the camera than I expected. She talks about volunteering, as well as the many animals that need homes. Once we're back in the car, her shoulders sag, her body deflating, as she lets out a heavy sigh.

"I really want to get eyes on them. There are so many animals there, and they have no space for any new ones that come in."

"I think putting up that video on your socials will help beyond what they—or you, for that matter—can imagine."

"Yeah?"

"Absolutely. The new princess of Formula 1 asking people to come and adopt dogs? Who is saying no to that?"

"I'm not a princess." She almost growls.

"That's not what the media is saying," I say as I throw my hands up in mock surrender.

"Fuck the media. I swear to God, if you or anyone working at Empress calls me a princess, I . . . I'll . . . be very un-princess-like."

"You're cute when you're flustered and angry, Ace." I wink.

"Nate . . ."

"What? I'm not hitting on you! I'm just saying you're always so sure of yourself, and when you're flustered, it shows a different side of you—one I'm sure rarely gets to see the light of day."

"And you'd be right about that." She sighs.

"I promise you will have to deal with worse than ''princess'. I know it's condescending as hell, but the media is viscous, and it will get worse. I don't want dumb nicknames to get into your head because they are not worth it. When they start going after your character and your driving, it's going to be really tough. It's important that we manage things like this from the get-go," I tell her, my tone more serious than she's used to hearing from me.

"I know."

"Honestly, I'd love it if you just avoided social media altogether, but I know that's not realistic."

"Oh, I've already blocked certain words from every platform, so I don't see the more critical pieces. Things get through, obviously, but I know I'm not strong enough to see all the bullshit people say about me every single day."

"Good. Keep that up, and if you see something that you struggle with, call me. I'd rather you call me at two in the morning than sit with it and let it ruminate in your head. That's what makes you have a shitty qualifier or race day. When you are too in your head, it'll affect your performance on the track."

"Yeah," she says quietly.

"It feels nearly impossible to separate it all out, I know. But you are in a position where you will have to. Protect your peace. Protect your mind."

"Yes, Obi Wan," she teases as we pull up to Empress headquarters.

"I mean it, Rem."

"I know. You're just fun to mess with when you get all intense like this." She pulls into the parking spot.

"It's not a game, though." I can feel myself getting irritated that she's not taking it seriously.

"I'm not saying it is." She leans back like she's shocked at my tone.

"Joking and having a good time has their place, but I need you to really take this to heart. Reading all of that shit online is nothing but a bad time. I almost lost Beck's career completely when he decided to read all the articles about him. He almost didn't come back, almost didn't win the championship. If it feels like I'm micromanaging, I probably am, but it's that important to me and for you," I plead.

"Heard. I apologize." She bows her head.

"Thank you. I know I'm a pain in the ass, but there's a method to my madness."

"Yeah, I'm beginning to see that."

The smile she flashes me is breathtaking. It's the one I've only seen a handful of times, and it makes me want to say "fuck it" every single time.

And then she's gone, walking into headquarters without looking back like she didn't just blow yet another hole in my fragile heart.

Chapter 14
Remi

Australia.

I can't believe I'm here, walking around our little section of the grid, checking in on everyone bright and early, as I get ready for Practice 1.

It's officially my first Formula 1 race.

And I'm freaking the fuck out on the inside.

Every doubt, every snarky comment, every person who has given me a judgmental look over the years runs through my head on repeat. Hell, every word my parents have said about my little "hobby" runs like a teleprompter.

A strong grip wraps around my arm and pulls me through engineering to my little office.

"What the hell?" I gasp as the door slams.

Nate looks every bit the protector I've learned him to be.

"I know this is how you like to run things, and I'm not saying you can't go through the whole fucking building and say hi to every single person, but I know you're overthinking right now. We need to fix that before you go back out there."

"Nate, I'm fine."

"No, you aren't. Hold your hand out in front of you."

I do as asked, my hand shaking on its own accord—something that has never happened to me before because you can't have shaky hands in this sport.

"Shit," I whisper.

"Yep. Sit down. I have an idea."

I plop down in one of the chairs while he shifts the other one to sit right in front of me, so we're almost knee to knee.

"Okay, close your eyes and give me your hands. I want to try something. Visualization is extremely effective to refocus yourself on your goals and what you need to accomplish this weekend."

My hands clasp his, his warmth sinking deep into my bones and instantly calming me.

"I want you to think about your bigger goals. What do you want to accomplish in Formula 1?"

Eyes closed, I take a deep breath and really think about it. "Big-time goal is to win a championship. I'd honestly love to win a Constructor's more than a Driver's right now, but any will do." He chuckles at that, making me smile. "Smaller? I'd like to win a race. Just getting here was huge, but I want to actually win."

"Good. That's really good, Remi. Next, I want you to visualize what it will take to get to that particular goal. What will it take for you to win a race?"

"It starts with having a good practice. To me, that means not being the fastest but learning the most. It's about learning my opponent just as much as it is about me racing well. Practice 2 is more of the same, except I need to be in the top five for time. By the time we get to Practice 3, I should be a clear favorite for Qualifiers. I get good rest in between, listen to music, journal, but I focus on what I need to do and what the rest of the grid is doing."

"So good. Then it's Qualifiers," Nate says, his voice low and calm.

"The goal with Qualifiers is pole position, always. It puts me in the best position to do well on race day."

"And what does the day after Qualifiers look like?"

"Dinner. Knowing me, room service. Spend some time visualizing the track and all the angles I need to hit. Then making sure I get at least eight hours of sleep."

"Perfect. What's race day look like when you win?"

My breath catches at his innocent question. He didn't phrase it *if* I win.

"I wake up, get a full meal with lots of protein and carbs. Drink my cappuccino—savor it, really, as it's the only time I can let my mind go completely blank—then head down to the paddock. Make my rounds then have my meeting with my engineers before holing up in here and waiting for the driver's parade. Then, I suit up to do our warm-up lap and anthem . . ."

"And then you lay it all out on the track," he finishes for me.

I take in a deep breath, soaking in the visual: what the Australian track looks like and what crossing the finish line feels like.

"You know, you're pretty good at this," I murmur after a few quiet minutes. My mind is devoid of the noise. In its place is the feel of the track beneath my wheels and rush of speed that always takes my breath away.

"So I've been told." His voice is just as soft as mine as my eyes finally crack open.

"I think I'm ready," I tell him with more surety than I've felt since we got on the plane to get here.

"You definitely are. It's time to get suited up for practice." His smile is supportive, confident. It's exactly what I need right now.

I stand up, heading to the cabinet where I keep my racing suit, and start stripping out of my shirt.

"Woah, I'll just go." Nate stands up abruptly.

"Please." I scoff and roll my eyes. "It's nothing you haven't already seen before. It's just a body, I promise."

"Jesus." He rubs the bridge of his nose before he starts pacing. "It's not just a body, and you fucking know that. This is an exercise in taunting if ever I've seen one."

"Are you saying you can't handle seeing me in my underwear and a sports bra? Not the most flattering, I won't lie." I chuckle as I start with my fire-retardant pants and shirt.

"You know I would drool over you in a fucking Mumu. Don't start with me, Remi." He growls, still pacing and still not looking at me.

I bite my lip, trying to decide how far to push him, before I realize I'm playing with fire. For him and me, honestly.

Quickly sliding on my race suit over my legs up to my waist, I let the arms hang down at my side, leaving me in just my long-sleeve shirt on top. "You can stop freaking out now." The dejected tone isn't lost on either of us if the look he gives me is anything to go by.

"I'm not freaking out. I'm trying to be respectful while also not jumping you because we're blissfully alone right now." The pain on his face as he swipes his hand down it makes me take a step back from teasing him.

It's not fair to either of us to play this game when I was the one who demanded professionalism.

"Right." I inhale one big breath before I blow it out. "Let's go then."

We stare each other down for an extended second before he moves to the side and opens the door.

Moment over. It's time to kick some ass.

***

Practice 1 was horrible. Practice 2 the same day was somehow worse. I was hoping a good night's sleep would help me reset, but the way Practice 3 is shaping up, no dice.

I have one last flying lap to improve things.

"Pick up the pace through Section 2," Jason says in my ear.

"Copy." I grunt, gripping the wheel so tight I know it's counterproductive.

I cross the finish line and do a cooldown lap before he speaks again. "That's twelfth overall. We'll take a look when you get back in."

"Yep."

I couldn't say more if I wanted to right now. I had so much hope yesterday after Nate and I did the whole visualization thing, but it hasn't translated to actual skill on the track. I don't get it either. Testing went so well.

Pulling into the garage, I can see my crew trying hard to keep their faces neutral, but they can't hide the worry. Am I just a dud? Am I really going to make waves this season? It's not just a driver's competition. These men and women work their asses off just as much as I do, and yet their success relies solely on my shoulders at the end of the day.

I've just unhooked my harness, climbed out of the car, and set my helmet on the side shelf harder than necessary when Jason steps in front of me.

"Just give me a minute. Can we do a meeting in, like, thirty minutes?" I ask—no, practically plead with him.

"Absolutely. I'll set it up in the main conference room. Thirty minutes, Remi."

"Heard." I nod and head out the side door, making a beeline to the main building and my office.

Blissfully alone, I slump on the couch and attempt to regulate my breathing. A knock on the door has my whole body clenching up tight, but I assume it's Nate. It's probably a good thing. I need someone to talk me off the ledge.

"Hey." Sawyer's voice is like a jump scare.

"Hi." He might just be the very last person I want to talk to right now, if I'm honest.

"I wanted to stop by and check on you."

"I'm good. Just needed a minute."

"You sure? I watched a couple of your laps, and if you focus on the middle sector and really hug those turns, you'd probably shave a few hundredths off your time." His voice grates on my nerves even though his tone is breezy and calm.

"Yeah, I just need some time," I repeat.

"I'm just saying. I know this is new for you and figured you'd want some tips."

"Heard, Sawyer."

"And Section 2 always trips drivers up."

"Sawyer." I wait him out, making sure he actually hears me this time. "Thanks. I just need a couple of minutes alone."

"Sure. Sure. If you want me to sit in on a simulator test or watch your laps from earlier, let me know."

"Yep. Great." I give him a tight smile.

He goes to turn toward the door but pauses. "Turning down help isn't going to get you far. I thought we had developed a kind of friendship, but if I'm wrong, please feel free to tell me to fuck off."

"Sawyer . . . I just need a minute to myself. If I want advice, you're the first one I'll come to." It doesn't do any good to isolate myself from my teammate. We should be working together as a team, not be at odds with each other—as much as this little display of superiority has irritated the fuck out of me.

"Okay, good."

Another knock at the door makes my skin crawl.

Nate pokes his head in, concern etched on his face, before he spots Sawyer and immediately steps into the room.

They size each other up, and I don't conceal my eyeroll this time.

Apparently, a minute to myself is too much to ask. It has to be interrupted by the never-ending dick measuring contest.

"You okay, Rem?" Nate asks, still firmly focused on Sawyer.

"Peachy," I deadpan.

He finally looks at me, and whatever he sees must be like a flashing sign about my mood.

"She's fine, man," Sawyer says, clearly not reading the room at all.

"Can you both get the fuck out?" I plead. My breathing is getting tight, and the panic is just below the surface.

Nate looks at me with a pained look on his face as Sawyer rolls his eyes and heads out the door. Nate hesitates a minute before following behind, the soft snick and click of the door letting me know I finally get a minute alone.

It takes longer than I'd like to calm down my breathing, to soothe the panic crawling underneath my skin.

My thirty minutes are over far too quickly as my alarm goes off for the engineer meeting.

This first race weekend is not panning out how I thought it would.

***

After a *very* rocky start, I've started to pick up my pace. I placed thirteenth in qualifiers and am currently up to twelfth during the race, so I have some work to do.

With twenty-eight more laps to go, I'm starting to doubt I can push hard enough to get in the points I need.

"2.7 to Alejandro ahead of you," Jason says in my earpiece.

"Copy."

I just came in for a pit stop, so now it's time to prove myself. I keep a steady pace, pushing as much as possible. Now is the time to go all out.

"Good. Decreasing the gap. First chance to pass is Turn 9," Jason says.

"On it." I speed up as I go into Turn 2, gaining on Alejandro and hoping I can pass him.

I keep pushing my pace, and my lines are perfect so that when I enter Turn 9, I pass Alejandro with ease.

"Perfect. Next target is only 1.9 ahead."

"Copy." My heart is pounding, and I try to slow my breathing. I know what to do; I just need to stay focused.

The steady rhythm of my own breaths is the only thing I hear as I gain on Acevedo. He's another rookie, and there's an entirely different competition between us because we're all fighting to stay here. We don't have a track record to fall back on, so every single race for rookies is kill or be killed. Shut up and put up.

I pass him with more difficulty, going too early on one corner before trying again on the next to finally surpass him.

I'm up to tenth with seven laps to go. The driver ahead of me is over seven seconds in front, so unless something happens to him or I pull double the pace out of my ass, I doubt I'll get remotely close to passing him.

The final lap of the race is here, and the adrenaline that's been fueling me the last two hours is quickly dwindling.

"Hold it there, and you'll be in the points."

I don't answer Jason, too focused on making it to the finish line safe. Once I pass the checkered flag, I let out a big sigh and can finally breathe normally again.

"Stellar job for your first race, Remi," Jason says.

"Great job to the crew. You all did a wonderful job today," I say instead of accepting his praise. I'm technically in the points, but one point won't get us very far this season. It's not where I wanted nor expected to be, and it's honestly crushing.

I had a delusional idea that I would podium on my first Formula 1 race and the year would start off as best as any of us could hope. The media would slow up on me, and the rest of the grid would immediately respect me.

That's not what happened at all.

As I pull into the garage after my cooldown lap, I quickly get out of the car, slamming my helmet down on the shelf.

"Great job today." Jason claps me on the back.

I give him a weak smile before heading back to the cooldown room.

Nate wordlessly joins me. He hands me my journal and plops down next to me.

A few minutes pass before I find the words I'm looking for.

"That didn't go how I thought it would." My voice is weak.

"I know."

"I was too confident and hopeful."

"No such thing. This is all new for you. You need that confidence and hope for every race. Don't even think about getting all doomy and gloomy because of one race."

"But I failed."

"You absolutely did not."

"I barely got tenth place." I roll my eyes and huff like a petulant teenager.

"And do you know where the rest of the rookies ended up?"

"No."

"Fifteenth, nineteenth, and did not finish."

"But one point doesn't mean shit in the grand scheme of things."

"One point is more than half the grid got," he counters.

"Your optimism is cramping my current pessimism."

"You'll get used to it." He turns his head and smiles at me.

"I'm disappointed." I sigh.

His finger taps the journal in my lap. "Write about it. I'll give you space, but I just wanted to check in and make sure you weren't drowning in defeat."

"Very astute of you. Guess that's why you're the best, huh?" I give him a sad smile, unable to pull myself out of the gloom just yet.

"Indeed. I'll hold everyone off for half an hour. Write it all down, Ace." He nods to the book in my hand.

I reach out and grab his forearm as he starts to get off the couch, halting his progress.

"Thank you. For knowing what I need before I do."

"Anytime, Rem." He leans down and presses a kiss to the crown of my head before walking out the door.

My eyes close, and I just take a moment to savor the feel of his kiss, no matter how platonic it was.

And then I pick up my pen and write a jumbled mess of thoughts.

Chapter 15

March 16th

A failure.
That's what I currently feel like.
I know Jason and Toni—hell, all of Empress—don't feel that way.
But I feel that way. As my very knowledgeable and not-at-all-annoying trainer told me, I'm being harder on myself than anyone else is. Which is pretty on par with the course.

But fuck, I wanted to do better. I think this whole weekend messed with my head a lot. I flew out here so fucking confident that I would own the whole grid. That I could be a winner in one race. As a fucking rookie.

So damn delusional. I'm mad at myself for not being more realistic. I wanted the cinderella story. I wanted to be great from the word "go" because it feels like so much hinges on me being great.

I know Roni, Sydney, and Daisy won't be upset. And even if they were, they wouldn't project that onto me, especially not after one race. I know, logically, everything I'm feeling is unfounded.

But I can't stop feeling disappointed.

Is this as good as it gets? There are only twenty racers in the entire world. Someone has to win, and someone has to lose. There's very little leeway within the season, so maybe I need to curb my expectations.

The problem is, I don't want to. I've never been the person who just accepts how things look. I want to challenge the status quo. I want to push harder, work more, and see better results.

Maybe I'm not working hard enough. Maybe I need to be in the gym more. Do more simulations. Maybe talk to Nate about how to drastically improve things.

Maybe it's my perfectionism or just insanity, but I don't think I'll be able to handle a race like that all season. I know there are drivers who do it, but I just don't see myself being one of them. Being in the middle of the pack and just being okay with it? No, that's not me.

I know I need to do a debrief with Jason and Toni after this, but I'm dreading it. To see the possible doubt or disappointment in their eyes is going to kill me. I know they had grand thoughts about the race as well, and I didn't deliver. Regardless of what they tell me, I know that's in the back of their minds. It's crushing to have so many people depend on me and fail. After today, I'm sure I'll see fewer smiles. Fewer conversations and less hope.

I fucking hate that. I hate that what I do on the track has the power to affect every single person I work with on a daily basis. But if I were to have won—hell, even podium—I wouldn't be writing this novel currently. I'd be screaming for joy with everyone in the garage.

Shanghai is next week, and that doesn't give me a lot of time to practice in order to get better, but I have to try. I'll get with Nate and see if we can pump up what we're already doing. Maybe it's doing more mental stuff, who knows. But I need more.

I have to do better.

I have to improve.

There's no other option. I won't make it a year in Formula 1 if I don't.

Chapter 16
Nate

We fly to China tomorrow, and I'm struggling with a way to break through to my girl.

Remi took the Australia race to heart. No, that's too tame for how she took it. It crushed every optimistic bone in her body, and I've been fighting like hell since to get her back in the right mindset. She can't go into another race with her head a mess like it is.

It's half of what brought me here. The other half? A connection I couldn't stop thinking about.

"Nate! So good to see you so soon!" Dee says as I walk into the animal shelter Remi and I visited just over a week ago.

"Good to see you too."

"You here to volunteer again?"

"Actually, I was hoping that Murphy was still here."

Her sly smile tells me everyone in this building knew I'd be back for the dog that adopted me before I even realized it.

"He is indeed."

"And what would I need to adopt him?"

"Come back to my office, and we'll get all the paperwork done." She gestures me back, and I spend the next hour filling out paperwork, having a formal interview, and then getting the rundown.

I learn that Murphy was given up because he wasn't in an active household and was tearing up things. No other reason. It makes my blood boil. He does great with people, okay with other animals, but loves to see new places. When I tell Dee about taking him to races, she looks damn near giddy at the prospect of Murphy being a world traveler.

Before I know it, Murphy's in my passenger seat, tail wagging and tongue lolling out of his mouth.

"Shall we go surprise Remi?" I ask him. "You're about to be shocked with your new lifestyle, my man." I chuckle as he seemingly nods at me.

Luckily, Beck came through with an apartment, and I moved in this week in between races. I still have to get a bunch of things for Murphy, but I figured getting Remi out of her routine is more of a priority right now. She's become obsessed with doing more, being better, and damn near working herself to death.

She'll burn out before she can blink at this rate.

I pull up her number as we head toward headquarters.

"Where are you? We're supposed to be in the gym."

"Remi, my favorite overworking squire—"

"Do not call me that."

"Get your ass outside. We're switching things up." I ignore her protests.

"I can't afford to switch things up. I need to do better in China, and we freaking leave tomorrow. Now is not the time to live your carefree life, Nathan Jude Murphy."

"Oh no, not the full government name."

"This is not a game!"

I pull into a parking spot just as she walks out the front door, throwing her hands up in exasperation.

"Remi. Margret—"

"Nate, I swear to God if you call me Margret, I'm firing you. And what the hell is in your car?"

I climb out, pat my leg for Murphy to come, and hang up my phone.

She stops in her tracks, phone still up to her ear, as Murphy bounds over to her, sniffing and licking her hand. Remi finally snaps out of it.

"Oh my gosh, are you on a field trip?" She falls to her knees, dropping her phone behind her to wrap her arms around a wiggling and licking Murphy.

"Nope."

"What do you mean?" she asks, scratching behind both of his ears and smooshing his face to hers. The smile on her face is exactly what I was hoping to see. It's been absent for far too long.

"I adopted him," I say, shoving my hands into my jeans' pockets.

When I look at the two of them together, it's like I can see the future: my woman and my dog, going to another race weekend where Murphy and I watch her kick some ass, then snuggle at the hotel after. Hikes when we're in Austin—hell, anywhere we're at, honestly. I'll find a little doggie pair of headphones for Murph or put him in the cooldown room for the race.

I can see it all, right before my eyes.

"What?" Remi jolts back, plopping her ass onto the ground, as Murphy practically sits on her lap.

"Murph, man, you gotta give her space. She's the kind of person who needs a second with big news."

"You adopted Murphy?" Her tone becomes shriller by the second, and I know I need to stop messing with her.

"Murphy, come," I call him. He's reluctant to leave Remi, and who can blame him, really, but I need her full attention. "I couldn't stop thinking about him when we left. About halfway through the Australian GP, I decided I'd go back and see if he was still there. It just felt like he was supposed to be my buddy. And now you get a built-in snuggle buddy when we travel. Although, if I'm honest, I'd rather that be me, but I know that's not exactly possible." *Jesus, I can't just shut up, can I?*

"Wait, you're bringing him to races?" Her eyes practically bulge out of her head.

"Well, I'm not going to just leave him somewhere for multiple days a week more often than not during the season. Acevado has a dog!" I add, like that's all the explanation I need. If another racer can bring his dog, I should be able to as well.

Murphy nudges my hand, so I pet him while I wait out Remi. I wasn't lying to him. She needs a little space and sometimes a lot of time to process things.

"You would get a dog with the same name as you. Well, it's lucky we use the Empress plane to travel then, isn't it?" She laughs before patting her lap for Murphy to come back. "Welcome to Empress Racing, little man. We're going to have to get you a whole kit. Purple everything," she says. "You'll be the new mascot before you know it. Won't you, good boy?" His tail is going crazy as she talks to him.

My visions of the future only get more vivid.

The three of us lying in bed as the sun rises, planning how the day will go. Murphy excited for the new day while Remi and I kiss until we absolutely have to get up.

"Nate?" Remi's voice sounds far away.

I realize I'm daydreaming.

"Yeah? Yep." I clear my throat and refocus on the two of them getting along like thieves.

"I just asked if we were working out before calling it a day to pack?"

"Oh, of course. You know what? I think we deserve a day off. How about lunch?"

"A day off? Have you lost your mind? Are you sick? You must have a fever." She pops up, stands before me, and places her hand on my forehead. "Nope. No fever."

Murph circles around us, trying to figure out what's happening.

"I'm fine, I promise." I pull her hand off my head. "I just think taking a minute, maybe reflecting on the last week without killing your body, would be a good thing to do today."

"Except, we're on a plane for a million hours tomorrow and could do this then." Her eyebrow arches.

My thumb swipes over her hand. "We could, sure, but you'll be focused on Shanghai and not in the headspace to talk about Australia." Murphy nudges our hands that are still connected, making Remi snatch her hand out of mine.

"I don't like how you know me so well already." She smirks and arches an eyebrow. "So, lunch. Are we finding a place where we can bring the handsome man?"

"Absolutely." But I can't take my eyes off of her.

It's in these little moments, where I get lost in the idea of actually being in a relationship with her, that makes me question everything. Everyone who knows me would think I've lost the plot because I've always been the playboy. There was never a reason to slow down. Why even have a home base when you travel as much as I do?

But it's been different since Japan last year. The idea of traveling from city to city with no connections rings . . . hollow now. It's why I have an apartment for the first time in damn near a decade. Why I adopted a dog because his big brown eyes called to me. And why, whenever Remi is around, my head always goes to images of a life I never thought I'd want.

I turn to go back to my car when she halts my progress. "It's cute you think I'm letting you drive."

"But Murphy . . ." I gesture to the mutt between us.

"Will love going fast in a badass car. Let's go." She twirls her keys around her finger as Murphy follows her dutifully.

Geez, whose dog is he anyway?

I find us a spot not too far away that has outdoor seating so we can bring along the newest edition to the Murphy family.

"So, Mr. All-Knowing, lay it on me," Remi says once we've ordered.

"How are you feeling about Australia?" I ask simply.

She sighs, dropping her hand down so she can pet Murphy. "I think I'm okay with it. I mean, I'm not because I expected better, but I think I'm past the bitter disappointment, ya know? I realize it was unrealistic to go into the race thinking I was going to podium when it was literally my first Formula 1 race."

"Having ambition isn't unrealistic. I think you just set a hard goal and aren't used to the disappointment of not achieving it."

"So I'm learning. Do you think I'll just always be like this? Setting higher and higher goals because I'm used to winning, used to breaking down barriers? At some point, it's all got to break, right? At some point, there isn't any higher to go," she muses.

"I think you see the world very black and white currently. You see the levels of racing, and you ask yourself how you can get to the next level. You happen to have a natural talent that has caught the attention of the right people and made that jump a hell of a lot easier—and faster, for that matter—but I also think, at some point, your priorities will change. It's not like you'll be racing for another thirty years. I mean, you'll need an exit plan eventually. An idea of what you want to do with the rest of your life."

Our food gets delivered, and my words hang thick in the air between us. Oddly enough, they apply heavily to me as well. How long do I keep this up? How long until I realize all the travel and fast lifestyle aren't all they're cracked up to be? And what the fuck do I do with my life when I close this chapter?

Whatever Remi wants to do.

It's a very clear answer from the corner of my brain I try to avoid getting lost in. My priorities have already changed. Murphy is a testament to that. They changed the second I read the report card she left on the counter in Japan. I just don't have the answers for what happens after all of this is over.

There's a very real possibility that the depth of her desire for me doesn't run as deep as mine does. It would crush the fuck out of me, but I would respect her decision.

Jesus, Nate, you're getting way ahead of yourself.

"What if I need that back-up plan sooner rather than later?" Her small voice calls out to me.

"You won't," I say vehemently. "It may feel like that now, but it won't always. You have too much skill to need that plan any time soon. Which is why I wanted to do lunch. Talking about how you're feeling a few days *after* a disappointment, once you've had time to sit with it, is important to keep you level. Not processing the loss, or failure in your eyes, just bottles up. It doesn't take much for that bottle to explode when you're in a high-stress career."

"You sure you aren't a psychologist?" Her head tilts.

"Nope. I do have a psych degree, though."

"Seriously?" She pops a french fry in her mouth.

"Don't sound so shocked." I chuckle. "I've always loved the field, but it's extremely hard to do anything with a bachelor's degree, so I got creative. Ran into the right people and somehow landed as Beck's trainer, which turned into so much more."

"Your life is so interesting."

Laughter bursts from my chest. "It really isn't."

"Lies. You just magically land Beck, a Formula 1 driver, as a client and then he ends up winning a championship? There's way more to the story."

There is, but I'm not willing to get into it. Beck doesn't even know all the details.

She sighs once she realizes I won't tell her more.

"Fine, keep your secrets."

"I promise it's not thrilling. When did you realize you wanted to be one of the elite twenty?" I ask, taking a huge bite of my sandwich.

"I always loved racing of any kind—karting, bikes. It didn't matter. If it went fast, I wanted to do it and I wanted to be the best. I don't know if you know this about me, but I'm highly competitive." She winks, making me laugh. "I started watching everything I could get my hands on, but Formula 1 is the best of the best. I remember when I was maybe sixteen, I was karting in senior class and a scout was there. He pulled me aside and started talking to me about Formula 4 but was concerned because I was a girl. I made it my mission right then and there to break every racing barrier I could. If a scout was telling me I was good enough and it was just about my gender, then I was going to do everything I could to succeed and prove the haters wrong."

Every single day, I find something new to be in awe of with this woman.

"You were sixteen?"

"Yep. He actually passed on signing me for that reason. It's fueled a lot of my ambition." She laughs, but I don't join her.

"What a fucking prick. Write his name down."

She tilts her head as she bites another fry. "Someone's protective. It was thirteen years ago, Nate. I did just fine."

"Doesn't matter. He shouldn't be scouting if he's going to deter girls like that. What a fucking joke."

"I've gotten to throw the big 'fuck you' at him, I promise. It was satisfying as hell too, so no need to chase him down and make him pay, Daredevil."

"Did you just make a Marvel reference?" Scratch that, every hour, I learn something that amazes me.

"Thank God you got it, or else we may not be able to be friends."

"What about your family, are they supportive?" She doesn't talk about them ever, so I'm curious if this is a point of support or contention.

"Nope." She pops the P.

"Care to elaborate?"

"My older sister and brother are a surgeon and high-profile lawyer, respectively. It's what my parents pushed all of us to do, and I was the lone sibling who wanted nothing to do with any of it. I was seen as the lazy one. The one who wanted to go the easy route and not work hard for anything." She pauses to take a sip of water. "We clearly don't have the best of relationships."

"And they still don't recognize your talent?"

"God no. If anything, since I signed with Empress, they've gotten more standoffish. I barely hear from them, and I never hear from my siblings. Honestly, it's better this way. I gave up on them a long time ago when I realized it was only hurting me privately and professionally."

"I'm sorry."

"Don't be. Some families are just that way. I try to create a new one with whatever team I'm with. They're usually better people, who actually like me."

"Doesn't make it easier. You can push it all down and move forward, but the hurt will always be there."

"Very true. What about you? Is your family supportive?"

I clear my throat. "I don't have a family." Murphy shifts his attention to me, placing his head on my leg for support like he knew I would need it. "My mom left my dad when I was a couple of weeks old. Then my dad was in an accident at work when I was eight. Died on the spot, and I spent the rest of my childhood in foster care."

"Holy shit, Nate, I'm so sorry."

"I appreciate that." I nod. It's always strange telling people where I come from. It usually makes them uncomfortable as hell, but for me, it's just a fact of my life. I don't know any other way. I lived and have succeeded for the most part. I'd like to think my dad would be proud, although he'd probably slap me upside the head for being so wild the past few years.

The atmosphere has turned somber, and there's no recovering it here. I flag down the waiter to pay, and in a matter of minutes, we're walking back to Remi's car.

"I'm sorry I asked," she says as we start the drive back to headquarters.

"I'm not. I've come to terms with it. It just tends to make all other happy conversation cease, so I apologize for bringing the mood down."

"I'm glad I got to learn more about you, though. It sometimes feels like I'm in a fishbowl and all the observation is on me 24/7."

"Well, I'm a mostly open book. Tit for Tat. Ask away whenever you feel like you need a break from all the focus."

"You are nothing like I thought you'd be, Nate Murphy."

I won't tell her I'm only this way with her. Some secrets have to be kept.

Chapter 17
Remi

Anxiety squeezes my chest as we land in Japan.

It's not about the race.

It's not about how much of a struggle this season has been so far.

Hell, it's not even about the fact that I'm waiting to hear back about an apartment in Austin.

No. It's about the fact that I'll be in Japan, in the same fucking hotel as last year on that fateful night that introduced Nate into my life.

All I can think about is how it felt to be with him. How good the sex was. *God, the sex.* I'd be lying if I said that the night wasn't playing on repeat in my head the entire flight over. Which is a problem, considering I flew over *with* Nate.

"Hey, you've got this," Nate says as he stands up to grab his bag. Murphy follows behind him, tongue lolling out of his mouth, tag wagging at a steady pace.

"Yeah. I feel good about tomorrow. I just need a good night's sleep before practice," I lie. No need for him to know what I'm really thinking about.

"You should be free and clear after talking to the media, so why don't you just order room service tonight and then crash early?"

"That's a good plan," I say as I stand up, my tone flat and staring off into space.

"Hey, you okay? Really?" He walks up behind me, leaning around to duck down and look me in the eyes.

"Just stressed."

"Do you want to try some meditation before bed tonight? I can stop by your room and do a guided one. Murphy won't even try to sit in your lap this time.

Isn't that right, Murph?"

I hear Murphy's tail slap-slap-slap against the airplane seats.

"I don't know, a Murphy cuddle might be a good option too." I smile down at the dog that's stolen both of our hearts.

"What am I? Chopped liver? No cuddling for Nate?"

"Talking in the third person generally gets you kicked out of the cuddle session." I smile up at him.

The cackle of energy between us cracks to life. It's like there's a television in between us, replaying that night a year ago. The hot kisses, the trail of fingertips against each other's skin. I can see in his eyes that it's all playing out in his mind like a movie, just like it is in mine.

"Nate . . ." I breathe out.

"I know. God, I fucking know, Remi, but damn, you can't blame me." Pain is laced in every single one of his words.

"We can't . . . we can't repeat that," I whisper.

"I know." His pinkie hooks into mine. "It'll be fine after this race." He doesn't believe that as much as I don't.

"Right. After this race." My words are too breathy.

His eyes shift between mine, and I count the seconds. I can't decide if I want him to kiss me or take a giant step back from this whole thing.

Two seconds turns into five. I'm about to step into him when he takes one back, severing the moment.

"I'm sorry."

"No, you're fine. That was good." I step back too, trying to get as much distance as possible since I was literally a second away from caving.

I grab my bag and turn to exit the jet. It's safer this way. But it's also painful as hell to not have him again.

***

Dinner has been eaten, and now I'm waiting for Nate to come over to my suite so we can meditate before bed.

I agreed because I'm a glutton for punishment, but I'm also willing to do anything to have a good race at this point too. It may still be early in the season, but I've got to start seeing better results.

Which means more time with Nate . . . whom I definitely don't want to have sex with again.

Sighing, I drop my head back and stare at the ceiling, trying to banish all thoughts of how hot Nate is from my mind. Maybe if I just forget how his body looks naked, things will just magically get easier.

Don't kid yourself. That body will forever be in your memory. Who will you think about when you use your vibrator?

I have a point; it would be sad to never get off to visions of Nate again.

A knock at the door interrupts my inner musings, and thank God for that because one more second of conversing with myself, and I might scream.

"Hi." I open the door to Nate wearing basketball shorts and a loose-fitting tank top. A tank top that shows off his colorful sleeves that I traced all night long a year ago.

"Hi."

That fucking tension from the plane is still there in full force. Maybe it's because we're back at the scene of the crime, or maybe it's just been simmering below the surface since the start of the season. Who knows. What I do know is that I can't cave, no matter how much I desperately want to.

Murphy breaks the tension, luckily, by trotting in and headbutting my leg for some pets.

"Hi, my love," I say, bending down and scratching both of his ears.

"Well then, let's set up," Nate says, stepping into my room and letting the door shut.

I'm still petting Murphy as he drops the bag that has the yoga mats in it and starts moving furniture around to fit both of us in the space. I could help him, but loving on his dog while watching his arms flex as he moves is much more entertaining for me.

"You done checking me out?" he asks as she straightens up and lays out the mats.

I open my mouth a few times like a fish out of water before clearing my throat. "Umm, I was just seeing where you were putting all the . . . all the, um, furniture," I stumble through my lie.

"Sure. Let's do this." He sits down on one of the mats, and Murphy goes to him immediately. I follow behind, so confused by everything I'm currently feeling. How the hell do I stop looking at Nate like I'm attracted to him? How do I stop *being* attracted to someone?

A heavy sigh escapes me as Nate breezes right over my clear turmoil.

"Okay. Begin to relax your body by first tensing a muscle group and then releasing to create a feeling of relaxation. Start with your arms. Close your hands into tight fists and tense your hands and arms . . . all the way up to your shoulders. Hold for a five count."

I sink into the flow of the meditation. We work through my whole body and work on breath control for God knows how long. But I start to relax and forget about the stress.

"Tell me about a time when you felt confident."

I don't think about my response; I just let the stream of consciousness fly. "Winning the academy. It felt like I had all the tools, and it was just . . . *easy*. Last year in Japan. You made me feel confident. I've never felt that way with a man ever." My voice gets softer as I talk.

He clears his throat, but it doesn't pull me out of the meditation.

"And a time when you didn't feel confident? Where you felt like you were failing?"

"This whole season. Formula 1 in general. Everything feels hard."

"Explain how it feels hard. Just work through it."

"Nothing comes easily. It feels like I need ten more hours a day to make a dent in the progress. Everything I do doesn't seem to affect my performance, and I'm at a loss as to how to fix it."

"What if it's not a problem to fix?"

"What?" My eyes slowly open to find Nate staring at me with a look I can't figure out.

"What if this isn't a problem to fix? What if it's a matter of letting go of the control? If you're holding the reins too tightly, it might be hindering your progress."

"But . . ." I can't compute his words.

"This is how you've always done things, and it's worked out. You said things have always been easy. Now, you're faced with something that isn't coming easily to you. Change the process. You're the kind of person who doesn't like to fail, so you avoid it at all costs. If you aren't good at something, you just don't put yourself in a situation where people see you fail. People only see you succeed. It's a high for you."

I blink at him, finally hearing him.

"Change takes time. Changing how you train, how the car works for you, it all takes time. Which you hate. You want instant change, instant progress, but it doesn't work like that here. You've got to slow down."

His voice is still so soothing that it reaches the deepest recesses of my mind, the part that is vulnerable and weak. He's right. I like instant gratification too much. I'm scared to death of failure, and I put too much pressure on myself.

But I can't be any other way. I don't know *how* to be any other way.

"How?" I croak.

"That's what we're trying to figure out. Journaling seems to be working well for you, but maybe we need to do more."

"Should I start weekly therapy? Journal more? Spend more time at the gym?" I offer, desperate to find a solution.

"Let me worry about that. I'll come up with some options to try over the coming weeks, but I need you to be patient. Nothing is a quick fix." He scoots so he's sitting right in front of me, knee to knee. "I need you to trust that I will get you there." He grabs my hands and holds them between us. "I will not let you fail." He leans into me, and our foreheads almost touch. "You don't have to be afraid to be vulnerable. Show it all to me, Rem. I can take it and protect it."

His words touch a part of me that causes my thoughts to stop altogether—something he only seems to be able to produce. Thoughts about racing, about winning and losing, disappear and all I see is Nate in front of me.

A man who is willing to dig deep, to support me in all my failures. A man who continually thinks of new things for me to try. A man whose mission is to guide me to success, all the while keeping me sane.

So, I lean forward until our noses touch. I wait a brief moment to see if he has any objections, but when he doesn't move . . . I kiss him.

It starts as small pecks to one corner of his mouth, eventually moving to the other side. Then he swipes his tongue across his bottom lip, and any sense of restraint either of us had goes out the window. He drops my hands and threads them through my hair, pulling me closer. I'm up on my knees without even realizing it, pushing my tongue past his lips and tangling it with his. It's not a battle for dominance; it's a dance of alike souls trying to find their way.

It's intoxicating. Addicting.

Next thing I know, I'm straddling his lap. Both of us are too lost in each other to register the line we've just crossed.

We make out like we're behind the bleachers at a high school football game. It could be minutes; it could be hours. Time loses all meaning while I'm kissing Nate Murphy.

Then a wet tongue laps across my cheek. I jolt away from Nate to see Murphy hovering by us, panting his hot breath toward my face and wagging his tail. I slump against Nate's body, pressing my head into his shoulder.

"We shouldn't have done that," I murmur.

"I'm not apologizing."

I sigh. Clearly, we aren't over this mutual attraction, and that's an issue.

"Whatever you are about to say, just don't. I'm not quitting; you're not firing me. I'm not going anywhere, Rem. I can be professional."

"Except for the part where we just made out."

"*You* started that one. Not that I'm not a willing participant. I've restrained myself this entire time, and I can continue to do so."

What I should say is that the risk is too great. How long before both of our restraints are tested again? How long until we slip up and it affects my job? How long until we both screw up and I lose everything I've worked for, hell, Nate too?

Instead, I say, "Let's just keep things to ourselves. No one needs to know we've done anything with each other. And we can't let it happen again."

I feel him tense beneath me, and I know he's thinking the same thing I am. I've never forgotten what we did last year, and I sure as hell won't forget about this make-out session. But this is what has to be said. It's just between us, and if we can keep things separated, then there's nothing to worry about.

I just need to find a way to push everything outside of Trainer Nate way down deep in my head, so I don't slip up again.

"Whatever you need, Remi," he whispers.

His words feel like a promise tattooed on our skin. He'll do whatever I need, no matter if it breaks him in the end.

And I don't know if I can live with that.

Chapter 18
Nate

After a twelfth-place finish in China and a seventh-place finish in Japan, Remi is still wound tighter than a spring.

That's why I'm knocking on her hotel room door with Murph at my side on a Wednesday evening, holding a bag of takeout.

"Did I miss a meeting?" Remi asks, eyes wide as she opens the door.

"Nope. I did bring fresh food, though, because I know you haven't eaten the one I put in your fridge earlier." Her guilty look lets me know I'm correct in my assumption.

Her reluctant eyes move down to Murph before she sighs and holds the door open for us. It's been like this since we returned from Japan. That kiss drove a wedge between us. We may not act like it did, but it's in every conversation. Every time we are around each other, there's this hint of holding back. Like we can't be our full selves around each other anymore because God forbid we kiss again. I get it, I do, but I can't stand the distance.

I follow her in, shutting the door behind me, and Murph follows her to the kitchen.

"I also brought something for us to do," I call out.

"Like a workout? Meditation?"

"No, like fun." I chuckle. She told me she didn't have hobbies all that long ago, that her sole focus was on driving, and I vowed to do something about that. Well, here I am, with a crazy idea that might blow up in my face.

But I have to try.

"Fun," she says, deadpan, as she grabs bottles of water from the refrigerator. "I don't know what that word means."

"Ain't that the damn truth," I mutter.

"I'm not that bad." She reaches for the bag and unloads all of the Mexican food I brought.

I don't respond; instead, I arch my eyebrow and snap my finger at Murphy to go lie down on his bed. Remi insisted that he needed one in her hotel room too. She's damn near stolen my dog at this point.

"I'm not," she says with more outrage.

"I'm not saying anything."

"Your face says everything." Her eyes narrow at me.

"Just eat your damn food. You don't need to fight me on every single thing, Ace. Having a little fun won't kill you."

She's quiet, unmoving. Her stillness makes me look up at her in question.

"Is this a new way to try to get me out of my head? A way to see if I can race better?" Her voice is low, shaky, like she truly believes she isn't doing incredible things.

I knew this, but it doesn't hurt my chest, my *heart*, any less to hear it.

"No, Rem. I just wanted to take a break from everything. I remember you saying you didn't have hobbies, and mine are extreme sports, so I thought I'd find something that's a little more travel friendly . . . for all the flights," I add, fumbling around my thought process like I've never talked to a woman before.

Her eyes shift between mine before she seems to accept there is no ulterior motive.

"So, tacos and what?" she asks, taking a seat next to me.

"And a card game."

"Like Solitaire?"

"No, like a . . . get-to-know-you game of sorts." I take a bite of my burrito, in hopes I don't have to explain that I went on the hunt for a game that would help us get to know each other while also helping me get her out of her head for a second. If it also means I get to learn more about the woman I'm completely gone for, who am I to complain?

"You're being cryptic again."

"Because I feel like you're going to shut down the idea of fun the more I talk about it."

"I let you in, didn't I?"

"I think you only let me in because I brought Murph." At his name being said, his head pops up off his pillow.

"He does lessen the blow." She purses her lips together to hold back her smile.

"Eat."

"Yes, sir."

I suck in a breath at the term; her smile fades fast. That sizzle that's always between us flairs to life. I have to shove a huge bite of burrito in my mouth to stop something stupid from coming out of it.

Dinner is a silent affair after that. I clean up once we're done, while Remi and Murph go sit on the floor in the living room.

"Pricetitution?" she yells from the floor.

"You have to say how much money it would take for you to do random, weird, and altogether absurd things," I explain as I join them.

"That seems . . . random."

I shrug, not wanting to get into how much research I did to find something that wouldn't give away my incessant need to know more about her.

"All right, let's tuck in." She opens up the package, reading the directions before laying it all out properly. She likes things just so, but I already knew that about her.

"Okay, you go first," she says.

"How much money would it take for you to get a tattoo of the last thing you ate?" I ask with a giant smile.

"Umm, like, a million dollars. I'm not getting a tattoo of tacos on me. That's like saying 'I love pussies, all are welcome'."

I wheeze and pound at my chest to try to get out the laughter that's caught up with my shock at her words.

"And I'm the one with the dirty mind. Jesus." I cough, finally calming down.

"Like that wasn't the first thing you thought of." She scoffs.

"Umm, it wasn't at all."

"Whatever." She rolls her eyes before doing hers. "How much would it take for you to delete all of your social media accounts?"

"Zero. I don't have any."

"What?"

"I don't have any. If I get sent things, it's usually from the PR team, so there's no need for me to waste a bunch of time on social media. My job is to help whomever I'm working with. Getting inundated with shitty articles or headlines about them hinders my ability to help them. It was just easier to never have it at all. That was made all the clearer when Beck had his meltdown."

"I had no clue, but that's . . . smart. I wish I could just disconnect sometimes."

"Put one of those apps on your phone that shuts down your access during allotted times. It really helps." I shrug.

"I can do that."

The next several are easy ones, then there are some outrageous ones that have Remi laughing so hard she rolls over with tears streaming down her face, and Murphy licks them off, which makes her laugh harder.

"Oh my God, I can't breathe," she says as she finally sits up.

"Okay, my turn." I pick up a card, but I don't read what's on the card. Instead, I ask something that's been on my mind since we started this. "How much money would it take for you to give up your career if it wasn't fulfilling anymore?"

She stops dead in her tracks and looks at me. "I— Does it really say that?"

"Just answer it, Rem." I sigh. She knows this isn't one of the cards. It's way too specific.

"I don't think it would take a lot of money at all. I think the harder part would be me actually recognizing that racing wasn't fulfilling anymore. I don't see any of what I do objectively at all. I just race to be better, to do better."

I nod, still digesting her answer, when she speaks again.

"How much money would it take to say 'fuck it' and deal with the fallout of us being together?" she whispers.

"Rem . . ."

"Just answer it. I know it's stupid."

"It isn't stupid. It's just . . . reckless. And zero. It would take nothing for me to say 'fuck it'."

My truth hangs between us, this living thing that we can't do anything about right now. Because our circumstances haven't changed. She still feels like she has so much to prove in Formula 1, and I'll never be the person to get in her way.

Chapter 19
Remi

Last two finishes:

Bahrain Grand Prix - 9th

Saudi Arabian Grand Prix - 7th

"Remi, have a seat. It's so good to see you," Toni says as I step into her office.

It's been almost two months since the start of the season, and while I have improved slightly, I'm still not placing where I'd like to be during races. A couple of seventh places aren't going to cut it the entire season.

"Oh, you know," I answer. I can't even pretend to feel happy about how my start of the season is going, especially when it's not a secret.

"You're doing great. I know you're hard on yourself but be proud. It's still early in the season, and no one is running away with it yet."

"I know. I just expected more, especially by now."

"And what does Nate say?"

My head shoots up at her question, making her eyebrow arch and a sly smile tilt her lips.

"Well, that is very interesting," she murmurs.

"What's interesting?"

"Oh, nothing. What's Nate saying about how you're feeling?"

"That I'm holding too high of expectations on myself. That I'm used to winning and being the best, and it's difficult for me to be—in my words—losing."

"But you don't agree?"

"I mean, I do. It's just not as easy to get out of that mindset."

"I don't think anyone wants you out of the winning mindset. I know we sure as hell don't." She chuckles. "But if being in your head is affecting your performance, then it's something to look at. I'm glad you have him to recognize all of this with you."

"Yeah, he's pretty awesome with that. So, what's on the agenda for Miami? Anything new?" I ask, changing the subject. She already suspects something, and if we continue down this line of conversation, I'm sure I'll say something or my face will give away that something else has gone on between Nate and me.

"Actually, yes. This sprung up at the last minute. Sydney got the invitation but forgot about it. There's a charity gala—"

"Another one?" *I didn't realize that dressing up and schmoozing would be more of my job than actually racing.*

"Yes. This one is a good one, I promise. It's for girls in sports. It raises a ton of money to provide scholarships equal to their male counterparts. No sport is off limits for the foundation."

A smile blooms on my face. "Amazing! Is it the ShePlay Foundation?"

"It is!" Toni's face lights up with a smile that reaches her eyes.

I take back all the annoyed thoughts I was thinking a moment ago. "They funded my karting for a couple of years. I'd absolutely love to go."

"Perfect. The ticket is you plus one. Do you think you're going to bring anyone?" She picks up a pen and goes to her checklist.

"Umm, probably not."

"You could take Sawyer again," she says without looking up.

"God no," I say without thinking then cringe. "I just mean I don't think he would enjoy this gala, and I really don't want him to think we're anything more than teammates."

"Oh. Well, I wouldn't want to waste the ticket, but none of us can go."

"Nate can go," I blurt out, immediately mortified that I basically just set us up on a very fancy date after we've set clear boundaries about only being work colleagues.

"He'd really enjoy that, I think." There's a twinkle in her eye that I refuse to acknowledge right now. Not when I have to figure out how to see Nathan *freaking* Murphy in a tux again in a couple of days without drooling.

"Well then, I suppose we'll see you in Miami on Wednesday. I've got a little to wrap up today, and then Felix and I are heading out early to enjoy the beach." She actually blushes, and I can barely stand how cute the two of them are together. It makes me giddy for her. And jealous that I can't have that too. "Oh, and happy moving day!"

"That sounds wonderful, and thank you. I'm excited to finally not live out of a hotel room." I smile. "Well, don't let me keep you, and I'll see you in a couple of days."

I leave, my mind rushing between the upcoming race and my date with Nate. *No, stop calling it a date, and it won't be so ridiculously overwhelming.* Fake date . . . Sure, that's better.

I sprint down to the gym in hopes that it's empty and I can run off some of my nervous energy before Nate gets here. On race weeks, when I have my weekly meetings with Toni early, Nate usually shows up with lunch, and then we get to work. So, I may catch a break.

"Woah, where's the fire?" Hands clasp around my shoulders, stopping me in my tracks.

Apparently, my luck is absolute shit. Might explain my driving, honestly.

"Oh, umm . . ." I stall, coming up with nothing to explain why I'm panicking. "I just wanted to get a run in."

Nate looks down at me with skepticism. "You hate running."

Shit.

"Maybe I decided to run a marathon," I snark.

"Your contract says you can't during the season."

"Goddammit, Nate. Let me have my freakout without an explanation really quick."

He releases me and holds his hands up in surrender. "Fair enough. I'll just go check in with Beck. Come find me when you're done freaking out." He doesn't say it sarcastically; he says it in his supportive way that undoes me.

I sigh and let my shoulders sag, thankful that I have time to come up with a reason why I blurted his name and now he's obligated to a night out with me when he didn't sign up for that. He's just my trainer.

And you just picture him naked every time you work out.

Jesus, maybe I need to get laid. That might work him out of my brain. I know that damn make-out session in Japan did not help any of my conflicting thoughts.

Or maybe you can fuck him again . . . Just saying.

Dear God, is there an off switch for my inner-hoe voice?

A run. That will definitely clear my head. Nate's right; I do hate running, but the struggle I usually feel while doing it may help me clear my head and come up with a solution.

Twenty minutes later, I've sprinted full out three times and can barely breathe. I collapsed on the ground an unknown number of minutes ago, and that's exactly how Nate finds me.

"Must have been a really bad meeting if you're sprinting willingly." He peers down at me, blocking the fluorescent lighting.

"Ughhhh, I don't want to talk about it, but I have to tell you anyway," I moan.

"That's not cryptic at all. Did you fire me?"

"What? No."

"Whew, I genuinely couldn't tell by all of this." His hand waves in my general direction.

"Where's Murphy? I need my support dog to deal with you right now."

"First off, he's my dog. Second, just tell me. It can't be nearly as bad as you think it is."

I stare at him, his navy eyes blazing as they look at me in question.

"Fine." I sigh. "Toni gave me two tickets to a fundraising gala in Miami, and I may have accidentally said you would be my plus one." I close my eyes tight, dreading his response. Hell, even the look on his face.

There is a very long pause before I peek through one of my eyelids to find him staring at me with a look I can't decipher.

"Do you want me to go with you?"

"I mean, out of all of my options—and there's really only, like, two options—I'd take you over all of them any day of the week," I say without thought.

"But do you actually want to go with me?"

The seriousness of his question makes my brain stop completely and give him a real answer for once. Not one that I overthink in an attempt to hide my attraction to him and keep him at arm's length.

"Yes."

"Then send me the details, and I'll be there."

I perk up, just a little. "Really? You aren't pissed I just volunteered you to wear a monkey suit and deal with all the people you won't want to talk to?"

"Not pissed at all. If you want me to go, I'll happily do far more than wear a monkey suit."

I stare at him, lost in the vision of what he looked like at Daisy and Luka's gala.

"I mean, I look fucking amazing in a tux, so any excuse to wear one, honestly." He shrugs. The cocky words instantly break the tension.

All the doubts I had skitter away as a giggle erupts from my chest. Once I start, I can't stop. The giggle turns into tears leaking down the side of my face and me clutching my stomach in a poor attempt to stop.

"Holy hell, did I break you? What is happening?" Nate plops down next to me, concern written all over his face.

"I"—I heave through a gasp as I try to calm down—"have no clue." The giggles finally slow down. My arms lay out beside me as I catch my breath.

"I gotta be honest, whatever that just was has me worried about you. You okay? Need to talk about anything?"

"Nope." I wipe the remaining tears from my face.

"Remi . . ."

"I'm just stressed out. I thought things would be better on the racing front, and then all these events I didn't expect added to my schedule is a lot. Add in trying to move today and tomorrow before we leave for Miami, and I think I'm just overwhelmed." It all comes rushing out.

"Why aren't you letting me help you move? Hell, hire movers. You can't have that much shit right now. The goal is to take things off your plate, not add a shit-ton onto it. You should only be worrying about racing."

His lecture nags at the part of me that wants to prove everyone wrong. Doesn't matter that what he says is logical, it's just ingrained in me that I need to prove I can do it all.

"I can handle it, Nate."

"Can you? Because this was a pretty clear display that handling it all has you on a very thin edge."

"You don't have to analyze every single move I make, you know. You're supposed to be my trainer and my support, not my therapist or parent."

"That's not fair, Rem."

I sigh. "I know. *Shit.* I know. I'm getting defensive because I know you're right."

"So let me help you. We were going to do a light work out anyway."

"I don't know . . . Maybe I just need a break. Can we call my neurotic choice to sprint my workout?"

"If you add in fifteen minutes of neck work, I will." He looks over at me, leaning back onto his hands, so calm and attentive.

It catches me off guard. I don't know if I've ever had a man care about my wellbeing as much as Nate does, and that includes the very small number of boyfriends I've had.

We stare at each other for a minute, that ever-present pull to him drawing me in like someone is pulling the string. Then he clears his throat, and the moment is over. Nate jumps to his feet, holding his hand out to help me up. I take one more deep breath before taking his hand and let him pull me to my feet.

"Deal."

***

An hour later, I'm standing in my empty apartment in awe. It's nicer than anywhere I've ever lived by myself, and it almost feels unreal that this is my life.

I've made it.

I'm a Formula 1 driver with a gorgeous apartment that overlooks Lake Travis.

The only thing missing is a partner. But as I discovered earlier, I may not have the bandwidth to deal with that right now. Besides, the only man I'd want is currently off limits.

"Do you have furniture?" Daisy asks as she places baby Evelin on the floor on a thick blanket she brought. Sydney walks in behind her.

"Umm, very little. Just a bed set. It should be here within the next half an hour. I probably need to shop." I cringe.

"Well, you're in luck because we bought you a cute little sectional as a housewarming present," Sydney says, like it's a bottle of wine and not an entire fucking couch.

"What?"

"We figured you didn't have a lot of furniture, given how much you've moved around, and thought this would be the perfect present from your Empress family," Daisy adds in.

"You got me a whole couch?" Tears well up at how thoughtful these women are. I've never had girlfriends. I don't work in a field where they are readily available unless they're the girlfriends of the other drivers. I've never connected to women. But these three? They go out of their way all the time to make sure I know I'm included in their group.

"Oh Lord, don't cry. My hormones are still so jacked up that I'll start up," Daisy says, waving her hand in front of her face to stop the tears.

"Sorry. It's just so . . . unexpected. Thank you so much."

"Group hug!" Daisy yells, and we all laugh as we come together. Evelin babbles as we huddle above her.

"Oh no. We interrupted the female bonding," a male voice says from my doorway.

I spring back and am shocked to find Beck and Luka at my door.

"Do not be jealous of the female bonding, Luka," Daisy scolds but with a smile on her face.

"What are you guys doing here?" I ask, shocked at yet another level of support I've never had before.

"This guy"—Beck leans to the side as Nate walks up to the doorway, stopping my heart in its tracks—"said you were moving and didn't have help."

I look at Nate and see worry in his eyes. "You called them to come help me?" My voice is small and cracks a little, betraying the emotions swirling around my heart.

He shrugs. "No big deal, Rem. You shouldn't have to stress out about stuff like this. I actually called Beck to yell at him for not paying for a mover for you, and it kind of snowballed from there."

"We offered!" Sydney throws her hands up.

I smile over at her. "When I refused, it was because I didn't have a lot of things, not because I thought all of you would show up and help."

"You can still hire movers for three things, Remi." Luka laughs.

The men walk into the space, and Beck gives Nate a funny look that I can't read into.

"The couch is getting delivered in the next hour, so all we have is what's in your car and the bed, yes?" Sydney asks.

"Should be it." I nod.

Beck clears his throat. "There's also an office setup coming in about an hour."

"What?" I screech.

"We can't let the women have all the fun," Luka says, bending down to pick up his daughter. "No, we can't. You are already taking over Empress, so we had to chip in too, didn't we, Ev?" he says to Evelin in a baby voice.

"You guys . . ." I gulp, trying to find the words.

Nate walks over to me, eyes serious. "Just nod and take the gifts, okay? You deserve this. Let all of us help you. Now, where's your car so I can go get all your shit?"

A bark of laughter leaves me. Nate always manages to cut the seriousness at the perfect time. It's an artform, and he's perfected it.

"In the parking garage Level 2. Right next to the elevator."

"Keys?"

"On the counter," I whisper.

He bends down to my level. "Thank you. Now, enjoy some time with your friends—well, bosses. I'll be right back." He kisses my cheek before snagging my keys off the counter and walking out of my open door.

"Boys, go help Nate. Us ladies apparently have a lot to talk about." Daisy's words pull me out of my daze.

Turning around to Sydney, Beck, Luka, and Daisy, I'm met with looks of confusion, interest, and shock.

And that's when I realize what Nate did before he grabbed my keys.

Beck and Luka turn and walk out my door quickly, like they weren't party to anything.

"There's nothing going on," I rush out before anyone says anything.

"Uh-huh. And I don't own Empress Racing." Sydney rolls her eyes.

"OH MY GOD, I freaking knew it!" Daisy bounces on her feet.

"We need that fucking sectional here so we can sit and talk because I have a feeling there is way more to the story." Sydney shakes her head.

"There's nothing to the story. Not a thing. That was a friendly peck. Yep, that's all it was," I ramble.

"How many guys do you let give you a 'friendly peck', Dais?" Sydney asks.

"Zero."

"You, Syd?"

"Nada. Hold on." She pulls up her phone and lets it ring on speaker before it clicks over to answer.

"Hello?"

"Toni, have you ever let a man give you a friendly peck before?"

"Jesus," I whisper.

"Absolutely not. There was that one time I let a friend help me with some stress relief. He's now my partner." Her laughter rings through my empty apartment.

"That's what I thought. Thanks, Toni. We'll talk to you when we get to Miami." Sydney doesn't wait for Toni to reply and hangs up.

My eyes flick between the women, trying to come up with anything to say. I can't rightly say that we hooked up in Japan over a year ago. That I think about that night every single day. That we decided to act like that night never happened. I can't tell them I think walking out on Nate early that morning was a mistake, but I can't change it now. Then we just coincidentally ended up working together here and had a very innocent make-out session that didn't mean anything a few weeks ago.

"Oh shit, this is deeper than we think." Sydney says.

"I—" I snap my mouth shut.

Sydney holds her hand up. "You don't need to tell us anything. What I will say, though, is if you need anyone to talk to, we're all here, okay? Whatever is happening or did happen between you two is just that—between the two of you."

"You are no fun. I want the juicy details." Daisy's shoulders slump.

"We're respecting her space. And from the looks of it, they don't even know what's going on between them," Sydney says.

I stand there dumbly. Not talking, not registering everything that just happened, but thankful to Sydney, who seems to have a sixth sense for whatever *is* happening between Nate and me.

"Look at the panic on her face; she's freaking out," Sydney says as Daisy nods her agreement.

"I am right here." I finally snap out of my daze. "You don't need to talk like I'm not standing two feet from you." Sighing, I try to give some sort of explanation. "I don't know what's happening currently. There may be a small . . . history, but I don't want to get into that. It's all just so . . . complicated." I cringe, knowing my explanation will just bring more questions. But I don't have any answers, and I'm sure as hell not telling them in great detail what Nate can do with his tongue. Or fingers. Or that incredible dick.

Jesus, Rem, get your head out of the clouds.

"Is it safe?" Beck calls out from the door.

"Yes!" I yell back, giving all the women a look that says they better shut it ASAP.

"We're good," Sydney reiterates, still looking at me with curiosity.

"Yep, good," I squeak.

I'll be good as long as I survive this day. That's what I try to remember as my empty apartment starts to become my home.

Chapter 20

April 29

Today was unexpected. The whole crew showed up to support me and help me move into my new apartment. I still don't think I can find the words to describe how it felt. While I've made friends in the academy, none of them were friends enough to spend time with outside of work. These people—my bosses, technically—showed up like it was common courtesy, not an incredible gesture of friendship.

And Nate . . . He called in the reinforcements too. He knew I would turn down help and made sure I wasn't alone. Although, he did fuck up and kiss my cheek in front of everyone. I don't even want to think about what the blowback will be. Sure, they all seem fine with it now, but that will fall apart in a second if things become a distraction. Even if Nate and I never do anything again, if the memories prove to be a disturbance to my racing, I don't think they'll be as unforgiving.

God. I don't know. My head's a fucking mess, especially after Japan. When I'm with Nate, it's like . . . it's like the world is right. There's no tilted axis; there's no asteroids coming to rain on the party. It's just . . . comfortable. I don't know if I've ever been comfortable a day in my life. Whether that's my own doing or just the job I have, it doesn't really matter at the end of the day. I'm not in a place where I can be comfortable yet. I haven't achieved my goals, therefore anything with Nate just ends badly. For both of us.

And I just realized that you, Nate, will actually be reading all of this so just . . . act like you didn't. Please. I can't handle a conversation about this right now.

In other news, I leave for Miami tomorrow, and I'm so excited for the gala and the race. I feel like Miami might happen for me. It's one of the tracks I have actual experience with, so I feel more confident overall there. I'm manifesting a podium finish. you heard it here first.

what a mess I am. This entry is all over the place. It's an apt reflection of my headspace, though. I have a week off after Miami before the Italian Grand Prix. I think I need to seriously think about a breakaway from everything. Just a couple of days. Because I don't know how much longer I can have all of this swirling in my head before I break completely.

Chapter 21

Nate

Remi lives in the same building as me.

What the fuck kind of karma did I earn to live in this kind of torture? Not only is she in the same building but the same fucking floor. At least we're not right next to each other. I'd probably try and listen to her through the walls, which is creepy as hell even for me.

I sigh as I collapse back onto my bed. Murphy jumps up and rests his head on my stomach, staring up at me.

"We're really fucked, aren't we, my man?"

Ever since the Japan race a month ago, things have been different for me. I've been trying so damn hard to hide it, but our little make-out session made it clear that my feelings for the woman aren't going anywhere. If anything, they're growing at an alarming rate. Every day, there's something new I find intriguing. It's the little things. The things she tries to hide from everyone else, the vulnerabilities she hates showing. I get to see them all, and it's a struggle to keep her at arm's length.

But I will respect her wishes. Even if it kills me inside.

Murphy huffs.

"It's rough on you too, huh? I know she jokes that you're her dog, but damn if it doesn't feel that way when we're all together, you traitor."

He pushes my hand with his snout.

"Yeah, yeah. I'm a sucker for her too, Murph."

Margret Bouchard. Who knew such an unsuspecting woman would fall into my life and knock me on my ass.

Even the guys noticed. Beck was very quick to point out the living situation, then Luka commented on the stupid fucking peck I planted on her cheek. What was I thinking? I wasn't. That's my only excuse. It was an unconscious action that felt so damn natural. I texted everyone to help her move in, and it all felt so domesticated that I had a lapse in judgement. Remi's shocked face still haunts my thoughts.

We're not even six races into the season, and I'm failing miserably at keeping my feelings for Remi separate from my job to train her. It's worrisome because she's relying on me. Am I the reason she's struggling so much? Am I a distraction? Do I need to quit?

Hell no. Even if I am, I'll figure out a way to make it right. Because I'll be damned if anyone else comes in here and trains Remi. Selfish? Maybe, but I would shrivel up into nothingness if I had to leave her to fend for herself. I wouldn't trust anyone else to help her reach her goals.

And that's what I need to focus on.

Super easy and not at all taking every ounce of patience I have on a daily basis.

***

It's Thursday, and now that Practices 1 and 2 are over, it's time for the gala.

I'm sweating. The last time I saw Remi at a gala, I almost drooled all over myself and the floor. Now, I'm her plus one. There's no escaping when her sheer beauty becomes too much for me.

As I button up my black shirt, I think about what color dress she'll wear. Maybe she'll wear something classically black, and we'll match. Maybe she'll match Empress and roll out the purple again. She does look fucking gorgeous in purple. Paired with her dark brown hair and fair complexion, she exudes beauty.

I put the cufflinks through my sleeves before heading to the bathroom to take care of my hair. The waves are unruly, which is never an issue any other time because they give off the surfer-vibe look that works for me. But tonight, it's time to tame them. I take some hair wax and distribute it through, combing all the waves back into something resembling "put together". My hair is almost to my collar when it's combed back, the side part adding a James Bond feel to it all.

The all-black tux I decided on should be sleek and match anything that Remi chooses to wear.

Now, I just need to go pick her up.

My phone buzzes in my hand.

Felix: Heard about your little living conundrum, as well as your date tonight. As a man who hid things with his woman for far too long, make sure you're both on the same page before you do something public. She has enough attention around her; she doesn't need more. I know you have her best interest at heart, but . . . sometimes *our* hearts override that logic. And Nate? Don't fuck it up.

I blow out a breath at Felix's words. He's right. I *know* he's right, and I hope to everything I can that I don't slip up again tonight. That kiss to her cheek in her apartment is haunting me. Not that I regret it, per se. I just wish that was something I *could* do. It was pure instinct. But he's right. We're not on the same page, and that's a recipe for disaster.

I can't dwell on that now, though, because I need to go see a woman about a gala.

The short walk makes me more nervous, if that's even possible. Memories flood my mind. Remi shoved up against the wall as I kissed her senseless. I was barely able to contain my need for her.

Reaching down, I adjust the semi I'm now sporting thanks to the visual, and I will myself to focus. I can't have a boner all night. I can control myself.

I snort. *Yeah right.*

Before I'm ready, I'm at Remi's door with my hand up, preparing to knock. She beats me to it, though, which means she must have been watching through the peephole.

"Hi," she says shyly as she rips the door open.

I would say hi back, but I'm speechless.

We do match, in a sense. The smokey dark grey dress she's wearing hugs every curve. The thick straps on her shoulder lead to a V that gives just a glimpse of cleavage. It's not too much, just a hint of what's beneath, but it's enough to do me in.

The purple pendant that hangs between her breasts surely doesn't help either.

"Nate?"

"Huh?" I pull my eyes from her chest.

"Do I look terrible? Shit. I don't have another dress." She panics and spins around, but I reach out and grab her hand before she gets far.

"You look fucking gorgeous. So gorgeous you rendered me speechless. Like my brain temporarily stopped working because you look so fucking hot."

She blushes before pushing my chest. "And there he is. The horndog we all know and love." She rolls her eyes in an attempt to play it off, but this time, I don't want to let her.

"Only for you, Rem. Jesus, I mean, have you looked in a mirror? How am I supposed to get through tonight and *not* want more?" I plead. I didn't plan on getting into this tonight, or ever. But she needs to know just how fucking beautiful I think she is. The need to make sure she never doubts how gorgeous she is takes over.

"Nate . . . please."

"You have no idea what you do to me. How affected I am by you every second of every day. How hard it is to act like nothing has happened between us."

She yanks me into her room and lets the door slam shut behind us.

"You cannot just say shit like that!" She throws her hands up.

"If there is a day where you think you are anything other than stunning, yes, I can."

"We agreed."

"Technically, you agreed, and I went along with it because I would quite literally do anything just to be around you." *World, swallow me whole because I did not intend to spill my guts to this woman tonight.*

She's not in the headspace to even have this conversation, let alone discuss anything about what happened or could happen between us.

I know this, and yet I couldn't keep my damn mouth shut.

Because I couldn't stand to see the doubt in her eyes.

Fuck. I'm so screwed.

She starts pacing. With every step she takes, the slit in her dress reveals ample amounts of her muscled leg, making it harder for me to focus.

"Nate—" She continues to pace. "I—" Her hand runs through her curled hair. "You can't—"

"I know." I stop her with my hand on her hip. "I know I can't just say all of that. *I know.* But fuck, I'm just a man, Rem. How the hell am I supposed to pretend that I don't see you naked in my dreams? That I don't imagine how things could be different if we both just said 'fuck it'? The worst part about it all? I could never actually do it because I can't ever put you and your future in jeopardy. There's no chance in hell that I put your career at risk, no matter how badly I want you."

She shoves me, hard. "What the fuck am I supposed to do with all that information?!"

"Ignore it. Pretend like it's all in an alternate reality. I don't know." I put my hands up in surrender.

"I can't just fucking ignore it, you ass. You think you're the only one affected by Japan? I never expected to see you again, and now I have to not only see you but be *around* you, next to you, touch you. Every day! You think that's not hard for me? But I manage because it's what we have to do. What good does it do to tell me all of this? To make me feel bad that my career is the thing that is stopping us from seeing where things go? To make me feel like I have to pick between you and racing?"

"No! God no!" I sigh. This is going downhill so fast.

"I can't do this right now." She sighs. "We're late. We need to go."

Remi breezes past me while I stand still in shock. She doesn't wait for me to follow her, but I do anyway as my brain desperately tries to catch up to the last ten minutes.

We don't speak as we get into the elevator. The static between us is muddled and sad. I fucking hate it. But I have no clue how to fix it. Does she even want me to fix it?

See? I'm no good at any of this.

When we walk into the event, Remi is immediately taken away by a group of women. As much as I want to follow her, I know the best move is to give us both space.

I don't know what I was thinking letting myself word-vomit my inner thoughts upstairs. I knew she wouldn't handle it well. I knew it would end up crushing me and pushing her away.

And yet, I fucking did it anyway.

I'll be lucky if she doesn't fire me after this next race. It'd be what I deserve. I'll find a way to help her from the sidelines if she does. I can't let her fail, even if it means working through Beck to make sure she has the tools that she needs.

I run through a million scenarios of how I could keep working with Remi, but none of them really matter. It's up to Remi if she wants to continue working with me.

The lights dim, signaling the time for speeches, so I make my way to our table. Remi walks up next to me, allowing me to pull out her chair and push her in before I take my seat. The smile she gives me doesn't reach her eyes, and knowing I caused her light to dim tonight is more painful than anything I've dealt with in the past, and I've broken my femur and lived in foster care.

I lean into her, my nose brushing her hair—*God, she smells good*—to say just loud enough for her to hear, "I'm sorry."

She closes her eyes and inhales deeply, taking a moment before she says on a sigh, "I know. Can we just . . . not talk about it tonight? Please."

"Of course." I nod and straighten up in my chair.

The rest of the gala is a masterclass in restraint. It takes everything in me to not put my hand on her leg. To not ask her to dance. To engage in conversation only when I'm directly spoken to because my brain left the gala before dinner was even served.

Tonight may go down in history as the night I lost the woman I'm falling for.

Chapter 22
Remi

"Fuck!" I yell as I hit the wall in Miami on the eleventh lap. The car slams hard into the barrier, and my hands take the bulk of the impact. It hurts like hell.

"Remi, are you okay?" My engineer, Jason, says into my earpiece.

I do a quick body check. "Fine. Hands hurt, but I don't think anything's broken. Shit, I'm so sorry."

Crashing in a race is something I wanted to avoid at all costs, and yet here I am.

I'd blame the whole situation on Nate, but that's not fair. It's not his fault he was honest. It's not his fault that I basically said he's not important enough to me. But clearly, it's affecting my driving, which is not good at all. I clipped another car and sent myself flying into the wall.

The stewards help me out of my car and drive me back to the garage. I take off my helmet and don't make eye contact with anyone. Cruz tries to stop me and make sure I'm okay, but I just hold my hand up while turning my head away and speed walk out to my makeshift office.

The second the door closes, I can no longer hold back the tears. They stream down my face and neck, leaving cold streaks in their wake and soaking the collar of my undershirt.

I thought things were getting better. That my head was finally focused on driving. Then things with Nate blew up, and I crashed my car. What a failure on so many levels.

The slow slide of tears turns into gasping sobs as every feeling I've tried to push down for the last three months breaks free.

Empress hired the wrong driver.

I'm costing them too much money.

I'm not a good enough driver.

Things just aren't clicking for me.

I'm failing the entire team.

I'm failing Nate.

Nate.

Fuck. I can't even think about how much I've messed things up with him.

A knee-jerk reaction to his words destroyed everything we've built over the last couple of months.

My door cracks open, and Toni squeezes in, coming to sit next to me.

"Oh, Rem, it's not that bad. I promise."

"It really is, though," I say as a new wave of sobs wracks through my body.

"You busted the front wing and tire, but we've fixed worse. Hell, Beck has done worse. This is not the end of the world. We can fix it, and in Italy, you'll kick ass and be the star we all know you are. There's nothing so dire."

I wipe my eyes. "Sure is feeling like it. I'm sorry I'm a mess. I think it's just the stress of everything hitting me." *Not to mention Nate.*

"Understandably. You put a lot of pressure on yourself."

I chuckle. "Understatement of the year."

She rubs my back as my eyes finally dry.

"I'm good. I just need another minute," I tell her.

"Heard. We'd love for you to come down and help us navigate the rest of the race with Sawyer.

"Sure, I'll be right down." I use my sleeve to dry my tears.

Toni gets up, hesitating like she has more to say but decides against it, before leaving me alone once more.

The door pops open again, making me groan. I don't want to have to talk about any of this out right now.

Murphy shoves his way in, immediately putting his head on my lap. His unwavering support makes fresh tears rise to the surface.

"Do you want me to just leave him and go?" Nate's muffled voice from behind the door makes me laugh.

"No," I croak.

The door eases open, and his head pops in, his concern written all over his face. "You okay?"

"No." Petting Murphy is helping, though.

He tentatively walks into the room, sitting across from me. "It's not the end of the world. Crashes happen. It's not ideal, but maybe it's a good thing to get one out of the way. The fear of crashing is almost worse than the crash."

You know what's stupid? That I'm more upset that he can just shift back into professional mode so easily. I was the one who shut him down at the gala, and yet I'm sad he's keeping it professional.

How fucking delusional am I?

This is what I asked for—hell, practically begged for. Now I just have to live with the consequences.

"Maybe," I tell him.

"How do your hands feel? Do we need to check them out?" He reaches out to grab one before pulling back.

"I think they're okay. Super sore right now, but nothing some rest won't help." I hold my hands out so he can check them over. I know he won't tell me, but he's worried about them.

The moment he takes them into his hands, an electric shock jolts through me—the same one I feel every time he touches me. His calloused hands are familiar yet tempting in a way I've tried to avoid for months. The care he takes to inspect every millimeter hurts my heart. I don't deserve his care. Not after how I treated him before the gala.

"Nate . . ."

"Just let me look. I need to make sure you're okay," he says without looking up.

He turns over my hands, manipulates my fingers, and gently massages my palm.

"I'm sorry." The whispered words might be too quiet for him to even hear.

"Nothing to be sorry for, Rem," he mumbles, still focused on my hands.

"There's so much to be sorry about. I'm sorry for how I acted, and for how

I treated you before the gala. It . . . caught me off guard, and I apparently don't do so well with being out of control."

He looks up at me, his brows furrowed in what looks like pain and his eyes full of desperation. "Can we just . . .not do this right now? I'm— I can't talk about it."

"Sure. Of course." I drop my gaze to our hands and clear my throat, fresh tears making it clog.

"These need some ice. Are you going back to the garage?"

"After I take a few more minutes and change, yes," I say softly.

"I'll be back." He gets up swiftly, leaving Murphy with me, gone just as fast as he came, and the only thing I'm worried about is that I broke us. Not even what could have been, but our friendship that was coming to mean so much to me.

"I fucked up, Murphy," I murmur, burying my head into his neck. "I don't know what I'm doing. Maybe I'm just in over my head with everything." He turns his head and licks my cheek like he actually understands what I'm saying.

Nate

I race out of Remi's office as fast as I can.

Her apology damn near broke me. Not because I didn't want to hear it but because my heart is still in my throat from watching her crash. I'm teetering on the edge, about to lose my shit and wrap her up in bubble wrap. The second she clipped Alejandro and spun, I thought I was going to die. I thought *she* was going to die. My heart pounded so hard I thought everyone around me could hear it. Then everything, all the sounds and lights around me, went blurry and staticky, like I was on the verge of passing out.

Beck clapped my shoulder, bringing me back to planet Earth and keeping me steady at the same time. The look he gave me was a knowing one. I don't know if I said something while I was freaking out or he just guessed, but either way, it's not great that he suspects something.

Then Murphy found me and tugged on my shorts, leading me back to the pathway between the pitlane and the mobile offices. He knew exactly where to find Remi and didn't wait for me to see if it was okay with her before he barged into her office and comforted her.

All I could focus on was making sure Remi was okay. When she started to apologize, I knew I didn't have the bandwidth to have the conversation properly. It's a theme with us, I think, not being in the right headspace when the other wants to have a real conversation about us. Hell, we may never get off the merry-go-round of bad timing, honestly. It sure as hell feels like we won't. But none of that is as important as making sure she is okay.

Her hands are more beaten up than she's letting on, or she just doesn't feel it yet. So my mission to get ice isn't a moot one, but if I had stayed in there any longer with her turning to Murphy for comfort, I would have picked her up and held her until she realized what I was doing and shoved me away.

It takes me a minute to get the ice pack and some meds to help with the inflammation that's already showing up. The time gives me too much time to think. But nothing I come up with lends any answers.

Do I need to step back?

Can I get Remi out of her head enough to race to her fullest potential?

Am I able to shove my *very* deep feelings for her down and focus on my job?

The answer to all of those is . . . I don't know. It's almost worse that I don't have clear answers. Maybe I need to start journaling.

Someone walks into the room I'm in, which forces me to focus on my task once more. I wave to one of the mechanics then head toward Remi's office.

I open the door to an empty room, panic seizing my chest immediately. Then I realize she is probably already back in the garage and there's no reason to freak out.

My walk back is on the verge of turning into a jog. I probably look like a madman, and I absolutely feel like one. Once I'm in the garage, Remi is easy to spot. She's changed into an Empress polo and her hair is loose, the waves cascading down her back. I swear the skies open up and shine a light down on her as soon as I step into the space. Yes, in an enclosed garage, the skies opened up. That's how fucking delusional and gone for this woman I am. I recognize it, at least.

Murph is between her legs with his headphones on. They make a cute as fuck pair, let me tell you, but I don't waste any more time admiring them together because Remi needs the ice for her hands ASAP and I've already taken too long.

I subtly hand her the ice pack and medicine before taking up vigil next to her. Cruz hands me a pair of headphones and smirks at me. Maybe he won't be a problem after all.

Thank you, Remi mouths to me before turning back to the monitors in front of her.

I listen to her give advice on corners and tire degradation. The whole team listens with rapt attention as she helps deliver Sawyer a first-place podium win. I pick up her journal that's sitting next to her and go through her latest ones as she kicks more ass. The more I read, the more my heart hurts, if that's possible.

She's so selfless, and yet she thinks she doesn't bring enough to the table. Remi's so worried about others' opinions and making sure she's a good role model that she's losing herself in the process.

I write a couple more notes back discreetly, then close it and set it back next to her.

I wonder if she's seen my notes.

Would it make a difference if she had and is just ignoring them, or hasn't seen them and probably never will? Who knows. All I know is that writing back is a compulsion that hasn't let up. I *have* to write, to refute her worries and doubts.

As I watch her command an entire garage of mostly men, nursing her hands so no one is the wiser, I come up with a very stupid idea.

I'm going after Remi Bouchard.

It may take me weeks—hell, months—but I'm going to win her over. I'm going to make Remi want me as much as I want her. I just have to figure out a way for none of it to impact her success.

Super easy.

Chapter 23
Remi

The crash in Miami made me step back and reevaluate things.

During the two-week break between that race and the Italian Grand Prix, I tended to my sore hands and focused my training on my mentality. Nate was on board and helped tremendously with my reset.

If only I could reset my dirty thoughts and reminiscence about the man in question.

Now, a few days after Italy and a fifth-place finish, I'm preparing to fly out to the Monaco Grand Prix, and my mind is calm and focused. I shove Nate to the deep recesses and pray I can keep him there. I can worry about him later, when I'm not out to prove myself as real competition in Formula 1.

A knock on my door means it's "go" time.

"Coming!" I call out.

I snag my backpack and carry-on, and grab my now well-used journal off the kitchen island as I walk to the front door.

"Muuuurph!" I call out, dropping everything I just picked up to pet my favorite doggo.

"What I wouldn't give to get that kind of a reaction," Nate says under his breath.

I look up at him with a cocked eyebrow.

"You aren't my emotional support animal, so keep dreaming."

"He's *my* dog!" Nate says, throwing his hands up.

"Are you really Nate's dog, or are you mine? What do you think, boy? Should we see who you would really choose?" I talk to Murphy before moving to stand, but Nate stops me.

"He'd pick you, and you know it. That's not a fair test. I'm the one who feeds him."

"Sounds like you need to bring it up with"—I throw up air quotes—"'your dog.'" I smirk.

Murphy nuzzles my cheek, demanding more pets, and I happily oblige.

"You two are a pain in my ass," Nate grumbles, but there is a smile on his face. He's dressed in jeans today and a plain grey V-neck T-shirt. It's a damn fine look on him, making my vow to not think about him as anything other than my trainer hard as hell.

"All right, traitors, we're already running late," Nate says. He grabs my backpack off the floor and hands me Murphy's leash. I can't help my smile as he accepts that Murphy likes me better, even if it's just for the trip downstairs.

I decide to write in my journal on the drive over and let Nate drive us for once. I really want to get my head focused before we even land. We make it to the jet with very little fanfare.

Once we're in the air, Nate grabs us both drinks and sits next to me.

"Talk to me. How are you feeling?"

I inhale a deep breath before letting it out slowly. "Good, actually. I think not working out hard the last few weeks and taking a break from any media appearances I had on the schedule really helped me refocus for this race."

"No obligations for a couple of weeks can really help. You guys run non-stop, and even if you're used to it, breaks from it all are necessary."

"Thank you. For letting me have space, and a break for that matter," I tell him, genuinely glad that I have him on my team. He just gets it without me having to explain things. It's one of the things that draws me to him, not only as my trainer but also as *more*.

"That's what I'm here for. The goal is always to get you to a place where you're producing, but not at the expense of your sanity. There's a balance there, and sometimes it just takes time to find."

"Yeah," I whisper, watching him. Nate likes to play the fun and goofy playboy, but there's so much more to him. He's too enticing, too *good*, even if he tries to hide it.

"Stop looking at me like that, Rem."

"Like what?"

"Like you think I'm worthy of something more."

He doesn't get that I'm constantly looking for things that throw red flags up. I need to find things that turn me off of the man because I cannot fall for him. But there are none, not really.

I clear my throat in an attempt to drag myself out of the pull that's something purely Nathan Murphy. "I have some brand stuff I have to work on, so I guess I'll just . . . work on that." "Oh, of course. Don't let me keep you. I'll just work on something for next week."

We spend the rest of the flight alternating between working and discussing my schedule for Monaco. Nate has pulled back completely from our flirting and innuendos. At first, I thought it was just to give me space after the crash, but we're going on three weeks and lots of hours together, and it's like he's a different man—professional to a fault—and I'm not sure how to handle it.

Obviously, I can't have things both ways, but I miss the flirty, fun Nate.

But maybe this is for the best.

***

Is it possible to get tinnitus because of your own screaming? I'm pretty sure that's what's happening to me.

Third place.

A fucking podium in Monaco.

I think that's cause for screaming at the top of my lungs.

I've just pulled the car into the spot for third place and am trying to unhook myself from the car as quickly as I can. Once I do, I sprint for the group of Empress employees behind the barrier and jump on top of them.

I can't hear anything, my ears still ringing from my screams in the cockpit. But everyone patting my helmet, shoulders, and back with excitement is a high I've never felt before.

I did it. I actually did it!

Tears stream down my cheeks and my heart is pounding, but I know I still need to weigh in. Celebrations can come after the ceremony.

I manage to right myself with the help of a few familiar faces. Cruz, Toni, Jason and Nate are front and center with nothing but pride on their faces.

Weigh-ins and the cooldown room are a quick process. It's not much different from the academy. Sawyer placed second, and David Acevedo managed to win. I'm not even upset that I didn't win because no matter the place, I'm the first woman to podium in a Formula 1 race. *Ever.*

I soak it in as tears flow down my face. A trophy gets handed to me, and that feels more surreal than anything else. As the anthems play, I look out into the crowd. The entire Empress team is there: Sydney, Daisy, Beck, Luka, Felix, Toni, Cruz, Jason. Anyone associated with Empress is standing together as one, smiles wide across their faces. Then my eyes catch on Nate and well with fresh tears. Light glossy trails of wetness streak down his cheeks with the biggest smile in between. The dimples that I've seen far too little of lately shine brighter than the trophy sitting in front of me.

He mouths, *You fucking did it!* It makes my smile grow wider, if it's even possible.

It's not possible to answer him back because I know there are a million cameras on me, but if I could, I would tell him that *we* did it. There's no way I could have done this without him. It feels so menial, third place, but right now? After so much doubt, it's everything.

And then the champagne sprays.

Tradition dictates you spray the winner, but the racers on stage and the constructor that won for today's race all turn to me and douse me. I hold out my bottle to the side, both arms extended out, and literally soak in the moment as well as the champagne.

I don't know if I'll ever get the chance to be up here again, and I don't want to forget any second of it.

It's all over too fast. We're ushered off the stage and moved back to our garages. The room erupts in cheers as I step through the doors. More shoulder slaps and congratulations are doled out as I make my way into the crowd.

"Thank you," spills from my mouth without much thought as I scan the crowd, trying to find Nate. There are so many people here it's impossible to find him. The crushing disappointment that he's not the first one I see is shocking, although it shouldn't be. I may be conflicted all around him, but the need for his approval will never go away, I think.

I finally spot him in the back, watching on with a very excited Murphy. A smile just for the two of them takes over my face. The crew organizes a photo, which is customary for a racer's first win, but this time it feels bigger. It'll be the first picture of a woman winning—proof that it's all possible, that we can have no limits and take on every challenge we face.

I'm still riding high on cloud nine as I make my way back to my office sometime later.

Once the door closes, I lean against it with my eyes closed and take what feels like my first breath since getting in the car before the race.

A wet nose touches my hand, and my cheeks hurt from how big my smile is.

"You were fucking incredible." Nate's soft voice reaches my ears.

My eyes open, but I can't find the words. Emotion chokes me as I nod, releasing a sob I didn't expect. He makes his way to me in two big steps, wraps his arms around me, and murmurs words of praise and support. He doesn't tell me to stop crying; he just holds me as a race weekend worth of highs and lows releases. His giant hand cups my head and holds me to his chest as my sobs turn into slow, quiet breaths and my tears dry.

"I can't even put into words how proud I am of you. I knew you could do it; you just needed to get out of your head. Now that you've podiumed . . . Look out, F1," he says into the crown of my head.

"I wouldn't go that far. I'd be thrilled with some consistency," I mumble into his shirt.

"Baby steps. This was a huge victory, but we'll take everything one race at a time."

I nod, trying to figure out the words I want to say to this man.

"Thank you." It's barely audible against his shirt and chest.

"It was all you, Ace."

"I would have been fired three races ago if it wasn't for you. I never would have made it this far." I pull back and look up at him so he can really hear me. "You are the reason any of this happened, and I'll never be able to thank you."

His eyes shift between mine. That ever-present energy that feels like an entire entity is between us again. It's like we're both restraining ourselves.

"Remi," he whispers, almost pained.

I can't take it. I can't handle not touching him how I long to, not truly *feeling* him. So, I stop holding back.

Raising up on my toes, I graze my lips over his. He has time to pull back or turn it into a simple peck.

Instead, he cups the back of my head and holds me to him tightly. I'm wedged between him and the door, and I honestly couldn't think of a better place to be.

His tongue traces my bottom lip, letting me decide how far I want to push this, but my logical brain isn't in sight. I open, hungry and desperate to taste him. The hand cupping my head threads through my hair. With a firm but gentle tug, he tilts me the way he wants. My hands grip his shoulders in an attempt to not maul him completely. But when his other hand slides down my side and grabs my ass, all bets are off.

My leg hitches up on his hip—well, as much as my small frame can with his height—and the kiss turns frenzied.

This isn't a kiss; no, this is two people claiming each other. Our tongues tangle languidly; no one's fighting for dominance, and neither of us is rushing. I nip at his bottom lip, shifting to kiss his dimple that's on full display before kissing his mouth again.

I missed this . . . I missed *him.*

But this kiss doesn't change our circumstances. He still technically works for me and Empress. The implications of us getting together, and the potential for it all to get in my head and ruin my racing year, isn't worth it. I pull back slightly, and he seems to know exactly where my head just went.

He sighs, putting his forehead against mine.

"I'm sor—"

"Don't," he whispers. "Don't apologize."

"We can't . . ."

"As you keep saying. It's fine, Rem." He shifts, releasing me, and takes a giant step back. I shiver from the loss—not just the loss of his body heat, but the emotional distance shatters me.

We've been dancing around each other for so long, but the risk is too great. One misstep, and I lose my entire career.

The disappointment reflected in his eyes hurts too.

"Nate, I'm sorry."

"It's fine, Remi. I get it. Really, I do." He gives me a small smile that doesn't show his dimples, and for some reason that's what I focus on. I'm hurting him when I cave, knowing we can't be together.

"I just can't—"

"I know. Trust me, I know." His voice gets sharper as he turns around, running his hand through his waves, and calls to Murphy.

I move to the side as they both head my way, making room for them to leave on a day that felt so special.

That was before I fucked it all up by kissing Nate Murphy again.

Chapter 24
Nate

Torture.

Making out with Remi while not being able to *be with* her is akin to torture.

I couldn't even tell you who kissed whom first. It doesn't matter. That was a kiss that proved there's something between us, and it's all that matters, even if Remi isn't in a place to accept it yet.

But it's hard to stand there and let her pull away from me. So fucking hard to feel everything for her and then simply walk away.

I have plans, though, and they start tonight.

Me:

Remi should be heading to her hotel room shortly. I'm going to change and then head to the restaurant. Toni, you still good to go pick her up?

Toni:

Hell yes! I'm so glad you organized this!

Sydney:

It was such a good idea. I'm sad we didn't think to do something like this. I've invited all the usuals, and everyone said they're coming.

Me:

Thanks, you guys. I think it'll mean a lot to her. I'm going to pick up the cake on the way there, and I'll see you soon.

A hastily planned dinner to celebrate the first woman to ever podium seemed like a good idea. Now, all I can think about is kissing Remi again, but I can't dwell on it. I need her to see that we could work. That being with me won't bring down her carefully stacked house of cards. It's an uphill battle, I know that, but if I can show her just how good it could be, it will be far and away worth it.

She'll think Toni or Sydney planned it. It makes sense, seeing as they both have made history as women in Formula 1 as well. I'll let her believe it was them too. My plan is to work behind the scenes to make Remi feel less isolated. To help her see that she has a huge team of people who will support her no matter what. It's the first step in her seeing that the world won't fall apart if we're together.

I'm making big assumptions too, but everything I've read in her journal tells me she's terrified of losing this shot in Formula 1. She believes she gets one chance to do well. One season to prove she has what it takes to not only drive but *win*. She's worked her whole life for it. Lost most of her family because of it. I just want to make sure she understands that this little family at Empress Sydney has built isn't like that. They aren't going to throw her out because she crashed once or isn't winning every single race.

Simply telling Remi all of that won't work, though. I know. Sydney and Toni know. We've all tried, but it's not getting through. So I'm going to show her that she isn't alone instead.

The key to winning Remi's heart isn't going to be showing her how good we are together. We both already know that's a fact. It's going to be creating an entire network that will support her on good days and the bad so she can finally *live* without fear.

Murph and I make our way to our hotel room, where he's got a sweet little setup. Sydney has made sure he has everything he needs at every Vanstone we stay in. I guess there are huge perks to being buddies with the owner of the hotel. I don't have to worry about Murphy when I need to leave or when I'm heading places where I can't bring him. He really is the best dog.

I change into jeans and a lightweight, light grey, short-sleeved button-up shirt. It lets my tattoos shine, but is nice enough for the restaurant we're going to. I know my tattoos are kryptonite for Remi. She looks at them every chance she gets, so I'm going to take full advantage and show them off.

It takes me fifteen minutes to get the cake before I head directly to the restaurant to start setting up. This place has a back room, which is perfect for the number of high-profile people who will be coming. I didn't want anyone to be constantly hounded for autographs while we try to celebrate Remi.

"Good evening, sir. We have the room set up exactly how you asked. Can I take the cake for you and put it in the back?" the host asks.

"That'd be great, thanks." I hand it to her and then follow her to the back room. They somehow found race car decorations. They're classy, not like the stuff you find for kid's parties, making me think they made them somehow. On short notice, I'm incredibly impressed.

"This looks amazing. Thank you so much."

"We're happy to have you all here to celebrate such a historic day." She smiles at me. "If you need anything else, don't hesitate to ask." Then she disappears.

I pace the room. Waiting is the worst part. Will Remi like it? Will she be embarrassed? Will this have the effect I'm hoping for, or will it backfire? Time will tell, but I'm an impatient little asshole sometimes.

"Damn, this turned out great. She's going to love it," Beck says as he strolls into the room, interrupting my overthinking.

"Yeah?"

"Oh yeah. You have doubts?" His smirk pisses me off. He sees right through all my bullshit, just like I can do for him, and I'm not ready for self-reflection right now.

"Always," I huff.

"Not going to lie, I fucking love watching this."

"Watching what? Me setting up a party?"

"The fall of Nathan Murphy. God, I've been waiting years for this." He sighs wistfully.

"You're an asshole."

"And you are very gone for *the* Miss Bouchard."

"We're not talking about this."

"Heard. I'll just sit back and watch the entertainment."

"You have too much time on your hands, old man," I quip, trying to get him on his backfoot like he did me.

"Nice try. I'm quite happy with how things have landed for me. I get Sydney mostly to myself, and I still get to boss you around." He smirks.

"And you're still as annoying as ever."

"Now, boys, I thought we had grown up a little bit." Sydney enters the room, walking straight to me for a hug. "This looks phenomenal. She's going to freak." She smiles.

"Thanks, Syd."

"Does she know you set this up?" she asks, walking back to Beck as he wraps his arms around her.

"No, and I'd like to keep it that way."

Sydney tilts her head as she scrutinizes me. I'm saved from further questions by Luka, Daisy, and Evelin walking in. Evelin steals everyone's attention, as per usual, and I'm grateful for the break. My friends already know me better than I want them to. They see right through my attempts to keep Remi at arm's length. What they don't know is how insecure Remi is, how worried she is about every little step she takes. If I have to take all the comments and gossip, I will if it means Remi gets to be oblivious to it all. Rem puts on a brave face, a confident face, and she wears it well, but everything is surface level. This podium means more to her than she'll ever admit, and I think it's the one thing that's brought her back from the edge of self-sabotage.

I don't have time to dwell on it as the rest of the group shows up, including Felix, Toni, Cruz, and Jason, with Remi following closely behind. I can't hear what she's saying, but she stops in her tracks once she's in the room.

"Surprise!" Sydney says with her arms out wide.

Remi looks around the room, taking in the decorations and the people, before her eyes land on me. Her head tilts in question, but I just shrug with my palms up in an "I don't know" gesture.

"Congrats on your podium," I say instead, dipping my head to acknowledge her.

"This is . . ." She swallows around the lump in her throat. "I have no words. Thank you." Her voice is clear, not like she's on the verge of tears. No vulnerability in sight except a slight stumble over her words.

But I know better. She has a hard time accepting praise. Probably from growing up in the household she did, and she rarely shows her emotions. Only the happy, appreciative Remi shows up in a crowd of people.

The host calls for everyone's attention to let us know dinner will be starting soon. I requested a few courses to be served. No menus and no decisions. The hint of relief on Remi's face tells me that it was the right move. *Thank God.*

Conversation starts up around the room, mostly about the race and some of the wild shit that happened during it that didn't affect Remi at all. Some logistics get brought up, but Toni nips that in the bud, saying it's too much work talk.

"So, Remi, you got a man?" Cruz asks. "Or woman?" he adds with an eyebrow raised, making Remi laugh.

"Definitely no woman. I have a hard enough time making friends with women, let alone dating one. And nope, no man either." If I hadn't been watching her every move, I wouldn't have caught the quick glance she shot my way.

"Would you like one?" Cruz asks with a furrowed brow.

"Umm, no. I happen to know you have a thing for Nina in analytics."

Cruz's cheeks turn pink in a second.

"I fucking knew it," Sydney says with a smile.

"It's nothing."

"It wasn't nothing when I saw you kissing her cheek last week in the office." Toni grins.

"Jesus. There's no privacy with you all." Cruz shakes his head. "We're taking things slow. And I swear, if any of you mention anything, I will make sure a piece of equipment hits you in Spain."

"Wow, testy," Beck says.

"Do you know how hard it is to date in this world?" Cruz throws his hands up, but Beck, Luka, and Felix all arch an eyebrow, making me laugh.

"You're asking the wrong group there, man."

"And how many of you snuck around?" Cruz asks in retaliation.

"Just Felix and Toni," Daisy says with a bright smile.

I forgot how much fun this group is when they get together.

My eyes catch on Remi's, and the topic of conversation isn't lost on her either. The fact that she's looking at me makes me think the idea of sneaking around isn't as off limits as she believes.

The problem? I don't want to sneak around with her. If I can't shout to the entire world that I'm with Remi Bouchard, then I don't want it at all. I won't treat her like a secret, and I won't be treated as one in turn.

"Have you dated anyone while you've been racing?" Daisy asks Remi, making me straighten a little in my seat.

"God no. There's so much pressure and time commitment; it's just not something I can see myself doing."

"So, if you saw a future with a guy but you were still racing, you'd just automatically shut him down and walk away?" I cut in.

"That's not what I said."

"Then break it down for me."

"I just don't see how you can have such a time-intensive job and nurture a relationship, especially in the beginning, without things like jealousy and feeling neglected setting in," she refutes.

"What if the guy is fine with that? What if he travels with you? To some races?" I add, suddenly realizing that everyone's attention is ping-ponging back and forth between the two of us.

"What if it pulls too much of my focus? What if my racing suffers because of it?" She tilts her head.

Her words hit on everything I know to be true, but they still piss me off.

"What if racing wasn't your entire world? What if you realized there's more to life than a trophy?"

She jolts back like I slapped her. It was harsh, I know that, but I just wish she could see the world a little less black and white.

I wish I could add some color to her life to make her see that it wouldn't be the end of life as she knows it.

"That's not fair, and you know it," she says in a low tone.

"Okay, who needs more wine?" Felix calls out loudly.

Conversation continues, but Remi and I still stare each other down. I can just imagine what is going on in that beautiful head of hers. She's probably cursing my name, annoyed that I called her out. Truthfully, I'm annoyed at myself for going there. I won't win her over by cornering her. I sure as hell shouldn't have done it surrounded by people who are our bosses.

This is only going to push her further away and remind her why she doesn't want to start anything with me.

Looks like I'm back to square one.

Chapter 25
Remi

What an asshole.

I can't believe he said all of that around the entire upper management at Empress. Like I don't have enough shit to wade through, he adds this into the mix. It doesn't take a rocket scientist to put two and two together with that conversation. Now, I'll have all the women up my ass for information and all the men looking at me like I can't keep it in my pants.

Exactly what I didn't want to happen, and Nate knew that.

The rest of dinner is fine. Everyone seems to know that the topic of my personal life is now off limits, and Nate rightfully keeps his mouth shut the rest of the night. When it's time to leave, we all pile into two vans that will take us back to the hotel—women in one car, men in the other. Yeah, this isn't a ploy to talk to both of us at all and figure out what's going on between Nate and me.

"Spill," Sydney says as soon as the door shuts.

"Nothing to spill."

"Lies." Daisy scoffs.

"You don't have a *very* pointed fight like that if nothing has happened. I'm not saying you're sleeping together right now, but there's something going on there," Toni says.

"It wasn't a fight. Just a difference of opinions," I counter.

Daisy snorts because the whole van cracks up.

I sigh. "You all are ridiculous. Nothing is happening between Nate and me. This is what happens when you work together and spend too many hours a day with each other. That's it."

"Sure. Sure. And none of us know what it's like to date someone in this field and all the pressures that come along with that." Sydney shakes her head.

"Except none of you had to fight for your job every single day while all of this shit is going on," I say without thinking.

The laughter and chatter immediately stop.

"First, your job isn't on the line, nor will it be this year. I can't comment on next season because that's not something we're discussing right now. So, please don't put that stress on yourself when that's not even on our radar," Toni says.

"And second," Daisy butts in. "So, there *is* shit going on!"

"Dammit, you guys."

"Look, we're not trying to give you a hard time. We just want to make sure you know we are here to support you. Formula 1 is hard enough. Add in the fact that you have placed the weight of all the women in the sports world on your shoulders, and you need people on your team. People you can vent to and turn to when it's all too much," Sydney says.

I gulp back the lump in my throat.

"I'm not good at the whole 'making girl friends' thing."

"Girl, none of us are. Why do you think we get along so well?" Toni says.

"Except me. I've never had issues making friends of any kind." Daisy winks at Sydney.

"That's true. You dragged me kicking and screaming into friendship, but I'm grateful for it." She smiles over to Daisy.

I think about their words, their support, and I see the value of it all. My only real friends right now are Nate and Murphy, and clearly that's getting out of control.

"I— Thank you, all. I really needed to hear that, I think."

"I'm setting up a group text. Please send all your bitching and juicy details about significant others, or trainers"—Daisy looks up at me with a smirk—"into this one spot so we can all stay well informed."

"I have a feeling that group chat is going to turn into blackmail really quickly," I grumble.

"Oh, absolutely." Toni cracks up.

The rest of the drive back is filled with laughter and friendship—something

I've been sorely lacking for most of my life.

And maybe I'm a little grateful to Nate for pulling that shit at dinner because it made me realize how much these women are truly here for me.

I'll never tell him that, though.

***

The flight home is uneventful, thank God.

I think Nate knew I needed a quiet break from everything. Murphy became my mainstay. His head is in my lap almost the whole flight. I don't care what Nate says; he's my emotional support dog, and everyone but Nate knows it.

Once we've landed, we rideshare back to my apartment.

"Sometimes, I wish Murphy could spend the night with me." I sigh wistfully as I pet the mutt, who is still cuddled up against me.

"Absolutely not. Nighttime is the only time he gives a shit about me because you're not around," Nate says.

"It's not my fault he likes me more," I tease and smirk over at him.

He doesn't get the chance for rebuttal because we pull up to my apartment complex. I get out and grab my luggage from the back. I'm not expecting Nate to join me since he has Murph with him, but when he starts pulling his luggage out of the trunk, I get more confused.

"I'm just walking you up and making sure you get home okay," he says.

"Then you're taking another ride to your house? Seems excessive," I mumble.

His head tilts in question, but he doesn't say anything.

They both follow me inside to the elevator, Murphy sitting like he's done this a million times. Once we get to my floor, Murphy heads in the opposite direction of my apartment.

"Murph, this way first."

My brow furrows in confusion as I walk down the hall to my door. Murphy sprints up to me, headbutting my hand for pets.

"What did you mean, 'this way first'?" I ask Nate before unlocking my door.

His hand scrubs the back of his neck, signaling he's uncomfortable.

"Nate . . ."

"I technically got my apartment first."

"What?

"I moved in a couple of weeks before you. Beck sent me the listing, and I didn't realize you were looking here until you were moving in and sent me your new address." He cringes.

"Why didn't you tell me?!" I scold.

"Because you would freak out, exactly how you are right now."

"I'm not freaking out."

"Okay." His eyebrows are almost to his hairline.

"I'm not."

"Yep, I totally believe you."

It's irritating how well he knows me because I am actually freaking out. I can't escape him, it seems, and this is just a cherry on top of an already fucked-up sundae.

"I don't have the bandwidth to deal with this right now," I say, unlocking my door, shoving my luggage in, and slamming my door shut behind me. I instantly feel bad and quickly open the door back up, bending down to Murphy's height.

"I'm sorry, Murph. I'll miss you tonight, but I'll see you soon, okay?" I scrub his ears. He licks my hand before I pull back and shut the door behind me again.

I swear I hear Nate mumble something like, "At least he can do no wrong."

For some reason, it makes me smile. I'll make him sweat a little. Lord knows he's made me sweat enough times to question why I'm so against seeing where things go, or hell, even just hooking up with him again.

"Good night, Remi. I'm so proud of you." I barely hear him through the door.

Tingles spread through my body at his words. Those last five words mean everything to me. Yes, he's frustrating. Yes, he's too tempting. But most of all, I admire Nate and want him to not just see me as a woman. I want him to see me as a success.

Chapter 26

May 27

I've been avoiding my journal.

I could say I don't know why, but I know exactly why. My podium win in Monaco, and the dinner celebration as a result, has given me too much to think about.

Nate, the women at Empress, racing, my life in general . . . There's too much in my head. Hell, there's still too much in my head, but I know this might be the best place to "talk" it out, so to speak.

I've been lucky in this sport. As one of the few girls in karting, my odds of making it here were slim to none. And yet, I worked my ass off. Put a thousand percent into every new level I've reached, and I met the right people. I don't discount the fact that knowing people is what landed me in Formula 1. If I had never met Luka and Daisy, I wouldn't have even been seen. I know that as much as I know the color of my eyes.

Never in all of my twenty-nine years have I created real and lasting friendships. I honestly have no idea how to handle these new people in my life. They all have this built-in group. They're all highly successful in their own right and can relate to each other. While Beck and Luka have driven, it's different. They were always destined to drive. Sure, they had hard journeys, but would they really understand how I feel, how much different it is for someone who is looked down on by every other team?

Is that what this all boils down to? I feel like I can't relate to anyone? Never have, so it's easier to just . . . not? Put on a face, talk to everyone, and make them feel appreciated, but never actually dig deeper to find real connections?

It spills over into other things too, now that I'm looking at it. Specifically, things with Nate.

I've learned a lot about him, and he's learned a lot about me. We've . . . been together . . . but I won't let things go further. Why?

It's not just that we work together, although it's an easy excuse to use—convenient because no one questions it. I don't know how to do relationships. If I said yes to all the things Nate wants and I fuck it up, which I absolutely will, it's not just losing a hook-up or a boyfriend. That's what scares me. Nate has the potential to completely wreck me, break my heart into a million pieces that I'll never be able to put back together again. I see so much more with Nate, and that's the real reason I push him away—I think. Because we could be so fucking good together. But what if we aren't? Is it worth the risk?

I'm not so sure it is.

And I do have too much on my plate right now anyway. This is a pivotal year, and getting my head wrapped up in a boyfriend is probably the worst thing I could do for my focus.

A boyfriend . . . Be so for real right now. You'd make him hate you, resent you, soon enough if we even made it that far. Well, this has turned into . . . something. I wanted clarity and instead got more confusion and self-loathing, so that's fun. Good job, Remi.

It's a good thing I have the Spanish GP this weekend. Distraction will be the name of the game since my head is apparently so fucked up.

Chapter 27
Nate

Spain has always been one of my favorite races. It's primed for drama with overtaking opportunities, and you can never really guess how the race will go. It's everything I love about Formula 1.

Today, however, I fucking hate this race.

I'm still on edge from everything that happened in and after Monaco. Remi's been distant, and I've let her. After the huge fuck-up during the celebration dinner, I haven't been able to come up with a plan to get her to really see me as more than her trainer or a distraction. I've also had the boys on my ass about what's going on between Remi and me. They won't get any answers from me, though, because we all know I don't have them.

I fucking wish I did, though.

Sighing, I pat my leg to make sure Murphy is following me. I look down briefly, smiling when my little sidekick is right next to me, and crash into someone.

"Oops, so sorry," I say immediately then look up.

When I see it's Alejandro Suarez, I'm mad as hell that I wasn't paying attention so I could avoid this asshole like the plague.

"If it isn't the outstanding boy scout, Nate."

"If it isn't the cheating asshole, Ale." I tilt my head. If he wants to be passive aggressive, I'll just be full-on aggressive. I quit his ass for a reason, and I'm not going to be friendly to him at all.

"God, you're so fucking uptight. Does that really work for you? Do the ladies like that? Does Empress? Hell, they must if they called you back here."

"Does that 'I don't give a fuck about anyone but myself' attitude really work?

I'm shocked to see you with a job after last year."

"Funny thing about racing. I can do a lot and still manage to keep my job. Can your sweet—and I do mean sweet as fuck—Remi say the same?"

"Shut the fuck up, Ale."

"Oh, touchy subject? That's very interesting."

"Stay away from Remi. If I see you even remotely close to her in person or in your car, I will absolutely do what I should have done last year."

He snorts. "What are you going to do? Run out on the track and get yourself killed because I got too close to your precious Remi?"

"You have no fucking clue what I'd do to protect her from your slimy ass."

"Thanks for the ammunition, bro. I really appreciate it." He claps me on the back, with a grin plastered on his face, before walking away.

Murph circles my legs before nudging my leg to pull me out of my anger.

"What a fucking prick," I mumble, scratching Murph's ear.

I compose myself as I make my way to the gym. A training session with Remi is on the schedule, and I can't let this bullshit conversation derail my job.

I send the door flying open and am across the gym in the makeshift office area behind the pitlane, tossing my keys down onto the workout bench, before Remi even lifts her head. "Neck rotation to start. I want two more reps than usual."

"Hello to you too," she says, heavy with sarcasm.

I can't look up at her, though. If I do, she'll see just how fucking pissed I am. This is not the time to explain any of the shit with Alejandro. She has a race in two days, practice in a few hours, and I can't be the person who distracts her.

"Your daddy is being moody, isn't he, my love?" Remi says in that almost baby voice she has when she talks to Murphy. "That's okay. We'll just get this gym session done, then he can go eat some food. I bet he's just hangry."

Her words crack the shell of hate surrounding my heart, and I can't stop the smile that creeps onto my face. I try to fight it, but she knows how to completely turn around my day without even trying.

"Sorry. Just had a run-in that pissed me off. I'm good now," I grumble.

"Want to talk about it?" She looks up at me, still petting my dog.

"Nope."

"Heard. Let's get to it."

God, I love her. Somehow, she just gets me.

I freeze at the thought. I don't *love* love her. I just . . . admire her skills. Yep, that's it. I may have feelings for her, but I don't love her after a hook-up and a make-out session. There's no way. That's not possible.

Jesus, I'm a fucking mess.

Remi starts her exercises without fanfare. Once she's done with the first set, I send her through the paces of our usual race weekend routine. The normalcy helps my adrenaline level mellow out after my run-in with Alejandro. His words are still in the back of my head, but they don't rule my actions anymore.

"Okay, I want to end with meditation."

Remi sighs, making me arch an eyebrow at her in question.

"I feel like meditation always makes me think about other shit when I need to be thinking about racing."

"Really?" First I've heard of this from her.

"Lately, I just sit here and listen to you talk, and my head decides it's a great time to overthink everything I've said in the last three months."

"Okay. I'll let it be dealers' choice then. What do you want to close on?" Every time I think I'm making really good progress with Remi's headspace, she throws a curveball at me that I have to dissect and figure out.

"Can we just sit and talk?" Her words are innocent, but the look she gives me raises my hackles. She doesn't just want to talk; she wants to pull the attention away from her. But I'll let her because I'm a glutton for punishment and will let her do anything she wants.

"Sure." She sits on the floor, Murph immediately walking over to her and putting his head in her lap. "Traitors . . . the both of you," I mumble as I join her.

"It's not my fault he loves me more," she faux pouts.

"Whatever. You start." I roll my eyes.

"What pissed you off so much before you came in here?"

"You're not as sneaky as you think you are, you know?"

"I wasn't aware I was attempting to be sneaky." She smirks.

"It's nothing for you to worry about, I promise. How are you feeling about this weekend?"

"Stressed. But something, or someone, got you madder than I ever thought possible. Do I need to go beat someone up?"

"You're a pain in my ass. What's stressing you out?" I ignore her other question because I will not be having two conversations at the same time, especially when she doesn't need to know about my history with Alejandro. It won't help her at all; if anything, it will just add stress for her. I'll never be the person who intentionally adds stress to her life.

"Everything is so fucking hard. Spain is a challenging track, and I'm not super confident on it. Getting Podium in Monaco is nice, but I need to keep up that level of driving, and I'm not sure I can."

"I've never known you to back down from a challenge. So why now? Why are you so doubtful of your abilities?"

She laughs humorlessly. "Do I have abilities? Because this season is showing me that maybe my 'abilities' have just been luck."

"For almost fifteen years, it's been luck?" I scoff. "Get real, Rem. No one is that lucky, and definitely not you."

"What's that supposed to mean?" Great, now she's angry at me.

"It means that you have worked hard as fuck to make it here, and suddenly you've lost the ability to be confident in your skills. You're doubting yourself at every fucking turn when you shouldn't be. How did Monaco feel?"

"It felt really good."

"The actual race, how did it feel in the car? Did you overthink it all?"

"No, it was probably the only race I've felt comfortable in. Like, I jumped into the car and muscle memory took over, and things weren't . . . easy, but they weren't complicated either."

I stare at her, willing her to see that she has all the pieces. It's not a good day for me to be patient with her, I know that, but I'm going to try like hell because this could be the breakthrough we've been fighting for.

"I don't know how to replicate that, though." She sighs.

"Jesus Remi, you are so fucking frustrating. You replicate that by *not* thinking. Stop overanalyzing every single minute in that car." So much for patience.

"You are being such a dick right now."

"I know, but I need you to hear this." I see the trainwreck happening, but I have no wherewithal to stop it. I'm flying at top speed, and nothing is going to stop the words from coming out of my mouth. "Block out all the noise. Me, Toni, Sawyer, Jason, every other fucking driver. Put on a pair of headphones and blast out some motivational shit or EDM—whatever does it for you—but stop thinking. Jump into that car and *feel* the turns. Feel the road, the force that the speed puts on your chest. Just fucking feel." I'm almost yelling, *pleading* by the end of it, and I know I've fucked up much more than my training session today.

That's one hundred percent on me. I let Alejandro's threats get to me, and now I'm taking them out on Remi.

There is a glossy sheen over Remi's eyes, and it crushes every ounce of anger and frustration I have.

"I'm sorry." I sigh.

"But you're right." Her voice croaks before she clears it. "I've never been so in my head before, but I don't know how the fuck to get out of it." She pets Murph's head.

"Let's start by doing headphones during downtime. It will keep people from talking to you. Then you avoid any interviews on the go. Duck, dive, dodge—whatever you need to do to feel the asphalt under your feet and the steering wheel in your hands, and nothing else." Every ounce of fight and irritation melts from me. There are bigger things at stake right now; I can see that.

I'm not sure when my mind turned back to work mode, but it feels good to focus on getting Remi back on track. Sure, the underlying anger is still there—the fear that Alejandro will pull some bullshit during the race— but is worrying about that going to solve anything for Remi right this second?

No.

But having a plan usually helps her, so that's what I have to do.

I watch her physically straighten her posture. Gone is the gloomy slump of her shoulders. Her resilience might be one of my favorite things about her. She should be so fucking pissed at me right now, but she's not. Well, she might be, but she's worried about other things first. She's pushing all the other bullshit to the background, and she's rising up to try this new approach. It's incredible to watch. Like every vertebra sliding into place is a symbol of her standing proud and confident. She rises out of the ashes of doubt to do the damn thing.

It brings a smile to my face.

"You ready?" I ask, already knowing the answer.

"Fuck yes. I don't have headphones, though, so if you could kindly find me some ASAP so I can keep this feeling, that'd be wonderful."

Her words almost make me laugh. I snag my bag that's just off to the side to pull mine out and hand them to her. She slides them over her ears, pulls her phone from between her legs, and hits a couple of buttons before closing her eyes.

Remi takes one deep breath before blowing it out as slowly as possible.

Then she smiles like she knows she's going to kill it today. And in this moment? This might be the moment that I actually fall in love with Remi Bouchard.

Because I can confidently say that no other person on the planet can handle me the way she does. And she looks damn good in my headphones.

***

Remi places fourth. Even though she had higher hopes, fourth shows consistency.

I buy her a set of headphones to match mine the second she crosses the finish line in Spain. We can build on this. I'll make sure of it.

Chapter 28
Remi

Canadian Grand Prix - 5th

Austrian Grand Prix – 4th

It's been a month since what I affectionately call 'my and Nate's heart to heart'. Whatever pissed him off that day during the Spanish Grand Prix induced some tough love that I was in desperate need of, apparently. I'm not exactly where I want to be, but I'm consistently in the points, so I'll take it.

Our next race is Silverstone.

I've been looking forward to this race, purely so I had an excuse to go visit the academy. Life in the academy was slower paced. I had time to do other things. In Formula 1, I've been sorely lacking that. The travel is intense, and with Nate on my case, I don't get a lot of downtime. Although, that's not fair either. I put more pressure on myself than Nate does. I haven't been able to volunteer as much as I would like or do other things that help me unwind. Card games and board games with Nate have come in clutch when I only have a handful of minutes to chill.

Media day is the best time for me to go visit my old stomping grounds, and I'm just biding my time. I'm not slotted for any interviews, but I'm going to wait for them to get underway before I leave. Everyone at the academy is getting ready for their race this weekend too, so it should be quiet when I get there.

I double-check my outfit in my office mirror before peeking out of my door, making sure the coast is clear. I'm halfway down the stairs when Nate's head pops up around the corner at the bottom.

"Where are you sneaking off to?"

"Did you put a bell on me? A tracker maybe? How do you always know when

I'm going somewhere?"

He chuckles, the smooth sound never failing to get my heart racing.

"We'll call it my sixth sense. So, where are you going?"

"I wanted to stop by the academy," I say softly. It feels too sentimental almost; that's why I wanted to sneak out.

"Sweet. Let's go," he says, and Murphy's head pops around his legs.

"You don't need to come. I'm good going alone," I tell him as I reach the landing.

"Remi Bouchard, do you honestly think I would offer-slash-invite myself if I didn't want to come?"

His smirk irritates me. "Shut up, and let's go." I sigh and smile back but walk past him, not waiting for the two of them to follow me.

"Yes, ma'am," he calls from behind me.

In truth, I'm happy he caught me. His presence has a calming effect on me. He grounds me and helps me focus on what I need to. Regardless of how we feel about each other outside our work life, he's always here for me on the job. Always making sure I have what I need and supporting me, even if he thinks it's a bad idea or unnecessary. He's everything I'd want in a partner, and it scares the hell out of me.

The drive is about an hour. We talk about the upcoming race more than anything, but nothing of true substance.

The minute I pull up to the academy's headquarters, it feels like I'm coming home after a *very* long trip. My chest releases, and it's like I can breathe again.

"You okay?" Nate asks as I make no move to leave the car.

"Yeah. Just . . . processing, I think."

And he lets me do just that.

My mind is trying to place puzzle pieces, like I'm so close to figuring out how to overcome this impossible imposter syndrome. But I'm not quite there yet.

Without saying a single word more, I get out of the car and walk to the front door. The passenger door shuts behind me, and the soft pad of Murphy's feet on the concrete catches up to me.

The moment I open the doors, I'm bombarded with memories.

"Do my eyes deceive me, or has our superstar come back to visit her humble beginnings?" Sandra Hayes, the managing director of the academy, calls from the front desk.

"Did you get demoted when I left?" I crack a smile.

"It's been a tragic decline, sadly. Luka has practically taken over," she says with a sigh as if it's a shame, before we both crack up with laughter.

I encircle her in my arms. "God, I missed you," I murmur.

"Feeling's mutual, Rem. How are you?"

"So good," I say before she pulls back and really looks at me.

"How are you really?"

My eyes blur with tears immediately. "Better than I was, but still struggling," I relent.

"Let's go to my office, and we can chat."

I nod, just as Murphy nuzzles my hand. He always seems to know when I need a little extra love.

"And who is this?" Sandra gets down onto Murphy's level.

"This is Murphy, Nate's dog."

"Lies. Murph loves Remi more than me," Nate says, sidling up next to us. I'm grateful he gave us a minute.

"What a doll. What kind of dog is he?" she asks, scratching his ears.

"We think he's a Rhodesian-Collie mix of sorts. He's great on a run, but can be a couch potato with the best of them." A smile plays on Nate's lips as he gazes down at Murphy with so much love.

"He travels with us," I say before I realize the implication of what I just said. "With Nate and me for races. He's Empress's mascot." I keep adding explanations like it will discount my words that made it sound like Nate and I are together. Maybe it's all in my head, though, because my feelings for the man are so all over the place. If anyone can wade through them enough to get a solid lead out of it, I'd pay big bucks.

Sandra's small smile lets me know she caught onto my entire thought process and now knows there is at least something going on between Nate and me.

"Well, come on. Looks like we have lots to catch up on," she says as she stands up and gestures for me to lead the way. Nate stands back, calling Murphy back to him. "You two as well," Sandra calls.

"Yes, ma'am," Nate says. They fall in step with us as we make our way to Sandra's office.

"Okay, spill. What's going on?" Sandra asks as soon as we get to her office. As I suspected they would be, headquarters are dead since there's a race this weekend, so we didn't run into anyone on the way here.

I sigh, but Nate beats me to answer. "She's overthinking everything and stressing out about her job, even though Toni and Sydney would never fire her this season."

"Thanks, Nate. So very helpful of you." I shoot daggers at him.

"Were you really going to be honest? Especially with me crashing?"

"Oh boy, do I love this," Sandra says, running her hands together.

"You love a trainer that butts his way in and thinks he knows me better than I know myself?" I tilt my head, but it's all true. Nate does know me extremely well. I just want to hold on to what little control I have around him.

"Hell yes, I do. You worked with Beck, right?" Sandra asks Nate.

"I did."

"Incredible work. I'm glad that Remi has you . . . in whatever capacity."

"I'm sitting right here. Jesus." My head falls into my hands; I'm feeling embarrassed. My emotional support dog makes his presence known by sliding between my knees and resting his head on my thigh, as per usual. I pet his soft head before looking back up.

"I can't believe we haven't met before. What you're doing at the academy is really incredible stuff," Nate interjects.

"Oh, we have lots of help. It's really taken off since Luka joined the team."

"I saw you picked up a handful of women this season. How are they doing? I'm embarrassed to say I haven't been keeping close track of your races," I say.

"Understandably. You're taking the Formula 1 world by storm. You have your priorities. And they're doing well. Adjusting well enough, but they lack the confidence you had, so they are having a hard time."

I feel Nate's stare. Sandra's words hit home more than I want them to. I was confident here. I was mostly happy here, and it's like that all disappeared the second I signed my F1 contract.

"I feel like I stepped on something there," Sandra says.

"You did, but I think she's trying to piece it all together," Nate says softly, still looking at me.

"I want to punch you sometimes, you know that?" I scowl at Nate. He's not wrong, though. How do I get back to the confidence I had at the Academy? I'm close, I can feel it just on the edge of the track when I jump into my car, but I can't seem to drag it out of me.

"I do." His goofy smile makes me smile, and the introspective moment is over. Like he does so often, he lessens the seriousness of everything, which I'm in desperate need of.

"You two are cute," Sandra says.

"And moving on." I roll my eyes.

We spend the rest of the time catching up on mundane things. She gives me advice, and I try to give her some ideas for the new drivers. Nate stays surprisingly quiet during most of it, only chiming in when he has some new insight. He'd do wonderful things here with his training if he ever wanted to be stationary for longer than a few weeks at a time.

"Would you mind if I just walk around before I head out?" I ask when we're getting ready to leave.

"You are always welcome here, Rem. Stay as long as you want. And don't be a stranger."

We hug before Nate, Murph, and I walk out into the large space.

We end up on the track before too long.

"What's on your mind, Rem?" Nate asks.

"I feel close," I concede. "Like I'm almost where I see it all line up, but I don't know how to fully get there, you know? Sandra was right. I had confidence here. I never doubted that I could make big things happen. It's not like that in F1."

"The sheer amount of money involved changes how people act. Team principals are at the mercy of owners, and if there aren't results, they move on to the next team principal, the next engineer, the next driver. Empress is unique in that they don't work that way, at least not yet. They'll give you at least a year to get your footing."

"I know," I say softly.

"You've been consistently getting points, and that's nothing to balk at."

"Sawyer's actually winning," I counter.

"Sawyer's been in F1 for years. You're a rookie."

"When I'm able to lose myself on the track, I do better. When my brain shifts into autopilot and just focuses on what needs to be done on the next turn or the next chicane, it's easier to drive."

"So how do we channel that every race?" Nate asks, his pinkie briefly touching mine as we walk.

"You're the expert here. You tell me." I arch my brow at him with a slight smile tugging up one side of my mouth.

"Making me really work for it, aren't you?"

"Can't let you get off that easy." My cheeks heat at my words, the innuendo clear as day.

Nate's bark of laughter makes me giggle.

"I'm pretty sure that is not a problem I have, Ace."

"Shut up! We're supposed to be focused on me right now!" My fake outrage is clear as day.

"So demanding." He tsks. "What about Murph? He has needs too."

"Who could forget about Murphy?" I pat his head as he continues to walk next to me.

"When we get back, I think we should go volunteer at the shelter again," Nate says.

"So you can get a best friend for Murph?"

"God no. Can you imagine two dogs on flights? I would lose my mind."

"I think it's a great idea," I say, intentionally brushing his hand with mine.

We spend another hour walking the track, playing with Murphy on the grassy areas, and talking about everything except the upcoming race.

I think this trip back to my roots might be exactly what I needed.

***

"All right, let's get started," Toni calls out to the group.

We hold a team meeting before every race to go over changes and conditions expected for the weekend.

"Looks like it'll be a clear weekend for once, so let's take advantage of that. We're looking at a one-stop unless the weather conditions drastically change on us."

Toni continues her usual talk before opening it up to the floor for anyone to add anything.

"I really think we need to focus on getting a strong race from both drivers," Sawyer says out of nowhere.

Toni arches an eyebrow but lets him continue.

"Getting points is all good and everything, but we need a double podium if we want to make a dent in the Constructor's." I jolt back at his very pointed criticism. "Remi, we really need you to push so we can make that happen. I don't know what the issues with your car are, but we need to figure it out sooner rather than later."

"Okay, that's enough. What we're not going to do is go after your fellow driver. Worry about yourselves, and your teams will worry about where you all are on the grid and plan accordingly."

"It was just an observation, Toni," Sawyer says, but we all see right through him.

"And if you have more observations, you can talk to your engineer or come to my office." Toni's tone leaves no room for interpretation.

"Heard." Sawyer sits down but smirks over at me.

Pure anger takes over once the shock wears off. The meeting ends shortly after, and I storm out of the room to my office.

"What an absolute prick," Nate says after he shuts my door.

"Nate . . ."

"I mean, he's not God's greatest racer or anything. I've never heard another driver speak to their teammate like that."

"Nate."

"Ignore his bullshit. I don't know what his problem is."

"Nathan," I finally yell to get him to stop pacing and look at me.

"Can I just be alone before practice?"

He stares at me, confused.

"Please."

With a small nod, he turns and leaves.

I don't know why I so desperately need to be alone, but this anger I feel toward Sawyer feels like the push I need. Sawyer's criticism was bullshit, but I want to stew in, sit in it, and really let it wash over me. I know what he said was technically true, although a dick move, but if he's ballsy enough to call me out in front of our entire team, then the rest of the grid is saying the same shit.

People doubting me is my bread and butter. It's what's pushed me to try so damn hard at every level of racing I've been in. It goes back to my parents and all their skepticism about my choices in life. And yet, the second I get to Formula 1, it's like that no longer factors in. Sawyer just reminded me of who I am and what I'm capable of.

Everything in my mind clicks into place.

I take in one deep breath and blow it out before I get changed into my racing suit.

It's time I show the boys what this woman is all about.

Chapter 29
Nate

I am stressed the fuck out.

After Sawyer's little show of cowardice behavior, Remi had requested she be left to her own devices. She even told Toni she would talk to her about everything after the race. Hell, she turned Cruz away, and he's usually the only one she does want to talk to when she's trying to get her head in the game.

Remi went through three practices and qualifiers before she would even talk to me. Even that was more about going over some stretches. She put her headphones on and shut everyone out. This will either be the spark she needed, or it will be her downfall, and I'm not ready to find out which.

She placed fifth in qualifiers, which is good for her, so I'm hopeful this means we're heading in the right direction. Sawyer managed pole position, which pissed us both off. I could see it in Remi's eyes when she watched his flying lap.

I'm frozen as I watch her bob her head to the music in her ears, completely in the zone. Cruz walks up and taps her on the shoulder, letting her know it's time to get in the car. She looks up at me once, winks, then puts her helmet on, covering her face.

What does a wink mean? Is that good? Do I need to plan a misery party in the hotel room after this? What the fuck do I do?

A hand claps my shoulder, startling me out of my spiral.

"She'll be fine. I heard what that asshole said in the meeting. She'll use it to prove him wrong," Beck says with a confidence I sure as hell don't feel.

"And you know this how?"

"Because when everyone doubted me, I used their doubts. It forced me to face what I really wanted when I was against a corner. Well, that and Sydney, but the people who are the loudest in the media were the ones I wanted to shut up. The only way you shut up the critics is to perform, and she knows that."

Her engine fires to life, stopping our conversation. I move to the back, where I'm out of the way but can still see the monitors.

The countdown starts, and before I have a chance to get my head on straight, the first lap is under way.

She has a phenomenal start, jumping up to third before the third turn. I'm on the edge of my seat and beyond grateful I left Murphy in the hotel room today. He has a dog walker coming by because I was too antsy to have him at the race today.

About halfway through the race, she's called into the pits. It's a fast as fuck tire change, and I have to give Cruz credit. He's trained his crew to the max, and it shows with their speed.

Amaro racing fucks up their pit stop, allowing Remi to slide in front of them, landing her in second place. Now, she just has to hold onto it for twenty more laps.

My leg bounces uncontrollably as I chew on my fingernails—a nasty habit I only have when I'm anxious as fuck.

Ten laps to go, and she's gaining on Sawyer. I stand up, leaning over the table as close to the monitors as I can get. I hear the radio messages in my ear, telling me they're allowed to fight it out as long as it stays clean.

My heart is in my throat as she gains on him.

Eight laps to go. She tries to pass him on Turn 4, but he outmaneuvers her.

"Fuck," I curse under my breath.

But she bides her time.

On the next lap, Remi wastes no time. She maneuvers to pass Sawyer on Turn 1, and I jump up, screaming, before she's fully passed him. The entire garage erupts at her move. Toni and Jason give her praise through her radio, and now it's just a number's game.

Six laps to go, and she still holds the lead. Sawyer can't keep up with her pace. She starts to pull away.

Four laps to go, and she's more than six seconds ahead of Sawyer.

Last lap.

As she comes down the last straight to the checkered flag, wetness graces my cheeks. I didn't even realize I had started crying until I cupped my face with my hands in shock.

Beck jumps up and down over to me. We both scream and try to talk, but there's so much noise we can't hear anything. Both of us are ecstatic Remi pulled it off.

Ripping my headphones off, I run out of the garage and watch her victory lap.

I have never been so happy and fucking proud of a driver before. Not even with Beck, although it was close.

She pulls into the winner's spot as everyone from the garage gathers behind the barrier. I try to keep off to the side because I know the crew wants to bombard her with congratulations. Sawyer pulls up beside her, angrily getting out of the car, weighing in, and heading straight to the cooldown room.

What a tool.

Remi gets her weigh-in out of the way then sprints over to the group. She completely bypasses the mechanics and flies into my arms.

"Oh my God, how did I just do that?" she says into my ear.

"Because you, Margret Bouchard, are a fucking badass, and I am so damn proud of you."

She pulls away to look at me. Her watery smile doesn't detract from her beauty at all.

I smack her ass before she climbs down, earning me an arched eyebrow as she jumps as best as she can without a running start into her waiting mechanics.

"You are so fucked with that one." Beck's voice is low in my ear.

"Happily so," I tell him, smiling at her in the throng of people cheering.

***

I think I took a million pictures and videos of the podium ceremony. I never want Remi to forget this day, so I may have gone a little overboard.

Now, I wait for her to finish up her debrief. I have thoughts on how to celebrate, but ultimately, it's up to her.

"Hi." She saunters up to me. "Where's my boyfriend?"

"In my room. Probably cozied up on the bed, snoozing the day away. I ran him hard this morning, so I thought he might be too tired for the actual race."

"And he missed me winning. He's going to be so upset." She shakes her head in mock shame.

"I'm sure we'll find a way to make it up to him—a bone, one of those cups of whipped cream you get him, whatever."

"How do you feel about heading up to your room and watching a movie or something?" she asks. There's a heat in her eyes, but that can't be right. It must just be the adrenaline in her system.

"You don't want to go out?"

"I absolutely do not want to go out. I'm fucking exhausted." She huffs out a laugh.

"Say no more. Are you ready now?"

"Yep." She holds up her little gym bag. I snag it from her, leading her back to the area where the hotel shuttles are.

I look over at her once she's buckled up. "I don't have words to express how fucking happy I am for you."

Her head lulls over to her shoulder, as she gives me a side eye. "Thank you."

"I knew you had it in you. What finally clicked?" I ask, curious what changed.

"Oh, you know, I remembered that I'm fueled by doubts and animosity—have been most of my life—and somehow I forgot that once I got to F1."

I laugh at her assessment, but from what I know of her family, it adds up perfectly.

"I'll take it, as long as it isn't directed at me."

"You do a fairly good job of not pissing me off most days. Too good of a job, actually." Her eyes shift to my lips, making my dick take notice.

"Remi . . ." I whisper.

"Just . . . don't overthink things."

I laugh because if anyone is the overthinker here, it's her. She leans over just close enough to touch, stopping my laughter in its tracks.

"Be very sure about this, Rem."

She answers me by softly pressing her lips to mine. It's almost innocent because we don't immediately maul each other, like it hasn't been fifteen months since we've done anything more than kiss.

I let her lead, though. I won't be pushing for more, no matter how badly I want to.

When she pulls back and looks at me with hooded, desire-filled eyes, I almost drag her into my lap. But my patience and willpower stand true.

I open my mouth to tell her as much, but the van stops in front of the Vanstone, prompting Remi to jump out.

I follow, like Murphy usually does, at her whim and happy to be so, practically wagging my ass.

The second we're alone in the elevator, she stares at me like she wants to jump me.

"Rem, I don't know if this is a good idea."

"I know."

"The reasons you didn't want to at the beginning of the season are still true today," I hedge.

"I know."

"You looked so fucking hot getting out of your car today as the winner," I whisper.

"I know." She blushes.

"One day, I want to fuck you in your racing suit." *What the fuck am I saying?*

"The jumpsuit does it for you?" She hooks her pinky with mine.

The elevator doors open, and I drag her down the hallway to my room. I press her against the door before leaning down to her ear.

"You do it for me, Rem."

I tap the key card and open the door, making us stumble inside.

Murphy greets us immediately, beyond happy to see Remi.

I let him have a minute before pulling Remi to me.

"What do you want to do tonight? The ball is always in your court," I remind her.

"I want to celebrate feeling alive for the first time this year. I want to celebrate being a woman."

I cup her jaw, fingers sliding into her chestnut waves. "Done." Not wasting another moment, I descend on her lips.

This kiss is nothing like the one in the van.

This kiss is over a year of pent-up sexual tension. This kiss is me begging her to see me as something other than her trainer. As a man who could be by her side, cheering her on from the sidelines, happy to be in her atmosphere every single day.

Her nails bite into my forearm. With an arm around her lower back, I haul her up to my chest. Her legs wrap around my middle, and I can't stifle my groan as she lands against my already rock-hard erection.

I walk, albeit slowly because I can't stop kissing the woman wrapped around me, to the bedroom. Kneeling on the bed, I shift us up to the pillows.

"Please be sure," I whisper as I pull back from kissing her, too much vulnerability in my words.

"Nate." She puts both of her hands on either side of my jaw. "I want this. Stop asking me."

I'll always do as my woman demands.

Holding myself up with one hand, I immediately place the other to her pants. I shove them down, but she has to help wiggle out of them.

Her barely there panties have me nipping her bottom lip. "Tease. What happened to practical underwear?"

"I wanted to feel invincible today, and silk usually does the trick." There's so much I want to say about that, but now is not the time. Now is the time to remind her how fucking good we are together.

"Does that mean you're wearing silk for every race from now on? Because I'm not so sure I can handle that." I kiss her jaw, down to her neck.

"Oh yeah? And how could I help you handle that?" she asks like the damn minx she is. This Remi is so much like the Remi in Japan last year. Witty, confident, not afraid to speak her mind. There aren't words to describe how happy I am to see her again.

"You could . . ." I trail off, nipping at the side of her breast before kissing her nipple. I pop off before meeting her eyes. "Give me every single pair later that day. I'll make sure they get dry-cleaned." I kiss down her sternum with a smile.

Her laughter fills my soul. "Sure, dry-cleaned. Is that what the cool kids are calling it nowadays?"

"It's what I'm calling it when I peel them off your delectable body every night."

Her laughter slows, but she doesn't say anything. I know better than to hint at doing more of this. She may have given in tonight, but that doesn't mean she's ready to date me. I may be ass over head for this woman, but I'm not stupid enough to think this lapse for her means anything other than a hook-up. I'm going to try like hell to turn it into more, but I'm also not delusional.

So, I do the only thing I know will get her out of her head.

I lick her cunt until she's dripping and writhing on the bed.

One day, I'm going to see if just licking and sucking her gorgeous pussy will get me off. Today is absolutely not that day, but I'd like to challenge myself at some point.

One orgasm turns into two. I'm shocked Murph isn't scratching at the door to help out his best friend, who is clearly screaming in pain—so he would assume.

I smile at the thought. Remi is loud as fuck right now, and all it's making me want to do is get her off again and again. See how many orgasms I can pull from her before she loses her voice or passes out from the sheer pleasure of it all.

Her fingers thread through my hair and grip it hard, yanking me up to her.

"Are you trying to kill me? Holy shit." She's panting, eyes wide. She's gorgeous like this.

"Death by orgasm doesn't sound so terrible."

"I have races to win; you can't kill me with pleasure right now."

My eyes shoot to hers as I pause. It's the second mention of the future, and for some reason, it stops me in my tracks.

"What?" she asks, eyes flitting between mine.

I can't tell her that the only thing I see in my future is her, and Murph. That the only thing I want is to be with her every single moment of the day.

Because she doesn't want the same.

I can't even fault her for it. She has bigger things to worry about, but it also means I can't just have sex with her and walk away. It'll crush me.

"I, um, I think I need to say good night." My whispered words are harsh in the quiet room.

She scrambles to sit up, still trying to catch her breath.

"What?"

My brain struggles to come up with the words to explain how I'm feeling, so I just tell her everything that's in here.

"I can't just have sex with you. I've tried for months to put you firmly in the friend and client zone, but no dice. I want you. I want all of you. And I don't think I can sleep with you until we're on the same page."

"So, you'll just eat and finger the fuck out of me instead?" She's outraged, rightfully so.

"I'll give you orgasms whenever you want them. I just can't . . . sleep with you."

My heart aches. I may have just lost the best thing to ever happen to me. But I can't pretend anymore.

"Nate . . . What the fuck?" she whispers.

"I like you, Rem. As more than a friend, more than a client. I fucking like you so much. I know that you have a lot to work through this year. I know your priority is racing. I'll be here in the wings, waiting, until you can make room for me. But until then . . . I have to draw a line in the sand. I have to protect myself . . . just a little bit." The pleading in my voice doesn't go unnoticed.

"I'm just getting to a place where I'm feeling comfortable in the car," she whispers.

"And I would never ask you to put me before your job. Never, Rem. I'm just asking you to think about it. When the season is over, see if this is something you could see for yourself."

I lean up, over her, and press a kiss to her lips. "I won't ever give you an ultimatum, and I want you to succeed in F1 more than anything. But I can't have sex with you and not want more, not need everything." I kiss her one more time before standing up and giving her space.

She lies there for a minute before standing up and grabbing her clothes to get dressed.

Walking to the door, I think she's going to leave without another word, but she turns around and shocks me.

"Thank you for giving me time. I see your . . . point and how you're feeling. But I need time."

It's not an absolute no. I'll take that tenfold.

"I have all the time in the world, Rem," I say softly back.

She stops to pet Murphy before standing up and looking back at me. "Oh, and Nate?"

I tilt my head in question.

"I already have an idea for that tattoo you owe me." She exits my room for the night, leaving me more confused than ever.

It was the right move even if it feels like shit. But she didn't completely write me off.

I'll take the win and keep showing her that I'm not going anywhere. Agreeing to let her pick a tattoo for me when she won tells that tale far more than I ever could express with words.

Chapter 30

July 8
It's been a wild fucking week. That's the best way to describe it.

I won my first Formula 1 race.

I think that still hasn't hit me yet, but it also feels incredible.

I feel free from the mud I was stuck in. I realized I can actually drive the car and do it damn well, if I can toot my own horn.

I told Nate it was people doubting me and animosity that helped me figure it out, and it was true. I needed to remember that people doubting me is all the reason I need to prove them wrong. I'm not sure why I started taking those doubts to heart this season, but no more.

It pissed off Sawyer to the max too. That was very enjoyable. Overall, I feel more focused, more secure with the car and driving in general. I'm not sure why I couldn't get a hold of it all earlier. I mean, almost five months is too damn long for a driver to get their shit together. We're fourth in the Constructor's championship, and frankly, for me that's not good enough. Sawyer's pulling his weight, as evidenced by him leading the Driver's championship. But it's time for me to help the team and get us into to position to take the trophy. We're not so far back that it's impossible.

I honestly feel like my focus is sharp. I feel fantastic about driving.

What I'm completely lost about is Nate.

The only thing that was better than winning that race was being with him again. Sure, I've been battling my attraction, but this . . . this solidified my feelings for him.

He told me he liked me as more than a client, as more than a friend, and I . . . I think I like him right back. I haven't been with anyone since him. Every single day we're around each other, I check him out, watching his tattoos move as he works out, watching his ass when he does squats. Those aren't friendly looks. Hell no. In my almost thirty years, I've never had someone affect me like Nate does.

It doesn't change how much is at stake for me right now, though. I have to respect him for just laying it all out there for me. It gives me time to really think about what I want, what I want my future to look like—all of it.

All I've figured out is that I can't afford to put more on my shoulders this season. Maybe we hang out over the holidays and see how things go. But I just don't see how there's a way to pull my focus off of racing right now. Who knows. I mean, what man is going to wait for a woman for another five months?

I clearly don't have the answers, but I feel like I'm closer to them. Now, it's time to buckle down and work hard to keep up the pace.

Chapter 31

Nate

The change in Remi has been noticeable. Ever since her win, she's been competing every single race. She's working harder than she has been, if that is possible, and she's still managing to find time for her new friend group and volunteer opportunities. I don't know how she has so many hours in her day, but I aspire to be her level of productive.

I'm also prepared for the day when she crashes. One day it'll hit her, and she'll need the break of all breaks, and I have plans in place for when that happens.

Today is a big day nonetheless.

Today is Remi's thirtieth birthday.

We're actually home for a change. So, like any lovesick fool, I've planned a surprise party for her—with the help of Toni, Sydney, and Daisy, of course.

"You don't think you went a little overboard?" Beck claps my shoulder as he walks into the space I've rented for the party.

"Nah. She'll like it." I should know; she's talked about this restaurant no less than seventeen times in the last two months. It's her favorite, and we get to-go food from here all the time when we're still training through dinner.

"What *is* going on between the two of you anyway?" Luka sits down at the table in front of us.

"Nothing." I shrug.

"That's not what Toni says. She told me that Remi didn't want to go out and celebrate her first win, but then she happened to see you both walking into the elevator back at the hotel . . . holding hands . . ." Felix arches an eyebrow.

"I thought your women were the queens of gossip. Did it transfer to you three?" I tilt my head.

"Deflection . . . They're definitely hooking up," Luka says like he just solved an unsolved mystery.

"Nothing is happening." At least that's the truth. Nothing is happening right now, even if I'm desperate for it. I meant what I said—I'll wait for her—but damn if it isn't killing me every single second.

Beck stares at me for a long second before he sits down and gestures to the chair next to him. The four of us get comfortable at a table before he speaks.

"You know we're all your friends, right? You can talk to us if you need to vent or just talk through some shit. Lord knows you've been that for me for more years than I can count."

"Really appreciate it, but there's nothing to tell."

"When Toni and I got together, she was worried about her job—understandably so—and I didn't fully understand it at the time. I mean, sure, I've faced scandals, but it's different for them, you know? Women in this industry have it hard enough as it is, and that's without adding anything like controversial partners into the mix," Felix adds in.

"You think I'm controversial?" I ask, affronted.

"I do not, but thanks for the information." He winks. "They have pressure on them that none of us have ever had. I don't know a ton of your history, but I know Toni, Sydney, and hell, even Daisy faced a ton of scrutiny over shit we would have never had to talk about. They have to answer personal questions, but they can't answer them with anything other than professionalism because it'll send the wrong message otherwise." He rolls his eyes.

"Sydney was so stressed when Pierce bought Empress. She was worried that everyone wouldn't respect her. That the only thing they would focus on was her dating a driver—retired or not. No one would look at her actual merit," Beck says.

"Daisy was mostly behind the scenes, but when Sydney got diagnosed, she stepped in a lot and had to do a ton of interviews. We were already married at the time, but she still got shitted on because of it. Media doesn't care if they are capable; they just want to find faults." Luka sounds disgusted.

"Why are you all telling me this?"

"Because any one with eyes can see that there's more to your relationship with each other. Not outside of our little circle, but we can see it. We also know that Remi is under a lot of stress and pressure because of her job. We just want you to know that we've all been there to varying degrees. Sometimes, it's nice to bitch about it with people who understand," Beck says.

I sigh. Remi and the women will be here shortly, but talking some things out doesn't seem like a terrible idea.

"I'm hook, line, and sinker for the woman, but she has enough to focus on. I won't be the one who pushes her just because I'm a needy prick." I could tell them the whole backstory, but that's not my story alone to tell.

"So, what's the plan?" Luka asks.

"Be here for when she's ready." I shrug again. "Train her, get her whatever she needs when she's stressed out, and wait for the time when she's ready to pull the trigger on us."

"Is that what the party is about?" Felix asks.

"Mostly. I wanted her to have a birthday where she could just be Remi. No stress of the job, no thinking about winning or training or diet. I just wanted her to have a memorable thirtieth."

"Yet you're letting the women take credit for it." Beck sends me a side-eye.

"What good would it do if she knew I set it all up? It would make her feel like she owed me something. And I can't do that to her. She doesn't owe me shit."

"I never thought I'd see the day," Beck muses.

"Yeah, yeah, you're the one who spread that playboy shit that still haunts me." I roll my eyes.

"If the shoe fits."

"I literally haven't had sex in a year and a half." I throw my hands up in annoyance.

The guys stop their joking and stare at me.

"Holy shit," Luka whispers.

"Mr. Playboy himself . . . taken down." Beck shakes his head in shock.

"What happened a year and a half ago?" Felix so wisely asks.

"Nothing," I say far too quickly.

"What?!" Beck yells. "You hooked up with Remi that long ago? How?"

"I'm not answering that."

"Wow. This goes so much further than I thought," Luka muses.

"You all need to chill out. I'm not gossiping about Remi, and I'm not telling you shit about *how* anything started."

"Damn, fellas, she's got him wrapped around her finger nice and tight. Was I this bad with Sydney?" Beck asks.

I bark out a laugh as Luka gives him a sad smile. "You remember when you almost punched me to get information?"

"Shit. Well, welcome to the club. We're all screwed when it comes to the ladies, and we love every second of it." Beck grins.

"Jesus, we should just throw on some pajamas and have a sleepover at this rate." Felix takes off his glasses and pinches the bridge of his nose.

"Not a half-bad idea. I'd have to bring Evelin, though, so Daisy can sleep in," Luka says.

My phone vibrates, saving me from this weird-as-hell conversation.

Sydney: On our way. She has no idea, just thinks we're going out for drinks.

Me: Perfect. Everything's ready.

I look up, and they're all giving me dopey smiles now. "They're ten minutes out. Please don't say shit. She doesn't need any of that tonight." I sigh.

Luka mimes zipping his lips, Felix just tips his head in a serious nod, and Beck is still giving me a shit-eating grin.

"What?" I ask him.

"Proud of you. All grown up and in love." He claps his hand on my shoulder.

"And that's enough of that. I'm going to get Remi a drink."

I walk up to the bartender and order her a vodka soda with lime and a whiskey for me.

Then I wait.

"How did you guys know I love this place?" Remi's voice is recognizable even over the noise of the restaurant.

"Oh, a little birdie," Sydney says, and I just know she can't hide her smile.

When Remi walks into the side room of the restaurant that I rented, she looks around in shock before her eyes meet mine.

"Surprise!" I say before handing her the drink.

She stares at me for a minute, like she's trying to piece everything together.

The table is set simply, mostly black and glitter as that's the common thread in her clothes that aren't Empress branded. And tonight, as if she knew the theme, she's in a tight little black dress covered in sequins.

She looks hot as fuck, and I'm barely keeping my shit in check.

There are also a few card games I used as a center piece. Some, she's talked about wanting; the others are her favorite that she brings on every plane trip. What started as something simple to clear her head has turned into a full-blown obsession, and I secretly love it.

Her eyes shoot back to mine, giving me a knowing look. Guess I didn't hide behind the scenes as much as I thought I could.

"This is incredible. Thank you all for coming and celebrating with me." She makes the rounds, hugging everyone and making small talk.

The waiter discreetly tells me the food is ready, and I nod in thanks before looking over to Sydney and nodding to her.

"All right, food's ready, so let's all take a seat. Once we get settled, we can start with the games," Sydney says, plopping down next to Beck, who kisses her shoulder. The only open seat is next to the birthday girl, and I know our friends did that on purpose.

Giant plates made for sharing land on the table. We immediately pass them around, loading up our plates with far too much food, and the room fills with hums of satisfaction and murmurs of "oh, that looks so good".

Remi leans in close to me.

"Thank you. The second we pulled up here, I knew you set this up."

"Every birthday girl should get the food she's been eating non-stop for a couple of months." I wink at her.

"I mean it, Nate. Thank you."

I nod. It would be so easy to close the gap between us and let my lips touch hers right now. And God, I want to. But it would just add fuel to the fire with our already suspicious friends.

The night is a mixture of drinks, *Cards Against Humanity,* and incredible conversation. I've never been shy, but I've also never had a friend group like this. It makes me wonder what all I've missed in my formative years, when all my time and energy was focused on getting out of foster care and making enough money to support myself.

My life could have been so different. Then my thoughts lead me down the road of never meeting Remi, and I can't imagine her not being in my life.

It's a night full of more laughter than I've ever heard from anyone in this group. Remi did that. She's the one everyone came out for. She's the one who drives people out of their comfort zones because she asked them to jump.

"Well, this was a blast, but we're going to head out." Sydney stands up.

"Us too. We're leaving for Hungary in the morning," Toni says with a sleepy smile on her face.

"We've got to tap out Ev's babysitter. This was awesome, though. We need to plan more game nights. Maybe once a month if we can manage it," Daisy says.

"God, that would be so much fun! I'll figure out everyone's schedule," Remi says, her face lit with pure joy.

Beck nods to me with a slight smile on his face, Luka claps my shoulder, and Felix leans down to murmur in my ear, "Take care of her. Tonight, and every day."

"Will do." I clear my throat.

We watch as our friends leave before Remi turns to me.

"This was the best birthday I've ever had. Thank you." Her eyes are a little glossed over, but she's holding her emotions back.

"It was all Sydney and the ladies," I deflect with a one-shoulder shrug.

"We both know that's not true. No one knows I love this restaurant except you. No one knows my obsession with card games. Except you. This has Nathan Murphy written all over it." She leans her head onto my shoulder. "Seriously, thank you. This was the best night." She sighs, and it's the most content she's ever sounded.

I wrap my arm around her and brace myself.

"I got you something," I whisper.

"What?" She jolts up, leaving her resting place on me and making me regret telling her. I'd love to hold her just a little longer.

"Just something small." I reach into my pocket and pull out the little cloth bag with a bow tied in a ribbon.

She carefully pulls the ribbon and opens the drawstring. The dainty gold chain twinkles in the lights as she pulls it up.

"Nate . . ." she whispers, cupping the small charm in her hand.

"You're hard to shop for," I admit.

"This is perfect." The Formula 1 helmet is an exact match to hers, including some pink tourmaline to mimic the pink swirls.

She sniffs, and panic hits my chest.

"I messed up."

"No! God no!" She wipes under her eyes, making me heavily doubt her words. "It's so perfect. I don't have words for how perfect it is. And thoughtful. Holy shit, Nate, this is the most thoughtful thing I've ever received." She flings her arms around my neck.

I hold her close to me, rubbing my hand up and down her back.

"Thank you for making turning thirty a little more bearable," she murmurs into my shirt.

I laugh at her words. "Your thirties are the best. You learned all the lessons in your twenties; now, you have money and can live however you want to. The world is your oyster," I reassure her.

"And what if I don't know how to juggle what I want right now? What if I end up losing what I want because I took too long to figure everything out?" She sits up and looks at me.

"Impossible," I mutter. "I think if you ask, you'll find that things—and people—are willing to do a whole lot to stay in your life and wait for you. You have all the time in the world, I promise." The double meaning isn't lost on either of us.

"I'm really trying," she whispers.

"There's zero pressure, Rem. I'll be here the entire time."

She buries herself in my shirt again, gripping my sides tight.

I don't know how long we stay there, but eventually the wait staff starts cleaning up around us, signaling our time is up.

We rideshare to our apartment complex, and I drop her off at her door.

"Tonight was everything," Remi says before lifting on her toes and pressing a kiss to my lips. "Thank you."

"Anything for you, Rem."

And I mean it. I'd do anything for this woman, and we're not even dating.

Chapter 32
Remi

Belgium GP - 3rd

Hungarian GP - 4th

The small three-week break we have in between Hungary and the Dutch Grand Prix is just what I needed.

In the academy, I didn't have these back-to-back race weekends, the never-ending training with no time to just breathe.

But I finally have time.

Nate saw that I was running past empty and gave me the first couple of days off of all things training.

Now, I'm sitting in my living room, bored as hell. I wanted time to do absolutely nothing, and it's taken me less than a day to be over it. I don't even have Murphy here to keep me company. A light bulb goes off, and I pick up my phone.

Me:

Can I borrow Murph for the day?

Nate:

I made a bet with Murph about how long it would be until you got bored enough to ask for him.

I chuckle to myself.

Me:

Who won?

Nate:

> Me, of course. Murphy doesn't talk.

I laugh more. I can just picture him saying that in a deadpan tone, like I was crazy for even asking.

Me:

> Of course, so obvious. Is that a yes?

Nate:

> You want me to drop him off, or are you coming to get him?

Me:

> I can come get him. Do you want lunch? My treat.

Nate:

> I still need to go for a run, so why don't I do that and bring you some food from that new Italian place down the street when I'm done?

I almost drool. I've been eyeballing that place for weeks, but pasta isn't exactly diet friendly when I'm racing.

Me:

> I absolutely won't say no to that.

Nate:

> Good. I'll see you in a few.

My heart rate picks up at how easy everything is with Nate. We're not together, thanks to all of my hesitations, but it doesn't stop him from doing small things for me. It doesn't stop him from going the extra mile whenever he can. I see it all, though. And it's starting to crack my resolve.

I run down the hall and knock on Nate's door.

When he answers wearing nothing but short running shorts, showing off that damn lighthouse tattoo and a backwards hat, I almost say "fuck it". He looks too damn good, reminding me of just how amazing we are together. It's not only sexual, although that's where a lot of my focus is currently, but we just click.

I barely notice Murph headbutting my shins until he licks my bare leg. My eyes drag up to Nate's, and I catch him trailing his gaze up my body. It's right this second I realize I never changed out of my lounge shorts that are cut high on my thigh and the tight tank top I put on without a care this morning.

Guess we're both getting a dose of look-what-you're-missing-out-on.

I quickly shift my focus to Murph. "Hello, my love. I've missed you." I kneel down and hug him—almost suffocating him, really.

"You never tell me you miss me," Nate grumbles.

I look up at him with a smirk to find his arms crossed over his very delicious chest, a smile on his face.

"Well, you would take it and run with it. Thinking it's cuddle time and that all other responsibilities don't matter."

"I truly don't see the issue."

"Go for your run, you ridiculous man," I tell him and grab Murphy's leash.

"You would be bored shitless if I wasn't ridiculous. What kind of life is that?" He scoffs.

What kind of life, indeed.

"Make sure you get some carbonara, please." Deflection is the name of the game for me. I'm still not ready to make a move for more with him, even if it is something I know I eventually want. I also know it's shitty of me to hold him at arm's length for so long, but I don't know what else to do.

"You doubt me? I know not to show up unless I have carbonara and breadsticks."

"Ugh. Hurry up and get your run over. I'm starving." I head to the hallway with Murphy right next to me, and Nate falls in step behind us.

"Do you want me to go there first? I can just grab your food then hit my run," he asks, tucking a tank top in the back of his shorts.

He seriously needs to chill on the hotness level. Or I need to just cave because the look on his face right now is doing a lot for me.

"No, no. Go for your run. I'll be fine." I wave him off, heading for my door.

"Jesus," he mutters behind me, so low I almost miss it.

"What?" I look back at him.

His eyes shift up from my ass quickly. "Nothing."

My lips roll between my teeth to stave off my smile.

"Shut up. I mean, can you blame me? Half your ass is hanging out!" he says with outrage.

"You're one to talk, Mr. Slutty Shorts."

He snorts. "Slutty Shorts? Is that an actual term women use?"

"I don't know!" I throw my hands in the air. "You look too hot to think properly. Put a damn shirt on or something."

We finally reach my apartment, and I very unwisely stop before I open the door.

Nate cages me against the wall with a hand on either side of my head and leans in close.

"You like what you see?"

"You've asked me that once before, and the answer hasn't changed in a year and half," I whisper.

"Shit, Rem." He pushes off the wall. "If I pop a boner right now, all of Austin will see it when I run."

"I'd pay a lot of money to see that. I bet you'd go viral on every social media there is," I muse.

"You are ruthless. And unfortunately for the lovely city, that view is only yours." He kisses my cheek. "Be back with your sustenance soon."

And then he's jogging down to the stairs.

"Your dad is going to get me in trouble, Murph." I sigh, opening the door and heading into my apartment.

***

Forty-five minutes later, a knock at my door sends Murphy barking his head off.

"It's me, you crazy mutt," Nate says through the door.

Murph doesn't calm down until I open the door, revealing the still ever-sexy man—this time with a shirt on, holding a bag of food bigger than my head.

"Did you order the whole menu?"

"I got options. And leftovers. You have three weeks off; you're going to want more pasta."

I have no doubts there's a dreamy smile on my face right now.

He rightfully ignores me, walking past us to the kitchen island and putting our food down. "Let's eat. It's getting cold."

"Yes, sir," I mumble as I turn around and follow him.

Nate looks back at me, and there's fire in his eyes.

"You liked 'yes, sir' a little too much, didn't you?" I roll my lips between my teeth to try to hide my smile.

"Dammit, Rem, I'm just a man. How am I supposed to *not* like you calling me 'sir'?"

I can't help it; I double over with laughter.

"It wasn't that funny." Nate rolls his eyes.

"It was pretty funny. And I gotta say, I'm not sure 'sir' is doing anything for me."

"Then call me an asshole. I truly don't care, Rem. I'll be happy with whatever you decide on."

"You're so dramatic." I smile.

Nate starts unpacking all the food he got—enough for a family of six, it seems—before he speaks again.

"I just want you to be happy."

"Feels like I'm getting there," I murmur.

"Good. Now, can you put on leggings or something so I'm less likely to maul you?"

"Absolutely not."

"Why?" he grumbles.

"Because if I have to suffer through a meal with you looking like that, then you have to as well. It's tit for tat, baby."

I dish up a heaping plate of pasta and breadsticks before sitting on a barstool at the counter.

"Is this my punishment for being wild in my twenties?" He looks to the sky.

"And a good chunk of your thirties." I shrug, taking a bite of my carbonara.

"Stop talking to Beck," he growls, shooting me a hard look.

I'd laugh, but I'm too busy savoring the deliciousness in my mouth. "Dear God, this is good." I moan.

"Rem."

"I'll share one bite with you, but that's all," I tell him, continuing to demolish my food in caveman fashion, moaning with every bite.

"Remi, I swear to God if you don't stop moaning, I'm taking the food away. I will literally strip right here and take you on the kitchen island. And I'm trying really fucking hard to respect your timeline on things."

"What if you still strip but instead of boning me, you just eat lunch?" I bite my lip. "Food and show? No?" I arch an eyebrow.

"Remi," he whines, collapsing into the chair next to me. "Please have mercy on me."

"All right, I'm done." I hold my hands up in surrender. "Promise." I put a spoonful of my food onto his plate before digging right back in.

We eat in companionable silence until he speaks again.

"This is really fucking good."

"Right? Can we find a way to put this into my diet, like, weekly?" I ask, batting my eyelashes.

He barks out a laugh. "Weekly, no, not unless you want your car to be overweight. We could swing biweekly."

"Stupid regulations," I mumble. "I'll take biweekly. Cut out the breadsticks if it helps."

"You make figuring out your meal plans hard as hell, woman. I'll do it, but damn."

"It's just because you're a sap for me and can't say no."

"That is absolutely true." He nods, taking a huge bite. He finishes chewing before asking me, "How was Murph? Needy as hell?"

"We spent most of the time cuddling, yes." I look over to said dog, who's giving me the sad eyes to get some table scraps. I won't cave because it's Nate's only rule, but I really want to.

"He missed you," Nate says softly.

"Is he the only Murphy who missed me?" I'm pushing the boundaries, I know I am, but I can't help it. Flirting with Nate makes me feel like a woman. Not a racecar driver, not one of the guys, but an honest to God woman with needs that I know for a damn fact he can take care of.

"Remi . . ."

"Dick move to ask. I know. Sorry," I concede.

"It's not a dick move. I'm just trying to figure out what you want."

"Get in line." I sigh. "It's not fair to you, I know. I just feel like I need this season under my belt before I start making huge life decisions."

It's more commitment than I've given him before. It's a timeline at the very least.

"Understandable. It's only, what, three and a half more months?"

Feels like an eternity.

"Something like that."

"Then let's see how we feel then. No pressure, no decisions."

"Okay."

"Hey." He grabs my hand and squeezes it. "I'm not going anywhere, I promise. And if you decide this isn't what you want, that's okay too." There's pain behind his eyes as he says it, and I just know it would crush him.

The problem isn't not wanting to be with him; it's making sure that I can figure out how to have a career and a relationship at the same time without sacrificing either of them.

Ever since my birthday, it's been the one thing I can't solidly overcome in my head. If I put too much of my time and focus on Nate, my racing could suffer, and vice versa. I haven't figured out how to feel confident in my ability to do both things yet, and that's what's holding me back.

"Thank you."

He takes off shortly after, leaving me with far too many thoughts in my head and no Murphy to cuddle.

So, I turn to my journal.

The sunset turns the light in my apartment into a gorgeous shade of orange.

For the first time since the season started, I have more than a few minutes to just sit and reflect. So, that's exactly what I do.

Instead of flipping straight to where I left off, I open my journal to the first page I wrote on and see something that wasn't there before—a note written in scratchy handwriting on the bottom of the page. I flip the page and find another similar note. As I flip through all the pages, on almost every single page I've written, there's a note from Nate.

Immediately, I'm annoyed that he even intruded in this way. Reading this is one thing. I can push that to the back of my mind and forget all about the fact that he sees far more of me than anyone else does. But him writing back? It feels intrusive.

That is until I read his responses.

February 2

What a fucking week. Somehow, I'm going to this damn gala with Sawyer of all people. I'm not sure how I really feel about it, but I also know I won't be pressured into anything I don't want to do. This is just friendship, possibly getting to know each other better, since we'll have to spend time together throughout the season. I'm thinking of it more like a friendship interview . . . at an event with all the bigwigs of the Formula 1 world.

That sounds so fucking stupid.

It's good for Empress, though. I know that. It's strategic for us to show up together. The two drivers getting along and forming a united front means we're an even bigger threat to other teams. If we aren't fighting each other, we're working together to win races. That's the biggest motivation for me: to scare the other teams with how well we work together.

I'm nervous for the big livery unveiling next week. It means I'm only a week out from testing, seeing everyone in Bahrain for their first big practice. It's where we all size each other up, and I pray to every single god I can think of that I don't make a fool out of myself. The pressure is unreal. I knew it would be a lot when I signed my contract, but now that it's really here? Now that I have to shut up and prove my worth? It's scary as well. I get one chance. It starts in two weeks. I need to show the other teams that I'm not just a pretty headline. I'm not just here to be a pretty face. I'm here to kick some ass and pave the way for other women.

I'm here to change the fucking world.

And I'm scared shitless I'll fuck it all up and ruin it for every girl after me.

February 2

What a fucking week. Somehow, I'm going to this damn gala with Sawyer of all people. I'm not sure how I really feel about it, but I also know I won't be pressured into anything I don't want to do. This is just friendship, possibly getting to know each other better, since we'll have to spend time together throughout the season. I'm thinking of it more like a friendship interview . . . at an event with all the bigwigs of the Formula 1 world.

That sounds so fucking stupid.

It's good for Empress, though. I know that. It's strategic for us to show up together. The two drivers getting along and forming a united front means we're an even bigger threat to other teams. If we aren't fighting each other, we're working together to win races. That's the biggest motivation for me: to scare the other teams with how well we work together.

I'm nervous for the big livery unveiling next week. It means I'm only a week out from testing, seeing everyone in Bahrain for their first big practice. It's where we all size each other up, and I pray to every single god I can think of that I don't make a fool out of myself. The pressure is unreal. I knew it would be a lot when I signed my contract, but now that it's really here? Now that I have to shut up and prove my worth? It's scary as well. I get one chance. It starts in two weeks. I need to show the other teams that I'm not just a pretty headline. I'm not just here to be a pretty face. I'm here to kick some ass and pave the way for other women.

I'm here to change the fucking world.

And I'm scared shitless I'll fuck it all up and ruin it for every girl after me.

I don't want little girls to lose hope because I can't get my shit together. I don't want little girls to give up on dreams because I couldn't succeed.

It's hard to sleep, knowing what's at stake.

I know that's dramatic as fuck, but it truly feels do-or-die for me.

One chance for every single little girl who has an interest in the sport. One chance to plant an idea in their head. One chance to show them they are capable of anything. No pressure and completely doable.

Now, time for a pep talk after all the dramatics.

You will kick ass at this gala. People will love you, and you will look hot as fuck while not looking slutty. You will be poised and intelligent. Then you will smile and do interviews at the livery unveiling like you've been doing it your whole life. Nothing to stress about at all.

Then you will kick everyone's ass on the track. Beat everyone's time and scare the shit out of them all.

Because you are a THREAT. You will WIN. And you will look damn good doing it.

When you feel overwhelmed and stressed like this, take a few deep breaths and count to ten. Repeat it until you start to feel more centered. Then remember you are Remi fucking Bouchard, and you are doing amazing things. You have no clue how special you are. Keep up the positive thinking because, at the end of the day, I can tell you that you can do this until you're blue in the face, but you have to believe it. Also, don't go with Sawyer.

March 2

It's been hard. I feel so fucking lost, and I just don't know how to change enough to make things better. How do you just suddenly get good at driving a car that you've been struggling with? How do you prove to people that this isn't all just a fluke? I'm past the self-pity stage. Now, I'm just angry. Nate's been giving me space, but it just feels like everyone is doubting me, talking when I'm not around and saying how I can't do this.

Maybe they're right

People are talking, Ace. They're saying how strong you are. How they're worried about you and how you're handling the crash. THEY. ARE. WORRIED. ABOUT. YOU. Fuck, I'm worried about you, Rem. I know you can do this, but if you can't get out of your head, if you can't stop second guessing everything, I'm worried I can't help you overcome it all. I just want to help you.

April 29

Today was unexpected. The whole crew showed up to support me and help me move into my new apartment. I still don't think I can find the words to describe how it felt. While I've made friends in the Academy, none of them were friends enough to spend time with outside of work. These people, my bosses technically, showed up like it was common courtesy not an incredible gesture of friendship.

And Nate . . . he called in the reinforcements too. He knew I would turn down help and made sure I wasn't alone. Although, he did fuck up and kiss my cheek in front of everyone. I don't even want to think about what the blowback will be. Sure, they all seem fine with it now, but that will fall apart in a second if things become a distraction. Even if Nate and I never do anything again, if the memories prove to be a disturbance to my racing, I don't think they'll be as unforgiving.

God. I don't know. My heads a fucking mess, especially after Japan. When I'm with Nate it's like . . . it's like the world is right. There's no tilted axis; there's no asteroids coming to rain on the party. It's just . . . comfortable. I don't know if I've ever been comfortable a day in my life. Whether that's my own doing or just the job I have, it doesn't really matter at the end of the day. I'm not in a place where I can be comfortable yet. I haven't achieved my goals; therefore anything with Nate just ends badly. Probably for both of us.

And I just realized that you, Nate, will actually be reading all of this so just . . . act like you didn't. Please. I can't handle a conversation about this right now.

In other news, I leave for Miami tomorrow and I'm so excited for the gala and the race. I feel like Miami might happen for me. It's one of the tracks I have actual experience with, so I feel more confident overall there. I'm manifesting a podium finish. you heard it here first.

 what a mess I am. This entry is all over the place. It's an apt reflection of my headspace though. I have a week off after Miami before the Italian Grand Prix. I think I need to seriously think about a break away from everything. Just a couple of days. Because I don't know how much longer I can have all of this swirling in my head before I break completely.

You know I just want you to be happy. If I can help you reach your goals, I'll gladly watch from the sidelines and cheer you on. If you want something more— and let me be very clear, I absolutely want more with you, Rem—then I'll ask where do you want me? If you don't? I'll still be your number one cheerleader, helping you achieve every single goal you have.

May 27

I've been avoiding my journal.

I could say I don't know why, but I know exactly why. My podium win in Monaco, and the dinner celebration as a result, has given me too much to think about.

Nate, the women at Empress, racing, my life in general . . . There's too much in my head. Hell, there's still too much in my head, but I know this might be the best place to "talk" it out, so to speak.

I've been lucky in this sport. As one of the few girls in karting, my odds of making it here were slim to none. And yet, I worked my ass off. Put a thousand percent into every new level I've reached, and I met the right people. I don't discount the fact that knowing people is what landed me in Formula 1. If I had never met Luka and Daisy, I wouldn't have even been seen. I know that as much as I know the color of my eyes.

Never in all of my twenty-nine years have I created real and lasting friendships. I honestly have no idea how to handle these new people in my life. They all have this built-in group. They're all highly successful in their own right and can relate to each other. While Beck and Luka have driven, it's different. They were always destined to drive. Sure, they had hard journeys, but would they really understand how I feel, how much different it is for someone who is looked down on by every other team?

Is that what this all boils down to? I feel like I can't relate to anyone? Never have, so it's easier to just . . . not? Put on a face, talk to everyone, and make them feel appreciated, but never actually dig deeper to find real connections?

It spills over into other things too, now that I'm looking at it. Specifically, things with Nate.

I've learned a lot about him, and he's learned a lot about me. We've . . . been together . . . but I won't let things go further. why?

It's not just that we work together, although it's an easy excuse to use—convenient because no one questions it. I don't know how to do relationships. If I said yes to all the things Nate wants and I fuck it up, which I absolutely will, it's not just losing a hook-up or a boyfriend. That's what scares me. Nate has the potential to completely wreck me, break my heart into a million pieces that I'll never be able to put back together again. I see so much more with Nate, and that's the real reason I push him away—I think. Because we could be so fucking good together. But what if we aren't? Is it worth the risk?

I'm not so sure it is.

And I do have too much on my plate right now anyway. This is a pivotal year, and getting my head wrapped up in a boyfriend is probably the worst thing I could do for my focus.

A boyfriend . . . Be so for real right now. you'd make him hate you, resent you, soon enough if we even made it that far.
well, this has turned into . . . something. I wanted clarity and instead got more confusion and self-loathing, so that's fun. Good job, Remi.

It's a good thing I have the Spanish GP this weekend. Distraction will be the name of the game since my head is apparently so fucked up.

If we're being honest here, I'm not exactly a poster child for relationships either. But people make mistakes; we learn from them and bounce back. What's important is knowing that and holding each other—me specifically—accountable to a higher standard. I would never break your heart, Rem, but you have the power to crush me. Chew me up and spit me out, and I'll gladly show up to work the next day to help you be the best racer you can be. I know the struggle. I understand the timing is completely shit, but I don't want things with us to hinder your driving. I'll be here. I'll be waiting for a time when you feel like you're ready. Never doubt that, okay? I could never resent you ... Ever. I just want to be with you. See if I can make you as happy as you make me.

July 17

My confidence is back. And it feels fucking incredible. I'm staying consistent, I feel like I can actually do this. I know I won't be winning Driver's, but I don't even care about that. I want to help us get the Constructor's. I want all the people that wrote me off to have to sit there and interview me as I hold the damn trophy in my hands.

Doubt and animosity . . . it's doing wonderful things for me.

I still feel like shit about Nate, though. I can't give him solid answers. I can't give into this craving for him. I want to, God do I want to, but I'm so worried it's going to mess up all the progress I've made. And what if he doesn't stick around? What if he doesn't want to wait until I'm ready? What if I take too long and he meets someone better? I think that would crush me.

Nate's the first man I've ever looked at and could see a future with. He just understands me on a level that no one ever has. I should probably learn more about him. To understand him more. Maybe that'll lessen the fear.

Who knows. I won't get any answers today, so I'm going to crash.

I didn't write back on the last one because my big-ass head got in the way of you saying you liked me. That it felt good to be with me. So, I went home and jacked off to the thought of licking you. Because I'm a terrible, horny bastard. I'm confessing because maybe you'll never actually see these, and it'll feel like a confessional of sorts. Who knows. If you do read this . . . I haven't been with anyone since you either . . . So basically, I'm fucked. I'll be waiting for you until the end of my days, I think.

Now, for this newest entry . . . I can only show you that I'm not going anywhere. Telling you isn't going to make a difference, but I'll show you every damn day, Rem. There's no one better than you. There's no one I could even look at besides you. There's no pressure. And just to add, you're the only woman I've ever met whom I could ever see a future with. You're the only one I want. And I'm willing to work for it. So put me through my paces, babe.

I choke on the tears that are now freefalling, a giant smile on my face.

He's been writing me back this entire time. He's been answering me, assuaging my doubts and letting me see more of himself since the beginning. I was just too focused on my own shit to even notice.

He's wanted me the whole time. Been on my side, no matter what I've thrown at him, with no complaints.

I sit back on the couch, reliving the past—all the little moments, all the pep talks, all the flirting, and all the patience.

It's been Nate since Japan last year. It's always been Nate.

My stubborn ass just couldn't reconcile how to have my career, that I've put blood sweat and tears into, and the man who's shown me nothing less than the utmost of support.

Holy shit, I'm an idiot.

I stop thinking—well, overthinking—and close my journal, racing to Nate's apartment.

I frantically knock, causing Murph to bark.

Nate opens the door quickly, looking panicked, even more so when he sees me.

"What's wrong? What happened?" He looks at me all over—checking to see if I'm hurt, I'm sure.

"Is what you wrote in here true?" I ask, holding up my journal.

"What?" He shakes his head, trying to understand what I'm saying.

"All the things you wrote, did you mean them?"

His eyes shift between mine before he grabs my elbow and yanks me into his apartment.

"Did you just now figure out I wrote back?" he asks, pacing around the room.

"Answer my question first."

"Obviously, Rem." He tosses his hands up in the air. "Of course I meant it all. I haven't exactly made it a secret that I want you."

I drop the journal to the ground and run.

The jump into his arms forces me to stop thinking about the what-ifs.

None of it matters. What matters is putting us both out of our misery. We've waited seventeen months. We've tortured ourselves—no, I've tortured us—for too long. Will there ever be a time where I feel like I can handle both my career and a relationship? I'm not so sure, so why not try to work through it all *with* Nate?

He bolsters my ass up with one arm and threads his other hand through my hair, kissing me like we've been separated for years.

It's life affirming, in a way.

But for once, I don't want to think about deeper meanings. For once, I just want to *feel*.

Chapter 33
Nate

Holy shit, am I dreaming? Is this all some weird lucid dream that I'll have to wake up from and be incredibly disappointed over?

My hand squeezes her ass hard, making her whimper.

Nope. Real as fuck.

I pull away from the kiss, pressing my forehead to hers.

"You're very pleased with yourself," she murmurs through a pant.

"Can you blame me?"

Her smile drops. "I'm sorry I took so long."

"I'm not. I told you I'd wait, and I meant it. Three months, three days, three years—I don't care, Rem. I'm in this."

"I am too. But I'm going to fuck it up," she whispers.

"I'd be worried if you didn't because I sure as fuck am going to mess things up." I brush my nose back and forth against hers.

"Can we have the whole talk about how we came to this point later? And instead, you take me to your bedroom and fuck the living daylights out of me?"

"*God,* I thought you'd never ask." I groan.

Thanks to my long legs, I eat up the distance to my bed in only a few strides and toss her on it. I tear my shirt over my head and drop my shorts like I'm up on stage to make money, and stare down at the woman in my bed.

"If you don't get naked in exactly two seconds, I'm ripping that shit off of you." I growl, growing more and more impatient by the millisecond. My hand goes to my hard cock, stroking it to take the edge off, as she frantically tries to undress. She gets tangled in her shirt and shorts somehow—her arms above her head, her shirt hiding her face as she tries to kick her legs to get her shorts off.

If I wasn't so far gone for this woman, I would absolutely make a joke right now, but I don't have enough blood in my brain to think at the moment.

My free hand grabs the fabric of her shorts, yanking hard and dragging her down my bed, but finally getting them off of her. Her lithe body is stretched out for me like the best present I could ever imagine.

"Uh, still stuck," she mutters. "Stop ogling."

"But you're so damn pretty to look at."

"Nathan Jude Murphy!"

I can't imagine it's possible for my smile to grow any bigger, but somehow, she manages to make it so. I kneel on the bed between her legs and lean over her to gently untangle her from her shirt. Her legs hook around my torso as I do. Once we're face to face, she blinks up at me like I hung the moon.

I have no clue what I did in this life to earn that look, but I'll spend forever trying to keep it there.

"Margret Ann Bouchard," I say softly in reply.

"Seventeen months."

"Worth every second." My hand trails up the outside of her thigh, the other bracing beside her shoulder. Goosebumps follow in my wake. I study them, her soft-as-silk skin reacting to my every touch.

The thighs wrapped around me squeeze, pulling me closer to where she wants me. Not going to lie, her strength is hot as hell.

"That damn smirk is about to piss me off if you don't touch me," she grumbles.

"Where do you want me to touch you, Rem? Here?" I brush the top of her pelvic bone, the trimmed triangle looking more enticing by the second, as her chest heaves with each panted breath. "No? What about here?" My fingertips move up her stomach, watching it suck in at my touch before I move to brush along the gentle curve under her breast.

Her hand moves to mine, jerking it up to her breast to cover it fully with my palm. My thumb moves back and forth over her nipple. It hardens under my hand and makes me lose some of my resolve.

"Nate..." Remi moans. "Why are you going so slow? I thought you'd already be done with one round by now."

I choke on my laughter. "Wow, such a vote of confidence in my stamina."

"You know what I mean."

"I do, which is why I'm taking my sweet-ass time. Call it a little retribution for teasing me in your gym clothes every fucking day." I lean down and nip at her jaw before moving to her collarbone.

"Like your slutty little thigh tattoo doesn't set me off every time I see it." She gasps as I pinch her nipple.

"The thigh tat does it for you? Good to know. I'll have to put something on the other one." I lick her neck, grinding down against her wet cunt.

She's definitely not wrong. I'm beyond close to blowing, but I don't want her to know that.

"You do owe me a tattoo for my win." She smirks before her face drops. "Jesus, I'll never survive if you have two. You'll have to wear pants every day." One hand wraps around my forearm by her shoulder, and the other holds my head to her neck as she grinds against me.

"I think I'll buy stock in running shorts. You couldn't take your eyes off of them." I nip at her ear.

"You're a menace."

"I am, indeed, but you like me this way."

"I'd like you a hell of a lot more if you fucked me already."

I chuckle into her skin until she angles her hips, and my cock notches at her entrance.

I suck in a breath and press up onto my knees. "I'm not wearing anything, Rem."

"It's fine." She moans.

But it's not fine. Look, I want to be bare inside of this woman more than possibly anything in the world, but there are bigger things at play here.

"It's not fine. I'm never going to put you in that position. Not with your career in Formula 1 just starting. I'm clean, but I'm not risking pregnancy at this point for you."

"I have an IUD, you chivalrous bastard. I'm clean. Now give it to me."

It's like my body hears her talk and takes on a life of its own. My hips hitch, pushing my head into her, and the sight alone makes me wrap my hand around the base of my dick to stave off coming.

"God, I forgot how big you are." Her eyes are wide, pupils blown.

"And you're going to take it all." One last squeeze, then I move my hand to her clit and circle it as I thrust all the way in.

"Fuuuuckkkk." I tip my head to the ceiling.

I'm not going to lie, I had hoped I could hold off. That I could Superman my stamina through this, but I fail.

Miserably.

Remi's already so worked up that it takes her minutes to start pulsing against me. My punishing rhythm sends us both spiraling. The second she arches her back and claws at my shoulder, I'm done for.

I want to tattoo those scratches on my soul.

I want to live inside of her, just so she remembers what I can do to her body.

My eyes don't leave her as she comes hard, eyes closed, head thrown back, looking so fucking sexy splayed out beneath me. I come with a gasp, gripping her hip so hard it's going to leave a mark.

Once we're both rung out, I press myself deeper inside of her before leaning over her again.

My forehead touches her as my nose trails up and down hers.

"Did I die? It feels like I died?" she murmurs.

"I'm glad you think that appalling show of endurance was good enough for you." I smile.

"I called it."

"You did. I'm not apologizing. I only got the one taste, and I've been jacking off a million times to the memory of it, but let me tell you, my brain did you and your incredible pussy zero justice."

She barks out a laugh. "Is this how you always are after sex?"

"Just with you, Rem."

She cups my jaw, looking into my eyes before pulling me to her and kissing me.

I don't think I've ever been so happy in my entire life. I don't know what this means for our future, but I don't care right now. Whatever curve ball she throws my way, I'll deal with, because this? This is something I'm going to have the rest of my life.

Chapter 34
Remi

I'm tracing the muscles of Nate's abs as we come down from round three, and my mind just won't shut off.

My hand moves up to the tattoos on his chest before I shift to sit up and trail my fingers to his thigh.

"What's it mean?" I ask softly. The lighthouse is different from his other tattoos. The others blend seamlessly into these bursts of colors. This one is by itself and strong.

"Perseverance." His voice croaks. He clears it before he continues. "It's a guide. Helps guide a person through challenging times and overcome obstacles. Some say it's a beacon of hope and a reminder to persevere through the toughest conditions."

I don't know much about his childhood except that he was orphaned young.

"Does this represent your childhood or adulthood?" I ask.

"Both. There was a lighthouse where I grew up. I was always drawn to it, but it became important after my dad died. At school, I read as much as I could about lighthouses and learned they have a much bigger meaning than just guiding ships. I clung to them and their meaning when I was in houses that were neglectful. Ones that were borderline abusive. Ones that had young kids who needed people to stick up for them. It wasn't all bad. A lot of kids had it worse than me, and I tried to remember that. But as soon as I was old enough and had the money, I got this." His fingers bump mine as we trace the outline together.

A tear falls from the corner of my eye.

"I'm sorry you had to go through all of that, and as a child."

"It took a long time for me to not be resentful. I won't say all things happen for a reason because my dad's accident sure as shit isn't that, but I think life is made up of all of these moments that feel unbearably hard. It's not until you step back or have time away from it that you see it all added up to something special. If my circumstances weren't what they were, however shitty, I wouldn't have the greatest job in the world. I wouldn't have gotten to see every single continent, travel the world, and see some truly incredible things. And I never would have gotten to meet you. If every bad thing in my life added up in the perfect way to align our paths, then I'll forever be grateful to them all."

"People underestimate you," I say, finally looking up, not bothering to wipe the tears off my face. "They put you into this box of the dumb-jock playboy, and all of that is so far from the truth. You're incredibly intelligent, caring, and one of the best people I know. I'm lucky to have met you, Nate Murphy," I tell him softly.

"All I care about is that you see me."

I lean forward and press a kiss to his chest, right where his heart is.

"I do."

His hand glides into my hair, pulling me up so we're eye level.

"Then that's all I need in my life. Well, that and Murph."

I smile. "I always thought having an unsupportive family was the worst. Not having people who have your back was hard growing up. You know what I'm starting to realize, though?"

"What, Rem?"

"I get to pick my support now. I get to surround myself with people who truly care about me. People who don't care if I win or lose, if I make a ton of money or am broke as shit. And you know who made me realize that?"

"Who?" His devastating smile nearly undoes me.

"You did," I whisper. "Everything I've put you through. The mess that is my head that you've had to wade through. And you're just here. No matter what, you're by my side. I don't think you know what that means to me."

"You'll just have to show me."

"Maybe I'll do something crazy, like get a tattoo." I wiggle my eyebrows up and down. It's incredible how we can go from serious conversation to playful.

And from playful to downright dirty. Nate is that person who can do it all, and I'm the lucky bitch who's in bed with him.

"Absolutely not. You get a tattoo because it's meaningful to *you*."

"Fine, Mr. Logical." I roll my eyes, my fingers dragging up the inside of his thigh.

"Speaking of tattoos . . . I owe you one for your win. You come up with anything yet?" He groans as I graze his cock. "Three rounds, Rem. I don't think I have a fourth in me."

I chuckle and plant a kiss to his chest. "Me neither, but teasing you is one hell of a drug. And I do have an idea. It took me a while, but I finally came up with something."

"I'll call my guy tomorrow."

"Just like that? You don't even want to know what it is? It could be something terrible!"

"And I'll still wear it with pride. You don't get it, Rem. I'll do anything for you and with you. There is nothing in this world that you could do that will change how I feel about you."

We may not have a round four, but we do spend the next hour making out like we'll never get the chance again.

***

Fourteen hours later, Nate walks out of his tattoo appointment with the outline of Murph's head and ears at the bottom of his thigh. I may have picked the tattoo, but he picked the spot—like the menace he is—and I'm wildly obsessed with it.

Chapter 35
Remi

Dutch GP - 3rd

Am I on a roll? Is that what this is?

Would I jinx it all if I say that I feel good about the car? About how I'm driving the car?

I don't care if I do jinx it because my confidence is back, and I feel like I'm finally on top of my game. I feel comfortable and like I'm a true threat on the grid. It doesn't erase how abysmal the start of my season is, but it should help us start making moves within the Constructor's Championship.

The struggles with Nate this year seem so damn pointless now. I know there's a chance this all bites me in the ass. I know there's a chance things will collapse, but right this second? I don't really care.

Nate's arm wraps around me from behind, and he buries his head into my neck.

"You're doing too much thinking," he grumbles.

"Well, some of us have been up for a couple of hours."

"Why? Dear God, I thought I fucked you to within an inch of your life. That should have been good enough to make you crash for at least eight solid hours."

I can't help but laugh.

"Does your ego ever not speak up?"

"Probably not. I'm much more fun this way." His hand caresses my exposed stomach.

"We have to be at the airport in forty-five minutes," I murmur.

"I can do a lot in forty-five minutes." His hand creeps up under my shirt.

"Nate." I stop his hand. "I still have to pack all my shit since someone kept me up too late last night."

"Just throw it all in. You can't have that much stuff." His teeth clamp down on my shoulder.

"I'm not a heathen." I gasp and place my hand over my chest, appalled. "And you only have one thing on your mind. You know, my training can't just be sex related." I turn around to face him.

"I think you just underestimate my skills. I bet I could make a whole training plan revolving around sex."

"It's truly inspiring how your mind works."

"Right?" His smile blinds me.

"I really do need to pack. We're only in Austin for two days before leaving for Italy. I don't like the hecticness of having my suitcase be a disaster when I only have a small amount of time at home."

While I would gladly do dirty, dirty things to this man, I know I would be distracted thinking about all the shit I still have to do. It would split my focus, which would only hinder my ability on the track.

"But when we get home? Or on the plane?" He gives me an open-mouth smile, and his eyebrows meet his hairline, letting me know he's teasing. But the gleam in his eye tells me he's a little serious too.

"Jesus. We're flying back with Sydney and Beck." I laugh.

"It's not like they haven't done it before." He looks properly chastised but still open to it if I am.

"We are not them! I don't own the entire team and am not able to do whatever the hell I want."

"A technicality, really." He shrugs.

"You're a mess." I shake my head and start to roll over to get out of bed.

He stops me before my feet hit the ground. "Forgive me. I've only had you for two weeks. I feel like I need to drastically make up for the time we lost."

"I'm not going anywhere," I tell him.

"I know, but we don't always have control over outside factors." His solemn words match his posture, and I know he's right, but it doesn't have to be this huge deal. We can take time and figure things out between us before those outside factors creep their way in.

I hope.

"There are only nine races left. It'll be fine." I pray my face makes my words believable because there's a lot that can happen in nine races.

Besides, we haven't even discussed what we are outside of screwing every chance we get in between racing and training. There's really not enough time in the day to talk about it, and I'm not in any rush to label things. If we label things, it makes everything real. It makes what's at stake that much more serious. I, for one, don't want to think about all the things that could go wrong due to Nate and me having a relationship.

A relationship. Can we consider what we're doing a "relationship"? Is my fear of the unknown and potential fallout from that title the thing holding me back from caving completely?

Nope.

Too many deep thoughts too early in the morning.

It's only been two weeks. We don't have to make any decisions yet.

Nate presses one more kiss to my cheek before finally letting me go. While I pick up everything off the floor—all the clothes that Nate so carelessly tossed everywhere after getting me naked—he rolls onto his back, the sheet falling low on his hips. His hands go behind his head, and the smirk never falls off his face.

"So, you're just going to lie there and watch me like some creep?"

"Is it really creepy if I was inside of you less than seven hours ago?"

"One-track mind," I mutter, opening up my suitcase, carefully folding the clothes I picked up.

"Only for you, Rem. But to answer your question . . . I can get packed in, like, five minutes. So yes, I will be just lying here, watching your hot self be all cute and neurotic."

"It's not neurotic to want my shit to not be a mess. We travel too damn much for me to just toss shit into a bag after every race. I mean, I would never find anything if I did that. What if I need my face moisturizer while we're on the plane? What if I need my charger? I would have to dig through a mess of crap, probably throwing it all over the plane just to get to it." My voice gets higher and higher as I talk, and I'm starting to realize that this isn't about packing.

"Rem . . . What's really going on?" Nate's concern as he sits up only makes me freak out more.

"It's just about packing!"

"Hey, hey, come here." He stands up, naked as the day he was born, making his way to me with his arms open.

I bury my head into his chest, trying to catch my breath.

"Are we freaking out about racing or us?"

"Is there an us?" I ask in a small voice.

"Oh, Rem . . . Maybe I haven't been clear enough. I'm all in. You can take as much time as you need. You can freak out and hold me at arm's length for as long as you need to. It's not going to push me away. The title is just that—a title. We don't need it if it stresses you out. If you need it because not having one is stressing you out, then title us away."

"None of that made sense," I mumble like the brat I am.

"Made sense to you, though," he says, running his palm over my back.

"I don't know what I want." I wish I had more answers. I wish I didn't second guess every decision of my life right now. I've always been overly confident, and then Nate freaking Murphy walks into my life and all that goes down the drain.

"And that's okay too. I'm along for the ride. Nothing needs to have a hard and fast deadline; we don't need all the answers right now. What I *do* need you to do, though, is focus on the rest of the season. If being with me starts to fuck with your head enough to affect your driving, then we need to have another conversation, but I don't think that's going to happen. You've been killing it. Your confidence has bloomed, and I really don't think there's anything that could deter that right now."

"I mean, there's technically a lot of things that could deter me."

"Stop being so fucking stubborn. My god, woman." He presses a kiss to the crown of my head.

"I just . . ." I sigh. "I've never done this before. I mean, I've barely had a relationship, let alone while I was driving in Formula 1. The most I've done is easy hook-ups." He growls, making me smile. "I'm going to fuck this up."

"Newsflash: we both will. I'm not exactly the spitting image of perfect relationships over here. You've heard Beck. You know my reputation. It might not be as bad as they make it seem, but there is a sliver of truth to it."

"That doesn't make me feel better."

"I suspect nothing will make you feel better right now. I just need you to know that there's nothing you can do that will push me away."

"Anyone ever tell you that you're good at this mental stuff?" I finally lift my head up to look at him.

"All the time. I am a highly sought after trainer-slash-sports psychologist-slash-best friend, after all."

I chuckle at that. "And always so modest." He winks at me as I sober up. "I'm sorry. I don't know why I panicked."

"No need to apologize. Shit happens. As long as we can talk it out, I'm never going to be mad at you for freaking out. It's perfectly normal, considering how much pressure you put on yourself all the time."

"I'm getting better!"

"Are you?" His head tilts in jest, but there's truth to his words.

"I'm trying to get better . . . Does that help?"

"Absolutely." He smiles that overly large smile that makes my legs clench together.

"Can you put some clothes on?" I ask, suddenly very aware of the vast amount of skin that's pressed up against me.

"Packing naked sounds like a much more entertaining game."

"Sounds like a nightmare. We'd not only get nothing packed, but we'd be late to board as well."

"One day, you'll naked pack with me."

"When that day comes, I'll . . . get Murph a best friend."

Nate's eyes light up. "Deal. Shake on it." He shoves his hand out for a handshake. When I make no move to shake on it, he grabs my hand and puts it in his, aggressively shaking them together. "I'm telling Murph about this too because you can't ever say no to Murph. He'll give you the sad eyes if you back out."

"You dare use your own doggo against me?"

"Abso-fucking-lutely."

I shove him, laughing. I'm not sure what I just signed myself up for, but it sure sounds like some long-term plans.

Chapter 36
Nate

Remi's stressed. Not her usual "will I fuck up this race?" stress. No, this feels directly related to our ongoing relationship.

Relationship.

She doesn't want to call it that, but I've been secretly calling her my girlfriend in my head and to Murphy since she knocked on my door, asking me if my responses to her journal entries were honest.

I don't care if it's delusional.

If I didn't think she'd freak the fuck out and potentially do some not-so-nice things in a Formula 1 car going over 200 kph, getting herself hurt in the process, I'd be shouting it out to the world already.

But I know she's not ready for that. Hell, she may never be ready for that.

I shake my head and refocus back on her doing some squats. She looks agitated, restless. It's a recipe for injuring herself, honestly, and I'm not liking it one bit.

"Take a break, Rem."

"I'm fine," she grunts, dipping down once more on the bench press.

"I said take a break." My tone is firm. Trainer Nate is not to be messed with, even by Remi Bouchard.

"What's up your ass today?" she asks, stepping out from under the bar.

"I should ask you the same."

"I'm fine."

"Are you stressed about Singapore?"

"No." Her answer is quick and curt.

"All right, sit down." I grab her water bottle and take a seat on the bench in the middle of the room. Handing it to her, I watch her slender neck as she gulps half the bottle.

She's procrastinating.

She finally puts the bottle down, looking over at me with eyes that speak so much more than her words will. Singapore scares her. I can't really blame her, honestly. It's notoriously rough for drivers, and with the forecast saying it's going to be one of the hottest races there in Formula 1 history, I'm worried for her.

Dehydration and heat stroke are both things we need to worry about with the upcoming race. That's not even talking about the street circuit being especially difficult for rookie drivers.

"Okay, I have a thought," I say instead of pressing her to talk to me.

"Okay . . ."

"Let's train outside. For the rest of the week."

"That sounds miserable." She groans.

"It will be." And I'm willingly subjecting myself to this torture for her.

"To what end?" she asks.

"To prep you for Singapore. It's still hot as fuck here. You can train in the heat, prepare your body for the sheer nastiness you'll have to endure, and maybe it'll help."

"Help me freak out less?"

"Help you prepare more," I counter. "And yes, it'll help you feel more in control of something you have no control over."

"It's supposed to be the hottest race, like, ever." Her voice is small, and her shoulders sag.

"It is. But you've handled worse. You've worked through harder things. It's just another race, and we just need to train accordingly."

"So, you're going to do this with me?" She stands up a little taller, like she enjoys the idea of torturing me.

I'd let her torture me in many forms, I'm afraid. A flash of her tits or a graze of her hand against my dick would go a long way for my willingness to put myself through hell.

"I am. I just need to drop Murphy off at home because it's too hot for him." I don't miss the dichotomy of my statement. If it's too hot for animals, it should be too hot for humans, but it's the name of the game in this sport, however wrong it feels.

"Okay, I'll come with you." She hops up off the bench, snagging her water bottle and heading to the little side room we've turned into Murphy's little area when we're in the gym lifting.

What I won't tell Remi is that I'm nervous for Singapore too. There's a lot that can go wrong. There's a lot that can happen in those tiny cockpits with the heat being as extreme as it's forecasted to be.

I'm worried for her health, but there's nothing I can really do about it. Training in like conditions is the only way I can have some semblance of control over what happens in Singapore, and it's not giving me much comfort right now. I have to show a confident face for Rem.

"Hey, you coming?" Remi pokes her head in, Murph between her legs, tilting his head as she speaks.

"Yeah. Yep." I walk toward them as Remi holds the door open for me. My heart is pounding harder than it should be right now because my mind is wrecked with worry still. But I do the only thing I can do: help Remi be the best she can be and hope it's enough.

We climb into my Jeep and head to our apartment building ten minutes away.

"What's going on in that head of yours? You normally talk my ear off," Remi says once we're almost there.

"Oh, just coming up with a plan for your workouts. If we can get some good training in for the next couple of days, before we fly out to Singapore, I think it'll make a difference."

The intensity of her stare makes sweat drip down my back. I can't let her see my anxiety about this race. She needs all her newly found confidence, and knowing I'm stressed about it will only make her second guess everything.

I will not be the person who causes more problems for her. I'm here to help her be the best she can be. But I'm also prepared for the day when she crashes. I have plans in place for when that happens. Contingencies upon contingencies for every occasion.

As I pull into the parking garage, Remi's hand on my arm stops me from getting out.

"Singapore sucks every year. It'll be fine."

When she believes that, I'll believe it too, I think.

"It'll be good, and you'll have a leg up with all this amazing training I'm putting your ass through." I smile, hoping it hides my worry.

"Ever so humble," she grumbles, rolling her eyes and getting out of the car. She pops open the back seat so Murph can climb out and heads to the elevators without waiting for me.

My tall frame allows me to eat up the distance once I'm finally out of the car, and I make it just in the nick of time before the elevator doors close.

"Sorry, my love, it's just too hot out there for you," Remi says, kneeling down when Murph whines.

He nuzzles her chest, and I'm suddenly very jealous of my own dog. He gets to stay in the air conditioning and has a front row seat to Remi's glorious breasts.

The elevator doors open, and Murph rushes out toward our door. Remi and I follow him, unlocking the door and crowding in the entry way.

Murphy seems to catch on that we're both feeling antsy, so he sticks close by. I pull on Remi's hand as she tries to walk further into my apartment. I bring her in close, wrapping my arm around her and tipping my forehead to hers.

"I have so much faith in you, you know that? I know you don't need me to tell you that you're killing it or that Singapore will be fine, but I need you to know that you are incredible. I am so in awe of you every single day. You're always going above and beyond in training, and it fucking shows, Rem. I'm so proud of you."

"Where is this coming from?" she asks as her hand snakes around the back of my neck.

"I just don't want you to be stressed out in the next race. We'll get through it, and then we move on to the next."

"I just have three practices, qualifying, and the actual race to get through." She smiles.

"And you'll do phenomenal in all of them. Of that, I have no doubt."

Remi presses up on her toes and kisses me softly.

"Sometimes, I don't think I deserve this much praise and hope."

"Why not?" I ask, stroking her back with a gentle touch.

"Because I just drive fast cars. There's nothing heroic or impactful about that."

"You don't think it's heroic to work your ass off and prove everyone in this sport wrong by being the first woman to race? You don't think it's impactful that you not only made it here but are actually challenging other racers for podiums? You don't think it's impactful that thousands upon thousands of little girls watch you on Sundays and have new dreams for themselves? You don't think it's heroic that through all the doubt, all the questions, you've never given up? You've never doubted you could do this?"

"You're going to make my head all big like yours," she whispers.

"I see no problem with that." I smirk, kissing her once more.

"I can't imagine both of us being your level of cocky." Her lyrical laugh makes me smile.

"Just . . . stop putting so much pressure on yourself. You are a role model, you have brand deals out the ass, you volunteer, and you travel an obscene amount. I promise, you have enough on your plate without adding more onto your shoulders."

"Easier said than done, I think."

"Then let me help take some of the weight. I'm a big man; I can handle it." I grin.

"And you are very unserious at all times."

"Rem, I'm dead serious. Use me and let me help take the load off. I don't care what it entails, just let me contribute."

I press a kiss to her forehead as she leans her weight into me.

"I don't really know how to do that," she says.

"Then we'll work on it."

"Add it to the list." She laughs.

"You ready to go brave the heat?"

She sighs. "No, but yes."

"That's the spirit!"

***

"I think . . . I'm going . . . to pass . . . out." Remi's bent over at her waist.

We're back at our favorite hiking spot, and I'm regretting the fuck out of starting with such a long hike.

"Like ,for real pass out? Or you're just exhausted?" Panic rises in my tone. Sure, I'm dripping sweat, my shirt long gone, and I've had less water than I should because I'm saving it for Rem. But if she truly is that close to heatstroke this far into the hike, my options are very limited on getting her help.

"Exhausted. This fucking sucks." She heaves in a deep breath and collapses onto the ground.

"It does. Drink some of this, slowly." I hand her one of the water bottles I packed.

She tries her hardest to not chug it, and I'm glad she actually listened.

"This is probably comparable to the car, though. There's no breeze, and the humidity is insane." Her chest rises and falls rapidly as she tries to cool down and catch her breath.

I sit on the ground next to her. "Couldn't have planned a better day for real conditioning."

Her head lulls to look at me. "I don't know if I can do this. I'll get no relief in the car."

"You can do it. We've been hiking for longer than the race is," I counter, hoping to assuage her doubts.

"But I'm not in a cramped car, in one position, unable to move for those two hours."

"Ace . . ." I give her the sternest look I can. "You've got this. If you can be up and ready to hike back in the next ten minutes, you'll be golden for Singapore."

"Sometimes, I wish you'd let me bitch and vent without all that positivity."

"Positivity is my middle name." I smile. I have to keep it upbeat for her because I know if I show an ounce of doubt or worry, she'll panic even more than she already is. She just got control of the car and her handle on it; I can't let her get tripped up by this.

"Ughhhh, you're annoying."

"I know. But will your annoyance lessen if I tell you I've got an ice bath with your name on it when we get home?"

"You tease." She sits up.

"I know the way to your heart."

She laughs. "That may be pushing it."

Don't I know it, because if I had the key to her heart, you can damn well believe I'd be using it immediately.

"One more sip, then we move," I tell her instead.

I stand up and hold out my hand to her once she hands me back the water bottle. She slowly stands up, stretches, and gives me a nod.

We wordlessly make our way back to the trailhead. Both of us are focused on breathing, not tripping, and our water intake instead of conversation.

Once I see my Jeep up ahead in the parking area, I relax a little.

"We're almost there, Rem." My throat is parched, but we're on limited water until we get back to the car, so I'll gladly suffer a little so Remi can have more hydration.

Her shoulders slump in relief, and her pace picks up. I blast the air conditioning once we're in, both of us sipping more water as the car begins to cool down.

"Holy fuck, that was hard," she says once she finally catches her breath. I'm trying desperately not to show her how challenging it was for me also. We'll call it dumb male pride or something.

"I will admit it's not one of my favorite things I've ever done."

"Just admit that was fucking awful."

I cringe. "It was pretty shitty," I relent.

"Thank God. I was about to think you were superhuman."

"Nope, definitely not that."

She looks over at me, eyes shining with emotions she's trying to hide. I won't push her to talk, though. Hard physical activity can bring up all sorts of shit—a release of feelings that sometimes don't make sense.

"I was promised an ice bath." Her chin wobbles.

"That you were. Let's go. I've got one set up on my patio that's already cold as balls."

"We're not going to the headquarters for theirs?"

Hell no. Not when she's in a sports bra and the smallest shorts known to man, dripping sweat. She looks like my every wet dream come to life.

"Nope. We're calling it a day. You can soak, I'm going to shower, and then I'll order us some food."

"Yes, please." She takes a deep breath, reining in her emotions and reverting back to the hard-ass Remi that everyone knows and loves.

I take solace in the fact that I get to see her undone in many different ways. I get to see the vulnerability she hides from everyone else.

By the time we make it back to our apartment, the sweat has dried on our bodies, and I feel like a day-old, wrung-out washcloth. Remi somehow looks more beautiful, with the slight sheen on her forehead and a slight pink tinge to her cheeks from the sun.

"Race you up there," she says before jumping out of my Jeep that I've barely turned off.

I follow her, like the sap that I am. "You don't have a key!" I call out.

"Damn you and your logic." She pauses by the elevator, arms crossed.

Maybe I should give her a key.

Woah there, Murphy, that feels like a very huge step for both of us.

Even though that's true, it doesn't make me want to give her one any less.

In the elevator, Remi leans into me, letting me wrap my arm around her for support.

"Are we doing that again tomorrow?" she asks weakly.

"The hike? No, but I think we should do some strength training outside. Less intensive and a lot shorter."

"I think I can handle that."

"I know you can."

She looks up at me. "You're a good man, you know that?"

I scoff, not used to much praise in general, let alone from Remi.

"I just mean . . . that was hard, and it completely sucked, but I think it helped my mindset for Singapore. If I can do that hike, two hours in a car should be manageable."

"Well, I'm glad."

The elevator doors open, and we slowly make our way to my apartment. We're attacked by Murph the second we walk through the door. Remi plops down on the ground to get some love. I head out to the patio and uncover the ice bath for her.

"It's ready for you whenever you're done with your lover," I tell her as I head to my room.

"Someone's jealous!" she calls outs as I strip out of my still damp shorts.

"Always!"

I grin and turn on my shower, not waiting for it to heat up before stepping in. It may not be an ice bath, but it does the trick.

Until the outline of Remi's naked body enters the bathroom.

"Rem . . ."

"The ice bath will be there. I wanted to show you my appreciation before that."

"Appreciation, huh?"

She opens the glass door, a little shy but no less determined. Who am I to stop my woman from doing what she wants? I sure as hell won't complain.

"Yeah. You always show me I'm capable of more than I think. And you do it all with me. I think that deserves something."

"Like what, Rem?" My voice is raspy with heated desire.

"Like this." She kneels down on the tile, and I wince at how much that probably hurts.

"Stand up."

"Nope." She pops the P before turning her focus on my dick that has no clue this position could be hurting her.

She takes me in her hand. My hand shoots out to brace me on the wall.

"Remi . . . Jesus."

"Just let me do something for you for once." She doesn't wait for me to say anything; instead, she licks my entire length, along the vein that's sensitive.

"Shit," I curse and watch a smile bloom on her face.

When she takes my tip into her mouth, I'm a goner. My stamina has always been shit with this woman, and that doesn't seem to be changing any time soon. It's a good thing I can still take care of her multiple times to make up for it.

She starts taking me deeper. My balls tighten up, and my hand threads through her hair, guiding her pace. It's my attempt to control how fast I come, although that feels pointless once I hit the back of her throat.

The pace I try desperately to lead stutters as my hand grips her hair tighter, my hips thrusting in short, shallow movements.

I realize my eyes are clenched tight, so I pop them open to find my little minx's hand between her legs, circling her clit in time with my thrusts.

"Hand off, Rem," I growl.

She startles, looking up at me in question.

"That cunt is mine. I promise I'll take care of you, but take your fucking hand off of it. That orgasm is mine."

Her legs close around her hand as her eyes close. She groans, the vibrations reverberating around my cock, and I lose it.

"Move your hand," I grit out, holding off until she listens.

Once her hand moves from between her legs, she looks up at me. That's all it takes to make me come. I'd be more embarrassed, but all I can focus on is getting her off. Hooking my hands under her arms, I haul her up my body and slam her against the tiled wall. Her arms loop around my neck as her legs wrap around my torso. My lips meet hers in a punishing kiss while my hand snakes in between us. I brush against her clit but move quickly to her dripping wet entrance.

Her head tilts back on a groan as two of my fingers slide inside of her. "Oh my God, Nate."

"That's right. Say my name, Rem."

She pants as I hook my fingers, rubbing along her front wall and hitting her G-spot with a steady rhythm.

Her legs tighten around me as she squeals, her pussy pulsing around my fingers as she explodes.

"Fuck yes," I hiss, nipping at her neck as she comes.

I'm already hard again, but we also just did a hard as hell hike. Recovery is a priority, even if I want to fuck her into the wall of this shower.

I keep kissing and nipping her skin as she sighs and slumps in my arms.

"Is this like cock-warming, except for your fingers?" she asks dreamily.

I burst out laughing as I gently remove my fingers.

"Just being greedy."

"Be greedy any time you want."

"Don't give me that power, Rem. You'll never get rid of me," I murmur against her skin.

"I'm not sure that would be so bad."

God, I want to believe her, but I know it's not that easy. It never is with us. We're hiding things between us, and until I can—very loudly—tell the world that I'm dating Remi Bouchard, things still aren't certain between us.

She could change her mind in a second, and I would stand here and take it. It would break me, but I'd break alone so she felt zero guilt. I would cheer her on as she took on the racing world.

I'd do anything for her.

It's nothing I haven't realized before, but somehow, I finally see the potential this has to demolish me.

Remi Bouchard holds my full heart in her hands.

And I'll gladly give up the organ for the chance to show her I'm worthy.

Chapter 37
Remi

Italian GP - 2nd

Azerbaijan GP - 2nd

The entire flight to Singapore, my head was on everything except racing.

The heat. The media. *Nate.*

God, Nate. I'm so conflicted. We're so damn good together, and yet I can't bring myself to be out in the open with him. There's too much at stake still.

And I feel like a bitch for not prioritizing our relationship . . . fling . . . whatever we are.

But I truly have no clue how to balance it all.

I should text Sydney, maybe Daisy—no, Toni. She understands the constant pressure and media coverage.

She's also my boss. I can't exactly have girl talk with her; however, she tells me to the contrary.

I'm a mess. A hot, sweaty, melting mess.

It's qualifying, and I'm just waiting for the last checks to be done before I get into the car. Even the ice pack vest I'm wearing doesn't feel like it's touching this heat.

"How are you feeling?" Nate asks, placing his palm on the back of my neck.

"Oh, just great. It's like a winter vacation in here," I say, sarcasm thick in my voice.

"Okay, smartass. How are you really doing?"

I sigh. "I'm hot and have sweat dripping down my boobs, and I'm already over it."

"If you weren't freaking out, I'd make a comment about the sweaty boobs thing."

My nose scrunches in disgust. "We need to talk about how gross that is and how you aren't going to be anywhere near my sweaty boobs . . . ever."

"Later, Ace. You can lecture me all you want later."

His hand massages the tension in my neck for a moment before he ducks down to meet my eye.

"You've got this, okay? You know how often you need to drink water. You know this course. Just stay focused and don't let any of the outside chatter get in your head."

"Yep." I wiggle out of his hold and grab my helmet. I know he means well, but right now, the pep talk isn't going to help. I just need to get qualifiers out of the way so I can figure out how much work I need to do tomorrow.

Nate gets the message and moves back toward the area he usually watches the race from, worry written on his face, but he's right. I need to focus. I'm here to do a job. If I can prove myself in the hottest race in F1 history, it would go a long way to prove my worth to this sport.

One deep breath is all I allow myself before hopping into the car and speeding off out of the pit lane.

***

Third.

It could have been worse, but I have some work to do tomorrow.

Now it's time to take a cold-as-fuck shower, avoid Nate like the plague, and try to get some good sleep before tomorrow's race.

***

I could only avoid Nate for so long. He came knocking on my door, freaking out that I had basically hidden myself away most of the day.

He thought I got heatstroke and was hiding it from him.

After this race, I'll analyze his concern for me. I'll think about what it all means and try to figure out my own tangled feelings.

But right now, I can't.

It's time to put some work in.

If I thought yesterday was hot, it's got nothing on this evening. It's somehow hotter and more humid, and I have a permanent pink tinge to my cheeks because of it.

Hands grab at my ice vest, throwing me off momentarily, before I realize it's Nate switching it out. He's been overly dutiful about switching them out often to keep my body temp lower before I'm stuck in the car for two hours.

Once the new vest is on, I'm directed to the track for the anthems and introductions. It's relatively quick, luckily, because I'm beyond ready for this race to be over. It's been so stressful.

My anxiety is through the roof, and the only way to temper it is to get in my car and feel the track.

I quickly walk to my car in the second row, Nate following me out of nowhere.

He spins me around, lifting the vest off my torso.

"You've got this. Drive hard, drink steadily."

I nod, searching his eyes for any doubts. There's nothing but encouragement and belief in them, though. I don't know what I've done to earn it, but I'm going to sear that look into my brain for the whole race.

I spin around, looking at the people and drivers surrounding me. Sawyer is ahead of me in pole. He doesn't even look my way. Alejandro is behind me in sixth. He catches my eye, sending me a look that I can't quite decipher. It's a mix of annoyance and . . . *anger*, maybe? I'm not sure because I've only talked to the man a handful of times, so I have no idea why he would be upset with me.

It doesn't take long for me and the rest of the grid to jump into our cars.

The look from Alejandro stays with me as the lights show the countdown. Once the fifth green light appears, I floor it, weaving around Malcolm Acheson to take over second.

I make it out of Turns 1 and 2 with ease, my sights set on overtaking Sawyer.

The team may want him to stay out front, but sometimes, you have to take matters into your own hands. He's mostly clear for the Driver's Championship, so stealing a win from him won't hurt. It would sure as hell help my overall confidence, though.

Things are smooth sailing until I take a sip out of my hydration system.

No water.

I try again, sucking harder this time, thinking there's a blockage or something, but still . . . nothing.

"Uh, guys, did we double-check hydration before formation lap?" I ask on my radio.

"Yep, it was good to go," Jason replies. "Is there a problem?"

"Yep, I have no water. Or I'm not getting any." I try to quell the panic I'm feeling, but all I can think about is two hours in this car with zero water. I can't get it through a pit stop. I just have to suck it up.

"Can you manage?" Jason asks in his no-nonsense tone.

"I'm going to have to." I try to match it.

"Just stay calm, keep your breathing even, and you'll be okay."

Not really hopeful if I'm being honest.

"Will do."

I take a deep breath, refocusing on the turn up ahead along with Sawyer. If I can make it through this first lap and make it to the DRS zone, there's a real chance I can pass him. Then I just need to keep my pace and lengthen my lead.

Totally doable.

I maintain my distance through the first lap, then the second I'm able to open up my DRS, I attack.

"Remi, let's not trade positions," Jason says.

"Jason, I have the opening, I'm taking it."

"Team first."

"If we're one and two, then it is team first. Doesn't matter who is in what place."

"We'll talk about this later."

I'm sure we will.

Sometimes, you have to take control of your own strategies. When the team is primarily focused on one driver, the other is forced to take matters into their own hands when they have the opportunity to. This feels like one of those times.

I'll apologize later, but right now is my chance.

I overtake easier than I thought I would, a bright smile on my face as I do. Only sixty more laps to hold the lead. I go to take a drink of water but realize belatedly that I have none.

The heat is already climbing in my cockpit, but I try to turn my focus onto my actual driving. If I focus on my lack of water, it'll make it ten times worse.

If I can push through until Lap 20, I can get a thirty-second breather during the pitstop. I'm not sure it will really help, but I'm telling myself it will for my own sanity.

"Box, Box. Box, Box." Jason's voice sounds eighteen laps later.

I take the exit into the pitlane, slowing my speed and pulling into our team spot. I take huge deep breaths as they change my tires and am off before it really makes an impact.

The heat is absolutely starting to get to me, but I'm desperately trying to think of something to distract me. Driving should be enough; hell, it should be my only focus right now, and yet the bead of sweat dripping down my back holds my attention instead.

I pull out behind a few drivers.

"Looks like they all still need to pit, so once they do, you'll regain the lead," Jason informs me.

"Thank you."

The next two laps, everyone trails off to the pits, leaving me yet again in first. Forty more laps to go.

My head starts to pulse in time with my heartbeat. It's not necessarily painful, but it's worrisome considering how many laps I have left. I try my water again, but still nothing.

It's okay. It's just a blip in time. You can do anything for an hour.

The affirmations play on repeat in my mind. If I can convince myself that the pain is temporary, the heat is temporary, then I can absolutely pull this off.

As the laps go on, the heat exhaustion gets worse. I'm starting to get lightheaded, which isn't a great sign.

Twenty more laps.

I just have to make it twenty more laps. That's nothing in the grand scheme of things.

The laps count down, Jason keeping me informed of where Sawyer is behind me.

With ten laps to go, I start getting stomach cramps, and my heartrate is off the charts.

Shit. I don't know if I'm going to make it.

"Alejandro just passed Sawyer. He's coming up fast on your tail. Now we need to push," Jason interrupts my freakout.

This is good, though. It gives me something to focus on instead of how badly the heat is affecting me.

I keep an eye on my tire degradation but push as full out as possible while still having a clean lap.

Six laps to go.

The end is closing in. I can do this.

Five laps to go.

"Alejandro is only a tenth back."

Can I hold him back for five laps? He's closing in way faster than he should be.

"Copy."

Four laps to go.

The cramping is getting hard to ignore. My muscles are tight and starting to spasm, not just in my stomach anymore. I look in my mirror, and sure enough, Alejandro is biding his time. There's a DRS zone coming up too, so I have to hold him off through that.

I turn the corner, and he takes his shot. I try to take my turn a little wider to block him, but it's useless. He pulls ahead. I watch as his hands tweak his wheel to the side in a jerky fashion. There's nothing I can do to stop it. There's nowhere for me to go to avoid him.

The back of his car hits my front wing and tire, sending me into a spin. I try to correct my steering, but I end up overcorrecting and crash into the wall.

The impact is immediate. My head that was already pounding feels like someone took a sledgehammer to it. My muscles are still clenched so tight, but I can't really feel any of it. My head is in a daze from the heat in combination with the crash.

"Remi, are you okay?" Jason's panicked voice finally registers.

"Umm, I think so. Shit, I'm sorry. I thought I gave him enough room."

"Don't apologize. We're putting a complaint in. Alejandro was way out of line. It looked like he jerked the wheel and purposely crashed into you. Are you sure you're okay?"

I can't really comprehend what Jason's saying. I do, however, take inventory of my body.

"Mostly. Wrists are killing me and my head is pounding, but I can still move my wrists, so I don't think they're broken. I need water," I whisper, emotion taking over as my eyes well up.

"We'll have it ready for you. Marshals will be there shortly, and they'll have some too. Just hang tight, and they'll help you out."

"Copy." My voice is barely above a whisper, but I don't have the energy for more.

Everything hits me at once.

The shitty race in the heat. No water, most likely heatstroke. And the crash.

I was just over three laps away from another win. I fucking needed this win. The tears start to fall, and I do nothing to stop them.

"Are you okay?" A man leans over my halo.

"Umm." I sniff. "Mostly, I think. I need to get out, and then if you have some water, I really need that first." I try to think logically. Give him what I think are clear instructions.

"Do you need an ambulance, or can you ride back to the pit? We need to take you to the med tent."

"No ambulance or med tent, just water."

I absolutely don't want the fuss. I'd rather head back to the pitlane and figure out how bad everything is first. If needed, Nate can take me to the hospital.

Nate.

Oh shit, I bet he's freaking out.

I start to lift myself out of the cockpit when hands hook under my armpits and help me out. I stumble once my feet are finally on the ground, but the man holds me up.

"Water." Another gentleman hands it to me. "And a ride." He gestures to the golfcart.

"Thank you both so much," I say, swaying as I try to hold myself together until I get back to the team.

"No worries. Just glad you're okay," one of them says as the other gets in the driver's seat and takes off. It's only a couple of minutes until I see the garage, and my relief is palpable. Taking small sips of water, I try to right myself before everyone rushes over.

I'm not even out of the cart yet when Nate rushes over to me.

"Are you okay? Are you hurt?" He cups my helmet in his hands, trying to see through my visor.

"I'm good." I grunt, his movement causing nausea to bubble up.

"Liar. Let's go." His tone is angry, but I know it's not directed at me. At least, I don't think it is. He carefully takes my helmet off before he wraps an arm around my waist and drags me to the back.

I barely register the mechanics and engineers who are probably all watching me like hawks.

Once we're in the back cooldown room, he plops me on the couch and kneels down in front of me.

The door behind him opens to reveal a pale Toni. She steps in and shuts the door behind her.

"Drink." Nate shoves a water bottle in my face, and I greedily take it. Forgetting that I should sip it, I down more than a couple of gulps before the cold water hits my empty stomach and starts to revolt.

"Shit. Slow down. Here." Nate puts a trash can underneath me, where I promptly puke up all the water I just drank.

"Oh my God." I moan, closing my eyes.

"You're freaking me out. Are you okay?" Toni's worried voice isn't enough for me to open my eyes.

I lean back on the couch with my head tipped up to the ceiling as it rests on the back.

"No. I think I have heatstroke. I have no idea about my wrists from the crash," I grit out, taking a sip of my water this time.

Nate's calloused hands grab my hand that's not holding my water and manipulates it around.

"Not broken but probably sprained. Sit up really quick," he murmurs, helping me sit up. He unzips my race suit, gently pulls my arms out of it, and manipulates it over my ass and down my legs by rocking me from side to side.

"We need to cool her down but not shock her system. I need to get most of your clothes off."

I open my eyes to see him grimacing, but I trust him to know what's best.

"I'm going to need a lot of help," I say, trying to joke, but no one is in a laughing mood.

With my racing suit off, I have on tight yoga pants and a long-sleeve athletic shirt, with just my underwear and a sports bra underneath.

He tugs on the tight shirt that's stuck to me because of all the sweat, using his strength to finally rip it off over my head.

Next are my pants—more difficult since I'm sitting on them—but he still manages within a couple of minutes.

"Okay, I'm going to leave your underwear on, but the bra needs to go. It's too tight and restricting. I'll put this right on you after, though." He grabs his own T-shirt behind his head and pulls it off.

"It's going to be a bitch to get off," I say, the fatigue starting to take hold.

Toni laughs but quickly covers her mouth. "Take a sip, Rem," she says once she's done giggling.

I do as I'm told, and then Nate manhandles my sports bra with surprising efficiency.

His shirt is over my head in record time, letting me breathe in the scent of Nate.

It calms me down more than anything has so far.

My breathing gets steadier, and I take small sips periodically.

"What now?" Toni asks.

"Now, we get her to the ice baths. It's going to hurt, but now that she's cooled down a little, we need to drop her temp drastically."

"We have one set up in the next room, so we don't have to go far. Do you need anything for her wrists?"

"Yes, please. If you can find some tape or wrap—anything like that—while I get her over there, that would be great."

Nathan Jude Murphy, always so great under pressure.

"Glad you think so," he responds, and I realize I just said that out loud. I'm too exhausted to care, though.

Then I feel him pick me up bridal style and move to the door. I close my eyes, taking another sip and curling up into his chest.

"This next part is going to suck, Rem. Do you want me to get in with you?"

"No. Just stay with me," I mumble.

"Always." I feel his lips against my temple as he kicks a door open. "Okay, love, this is not going to be a good time," he reiterates.

"Just do it." Another sip.

The second my feet hit the ice-cold water, I shriek. It's nothing compared to being mostly submerged, though. It's a jolt to my entire body. My muscles clench, and my teeth immediately start chattering, the breath stolen from my lungs.

"I've got you. You're going to be okay." Nate's soothing words do nothing to stop the violent reaction of my body.

But I don't climb out. I know this is the fastest way to combat heatstroke.

Soon, the cold isn't so terrible. It becomes soothing after being so hot for so long.

I hand Nate my water and submerge my head. It's the area that's been hurting the most, and the moment I'm under the water, it's like the pressure release valve opens.

I push myself up, gasping but starting to feel better.

"How do you feel?" Nate asks, handing me my water bottle.

I can finally focus, so when I look at him, I'm shocked to see the pain and worry dominating his features.

"Better. I feel better. I'm sorry," I whimper, those damn emotions taking hold once more. The tears drip down my cheeks at a steady stream.

"Don't apologize. That was the crew's fuck-up, and Alejandro's."

I open my mouth to counter his statement when the door opens again and Toni rushes in.

"I got you everything I could find, but I need to go talk to the stewards about that crash. You okay?" she asks me, the same worry in her eyes as in Nate's.

"Much better, thank you."

"Good. Don't stress anything. We'll chat once you feel a hundred percent."

Her words make the tears worse, and Nate looks beyond stricken.

"How do I help, Rem?" His voice tortured, but I can't offer reassurance right this second.

"Just stay with me," I hiccup through my crying.

"Always. I'm not going anywhere." He kneels forward, pulling my head to his chest and kissing my temple. "I'm by your side forever."

Chapter 38
Nate

Fear like I've never known is ripe in my bloodstream.

The moment I heard her water wasn't working, I started pacing. She was saying all the right things, but I could hear it in her voice that the heat was taking its toll.

Then the crash.

Never in my life have I been as scared as in that moment. And I watched Luka crash in person. No, having it be Remi—*my* Remi—was too much for me. Felix had to physically restrain me from sprinting out onto the track to get her myself. I'll have to apologize for that later.

Now, as I hold her the best I can while she's in the ice bath, the adrenaline dump is dispersing, leaving me wrung out and weary.

Her tears mingle with mine, both of us scared for very different reasons.

When I saw her crash on the monitors, everything flashed before my eyes—our relationship, or lack thereof, her career. Hell, my career. Every decision I've ever made involving Remi and the ones I desperately hope come to fruition in the future.

It all led me to one very obvious conclusion.

I love Margret Bouchard, and I will do absolutely anything just to keep her in my life. I'll do anything to show her that a relationship with me won't hinder her racing career at all. I have no clue how to make that happen, but I'm on a mission.

There's no time to waste after the heart attack I just had watching her crash.

I've been working up to this, sure, wanting to keep it at a pace Remi's comfortable with, but now *I'm* not okay with it. This bout with mortality took its toll on me, and I refuse to let her lead anymore. That's not to say I'll force her, because I sure as hell won't be doing that, but I will be taking her out on actual dates and having more sleepovers. Maybe more . . . I don't even know. My brain is moving too fast.

Holy shit, I need to breathe.

My thoughts are all manic and jumbled. They're no less true, but if I accidentally spew all of this to Remi right now, I know it'll push her away. She's sick and hurt, and doesn't need my impatience to be involved at all.

"Hey, I'm sorry," Remi's scratchy voice murmurs in my ear.

"Never apologize for that. None of that was even your fault."

The crash was Alejandro's fault.

Memories of him pulling shady shit last season flash in my mind. My heart drops, and my skin gets clammy.

Did he intentionally crash Remi?

Did he pull the same shit he did last season and somehow managed to get away with?

And for what? To let Sawyer win?

Is this all just a petty game to them both?

They could have fucking killed her.

I abruptly stand up, Remi's arms dropping from my shoulders.

"Nate?"

"I need to go talk to someone really quick. I promise I'll be right back."

"But—"

"Rem, I just need to do this, please. I'll be five minutes," I plead, handing her the water bottle and encouraging her to drink more.

She nods, resigned to me leaving, and the crack in my heart from earlier deepens just a little.

I walk out and damn near run into Felix.

"She okay?"

"She will be, but I need to talk to Toni," I rush out.

"She's at the podium ceremony because of Sawyer. What's up?"

I make a decision that waiting for Toni to come back will take too long, so I pull Felix away from the door and tell him my suspicions.

"Do you have proof of Alejandro doing this last season?" His jaw grinds in anger.

"I . . . I have notes from conversations and can tell you which races he pulled some shit at, but hard proof? No." I sigh.

"Send it to me when you get a chance. Toni already put in a complaint to the stewards for this crash. We all saw Alejandro jerk his wheel for no reason, so we should hear back from them shortly. If I can connect them or find a pattern, it'll give us more ammunition against him."

"You're going to do all of that?"

"I suspect you won't be leaving Ms. Bouchard's side for a very long time after this, so yes, I can handle investigating it."

I don't think; I just react. My arms fling around his shoulders in a hug.

"Thank you," I mutter.

"Does Remi know you love her?"

"Not yet." I step back.

"Then don't worry about any of this. Go show that woman what she means to you. And please make her take care of her wrists. We really need her healthy for Austin."

"Working on it, and done."

"And text Beck when you get a minute. He's worried about both of you. He and Sydney, I suppose. Just keep them filled in until we get home, please."

"Will do, sir. Thank you." I clear my throat realizing how unprofessional I've been.

"Oh Jesus, please don't start that. I'm not that old."

The corner of my mouth quirks up in a smile. "You are a little bit."

"I'll get Toni to fire you." He arches an eyebrow.

"Damn, using your connections for evil . . . I like it." I chuckle.

He smiles but then gets a serious look on his face. "I can't imagine a better partner for Remi. You are good together."

"Thank you." I tip my head.

"Now don't fuck it up."

I do laugh at that. "I'll try not to."

"And Nate?"

"Yeah?"

"Don't hug me shirtless again please." He smirks.

Spinning on my heel, I laugh and call over my shoulder, "No promises!" I have a woman waiting for me, and it's now my job to take care of her.

"Hi," she croaks when I walk in.

"How are you feeling?"

"Better. Still very shaky and weak, but much better."

"Good. I think we can get you out of the bath and work our way to the hotel."

"My clothes are in my office." She cringes as I help her stand up, the water bottle she's been working on falling to the ground.

"I'll grab them while you work on another water."

She hesitates.

"Rem, you can't walk across the walkway with just a wet T-shirt on. There are too many cameras," I try to reason with her.

She walks over to the chair in the corner, slumping down into it in defeat.

"Well, just . . . be quick please. I don't want to be alone right now."

"Do you want me to call someone? I can probably grab Cruz."

"Yes, please." She looks so thankful at such a simple thing; I don't even care that Cruz will see her dressed like this. I know he's not going to do shit, and he's just as worried about her as I was. Well, maybe not *as* worried.

"I'll send him in, and then I'll race over to get your clothes." I wrap a towel around her shoulders.

I don't waste time, heading for the door and shutting it behind me. I swear I hear her say something, but it's too faint, and I'd rather get this all done so I can come back to her.

As I reach the front of the garage, Cruz is walking back.

"Hey! Can you go sit with Remi until I get back?"

He starts to jog, not slowing down as he passes me. "Of course."

"Thanks, man!" I call out, but he's already in the back area.

I sprint out the door and to the temporary offices. No one's here since Sawyer won, and I'll take the blessing as something that doesn't slow me down.

Once I reach Remi's little room, I dig through her shit, pulling a random Empress shirt and the first pair of shorts I can find. I turn to leave but realize she'll probably want new underwear and a bra. Digging to the bottom of the drawer, I pull the first ones I find and sprint back downstairs and across the walkway.

I open the door. "Hey." Her coloring is better, and Cruz looks less stressed as well.

"Ready to change and head out?" I hold up the small pile of clothing.

"Yes, please. Thank you for staying with me," she says to Cruz.

"Anytime, girlie. See you back in Austin. Text me later." He stands up and claps me on the shoulder.

"Thanks, man."

"Anytime." He gives me a look that says he knows I'm full of shit, but I'm not threatened by their relationship anymore. He's a friend—a damn good one, at that—and I'm glad more than one person has her back.

Once the door is shut, Remi reaches out to grab her things, but she winces and grabs her wrist, making herself grimace more.

"Okay, let me do it."

I grab the hem of the soaked T-shirt, carefully lifting it up, drawing her eyes to mine.

We stare at each other as I slowly take my shirt off of her.

"Nate . . ."

"Rem."

"Thank you for being here with me." Her voice is meek, and I hate it.

"I wouldn't be anywhere else. My place is with you, Rem. All day, all night, and every single day."

"You really mean that, don't you?" She raises her arms up to let me slide the T-shirt over her head.

"Absolutely." I toss the wet shirt to the ground, and her hands slide along my shoulders, careful not to put pressure on her wrists. My hands glide down her torso, and goosebumps pepper her skin. Then I hook my thumbs into her underwear.

"That . . . This whole race scared the shit out of me. I don't really want to admit that."

"Scared me too," I tell her. She steps out of her underwear. I grab her clean pair and kneel down to let her step in. "I felt . . . helpless. I just had to sit there, knowing you were getting wrecked by the heat. And then the crash . . ." I swallow the lump that formed in my throat. Sliding up her underwear, I press a kiss to her stomach before standing back up and grabbing her bra.

"I feel like you could have picked something more practical." She smiles weakly. I look at the bra I'm holding and realize it's super lacy and see-through.

"I feel like I'm definitely not apologizing for this, however accidental."

"You just want to daydream about my boobs."

"A million percent." I smile as I hook it around her arms. She adjusts it to fit comfortably before I reach back and clasp it. Leaning forward, I kiss her softly before pulling back and grabbing her shorts.

We do the whole dance again as I get her dressed. Once we're done, I put yet another water bottle in her hand.

"You ready to go to the hotel?" I already have her phone and room key, which is all she brings to races normally.

"God yes." She sighs.

I cup her jaw, waiting until her full attention is on me.

"I don't want you to panic or freak out, or feel like you need to say anything. I just . . . have to tell you this."

Her eyes shift between mine, brow furrowed in confusion.

I kiss her again before pulling back. "I love you. And I'm not saying this because you just crashed and it made me freak the fuck out. I loved you long before today. But I feel like if I don't tell you right this second, I may never do it, and I promised myself I would take more risks with you." I sigh. "I'm rambling, but to sum all that up: I love you, Remi Bouchard. You're stuck with me for the long haul. Unless it's something you really don't want." I rush to add that last bit, second guessing my decision.

She opens her mouth, but I stop her.

"Don't say anything right now. I've sprung this on you, and I just needed you to know. I'm not trying to force your hand."

Remi pushes up on her toes, kissing me hard before dropping back down. "Take me back to the hotel, please."

Chapter 39
Remi

I love you, Remi Bouchard.

The words run through my mind on repeat. Nathan Murphy loves me.

Between the hellish race and the declaration of love, I feel pulled in too many directions, unable to properly digest anything that's happened today. Add in the exhaustion already seeping into my bones, and I'm ready to close my eyes and be done with it all.

"You want me to stay with you tonight?" Nate asks in the elevator.

"Please." I lean into his side, hoping I'll absorb some of his strength.

Luckily, Murph stayed home for this race because of the heat. Beck and Sydney are watching him, so we don't have another thing to worry about.

The elevator opens, and without hesitation, Nate swoops me up into his arms and carries me to my room. He taps the key he holds onto for me to the door, and we're inside before my head can catch up.

Nate sets me down on the bed, removing my shoes and socks before moving to my shorts. The simple action of just taking care of me has my tears welling up. The impact of the day is hitting me hard.

"Oh, Rem, do your wrists hurt? Do you want some ice? Pain killers?"

"Yes, but I don't think that's why I'm crying," I say through my tears.

"Okay. Shit. Okay. Let me get you that stuff, and then we can figure out what else is going on." He's frantic, I realize, which only makes me cry harder.

Nate comes back in record time, handing me the ice packs and then shoving a couple of pills and a bottle of water in my face.

"Swallow. Drink."

I do as directed, but his words make me smile. "Usually, you buy a girl dinner before issuing demands like that."

"Remi . . . you are literally bawling your eyes out. Now's not the time for banter."

My watery laugh doesn't appease him, so I grab him by his shirt and pull, telling him wordlessly that I want him to lie down with me.

I curl into his side, adjusting so there's no pressure on my wrists. His arm wraps around me.

"Talk to me, Rem," he mutters into the crown of my head.

"I crashed today."

"Technically, Alejandro crashed into you." I feel his muscles bunch up tight when he says Alejandro's name.

"And my water didn't work."

"Cruz won't let that happen again."

"I was so worried about the damn heat. We trained, and I felt so good, like I could handle it, and then I didn't have any fucking water." I am starting to get pissed now. The many fuck-ups of the day seem to not land on my shoulders at all. I just happened to be at the wrong place at the wrong time.

"I'm so sorry, Rem." Nate's hand slides against my shoulder and arm, trying to comfort me.

"None of this is your fault." I sniffle. The emotional side of everything is tapering off because the anger is starting to come out.

"How do I help?" he asks.

"Just keep doing this." I press a kiss to his chest, right where I know there's a tattoo of a watercolor bluebell.

I think about what this race means in the overall standings. What this means for the team, for Sawyer, for *me*. All I come up with is that I need to produce in the last six races. Try my best and hope it's enough.

"Are my wrists going to be okay for Austin?" I ask.

"Should be. They'll hurt for a few days, but they're sprained, so as long as you aren't pushing your body to the max and actually letting them rest, they should be good to go. Although, getting an X-ray when we get home wouldn't be a terrible idea, just to make sure."

"Whatever you think is best," I murmur.

"I just want to make sure you're okay, Rem. Anything I can do to help, I'll do it."

"This is helping."

"Good. You hungry at all?"

"Not really. I think I'm going to crash soon." I cringe at my choice of words. "Fall asleep."

"Hey, everyone has crashes, I promise. It's how you move forward after them that really determines your fate in Formula 1."

"You're right." I sigh, making a mental note to call Luka when we get back to town and see if he's up for a chat. If anyone knows about crashes affecting their future, it's him.

"Why don't we just call it a night? Get some sleep, and we'll talk about everything under the sun on the flight back tomorrow."

I nod but end up staying up into the early morning hours, listening to Nate's beating heart. The exhaustion isn't enough to pull me under.

Because the one thing I can't get out of my head is this incredible man being in love with me.

And I think I might love him right back.

***

I'm quiet for most of the flight back to Austin, too busy playing out a hundred different scenarios about Nate and me openly being together.

And the only solid conclusion I have is that we lie low for the last six races and then go public over the winter break. Or not even make a statement because who the fuck cares? Paparazzi can get whatever photos they want and speculate like they will whether we release a statement or not.

"Where's your mind at?" Nate sits next to me, handing me an electrolyte drink since I'm still not one hundred percent after my heatstroke scare.

"Everywhere." I laugh.

"That doesn't exactly help me help you." A soft smile lingers on his face as he takes the seat next to me. We're lucky to have the plane to ourselves today since Toni and Felix stayed in Singapore for a few extra days.

"I think I'm still trying to process things. Like, I saw an article that said the crash was intentional." I deflect what I'm really thinking about.

"Stop looking at articles."

"Funnily enough, you're not the boss of me." I tilt my head as I look at him. What I see shocks me. Does he look guilty?

"What do you know?"

"Nothing," he quips too quickly.

"Nathan . . ."

"Gah, never call me that again unless you say the full damn thing, and even that . . . Stop doing that."

His hyperfocus on me calling him Nathan gets my attention more than his words.

"Tell me what's going on. If you don't, I'll just hunt around online, reading all the speculation, and will probably get a wide variety of answers."

"God, you play so dirty sometimes."

"No, playing dirty would be withholding sex until you tell me. I'm not that cruel . . . yet." I grin.

"Keep it up, and I'll show you exactly how empty that threat is." His hand slides up my outer thigh.

"So cocky." I shake my head.

"You're telling me if I were to tease the ever-living fuck out of you for hours, you wouldn't cave?"

"Now, that's playing dirty," I mumble, admitting defeat. I don't think I could last thirty minutes of his teasing without caving. I think that says more about me than him, but whatever.

His hand moves up to cup my jaw, forcing me to look at him.

"I don't have anything definitive. Just a gut feeling and evidence of past transgressions."

"What does that mean?"

"It means that Alejandro jerked his wheel into you and most likely did it on purpose. Toni and Felix launched a complaint, but I haven't looked to see what the findings were."

"And what past evidence do you have? Why would he even do that? It'll ruin his entire career." I try to grasp onto what Nate's saying.

"When I was training him last season, he crashed a couple of times. I didn't think anything of it until we were in the gym one day, and he was talking shit about Malcolm Acheson and how he better watch himself in the next race or he'll end up like Luka. Nothing happened for a couple of weeks, and then Malcolm did something that really pissed him off, and he sent him flying the next race. He was subtle, so there wasn't any way to prove what he did, but I called him on it after the fact. Alejandro basically said I was his lackey, and I better shut up and do as I'm told, or he'll make sure I lose my job. I quit after our training session."

"Holy shit." My eyes widen.

"He's an asshole."

"Understatement of the century. Why would he take himself out of the race, though? If he hadn't crashed me, he could have overtaken me and won. It was that close." Something isn't adding up.

"I have my suspicions."

I stare at him, waiting for him to talk, but when he doesn't, I throw my hands up. "Well?"

"I don't want to speculate. I could be wrong, and then that creates problems for you."

"Newsflash, Nate: it's already a problem! I stayed up half the night, analyzing the crash and what I did wrong. What I can do differently so it doesn't happen again."

"You should have woken me up," he says, face stricken.

"That's not the fucking point!"

"What good does it do for me to spew all this shit at you? It's only going to make you madder than hell."

"Good! Maybe it'll help me race harder," I counter.

"You are a goddamned firecracker. Jesus." He shakes his head. "Fine. I think it was to set up Sawyer to win. They've stayed fairly good friends over the years, and I think that maybe this was payback because Sawyer felt slighted by you. I don't know if it was Sawyer's idea or Alejandro's, but either way, if I'm right, it doesn't matter. They both need to deal with the repercussions."

I jolt back when he says Sawyer's name. My own teammate. The man who wanted to go to galas together because it's good for our image. The one who gave me unsolicited advice that I didn't really like, but I didn't think he'd stoop to this level. I thought he was just a grade A douchebag. This is next level, though.

"What the fuck?" I whisper, trying to wrap my head around someone, let alone two people, being this vindictive. There was no guarantee that either of us would have stayed safe. We both could have been seriously injured. Not to mention, we could have gotten Sawyer caught up in our crash as well. There was so much that could have gone wrong, and Alejandro just accepted that? He was totally fine putting himself in danger, as well as another driver?

It's unfathomable.

"Say something," Nate mutters, worry written all over his face, as he takes my hands in his gently.

"Who would even think to do something like that? I mean, hell, have we not all worked incredibly hard to get to this point? Who would intentionally pull that shit?" I shake my head, still unable to comprehend it.

"Who knows, but he needs to be out of Formula 1. I gave Felix some information while you were with Cruz last night, so hopefully that helps them figure out how far this all goes."

"And I'm just supposed to go out on the track and race next to these fuckers in a couple of weeks?"

"I don't have an answer to that."

"I don't expect you to. I'm just trying to process all of this. Maybe I should just quit. If I'm going to be a target of this level of shit, I don't want to do this anymore. It's not worth my safety."

"No! Fuck no! You know Toni, Daisy, and Sydney aren't going to let them get away with this shit. They're just gathering everything they can get to make sure he never hurts anyone again. A lot can happen in two weeks, so just give them the time to make it happen.”

I sigh, knowing he's right. I still don't trust Sawyer, but maybe he didn't have a huge part in this. Maybe he bitched about me and Alejandro took it upon himself when the opportunity arose.

“Be a Formula 1 driver, they said. You'll change the sport, they said.”

“If nothing comes from the investigation, I will take things into my own hands,” Nate continues like he's ready to go to battle for me. It brings a smile to my face, and I know for a fact I'm going to figure out how to make things work between us.

“I'm not going to let you do that.” I sigh.

“Hey, I don't want you to stress about this. Our friends will get this all figured out. I just want you to focus on racing.”

“Fat chance of that.” I scoff.

“Well, lucky for you, I already have a plan in place.” *There's that blinding smile again.*

“What did you do, Nate?”

“Changed our flight.”

“What?” I screech.

“Relax. You have two weeks before the next race. We're only going to be here for a couple of days while your wrists heal, and then we can go back to Austin, where you can proceed to show me exactly how much of a badass you are.”

“You enjoy this too much.”

“I do. But doesn't a couple of days off in the Bahamas sound so much better than stressing?”

“I'm probably still going to stress.”

“Well, I happen to be an expert distractor.”

“You distract with sex.” I side-eye him.

“Exactly.”

“Thank you,” I murmur. “A break sounds really fucking good, actually. And if I have access to the gym, I'm going to work out so at least you can be assured that my wrists will still be good to go.”

“Oh, I called a place that's going to do X-rays really quickly once we're there, just to double check."

"You really thought of everything."

"I tried." He shrugs.

Yeah, I think I'm in love with Nate Murphy.

Chapter 40

October 8

Day one in the Bahamas, and I thought I would absolutely hate the warm weather after Singapore, but it's gorgeous here. True to form, Sydney had a bunch of stuff waiting for us in our room, like swimsuits and other necessities we didn't necessarily pack for a race weekend.

There are incredible perks to being under the Vanstone umbrella, I'll say that much.

Nate's been beyond attentive. My P-rays came back clear, but he's still wrapping and icing them whenever he sees me getting a little too wild and loose with my wrists.

He's a good man. The best, honestly. I'm not sure how I would have handled any of this without him. I've felt so lost this season, not myself. Yet he manages to come in and know exactly what I need. Training and meditation—hell, even journalling—have become one of my favorite things. The latter gives me a place to ramble and not make sense, but in my head, it's unscrambling all of my confusion one page at a time.

One day, I'll tell Nate how fucking good he is at this job. How incredible he is at motivating anyone he's around. No wonder Beck won a championship with him at his side. He's the special ingredient, the ace in the hole. And I'm just the lucky bitch who gets him on my team.

But I'm lucky in other ways too.

who knew a one-night stand to blow off some steam would manifest itself into a relationship with one of the best men I know. And yes, I'm officially calling this a relationship. I think it's always been one, in some fashion. It's not like we ever stopped being attracted to each other. I just needed time—more than him, apparently—to wrap my head around . . . having it all.

Is it possible to have it all? The career, the friends, the boyfriend?
It honestly seems too good to be true. I'm not the person who gets all of this. I'm the one who puts her head down and works hard. Sure, I make friends along the way, but we don't keep in touch or do things outside of the job. But suddenly, I have a built-in friend group, who group texts me, checks in, and throws birthday parties for me.

If I step back and look at my life now with a wide lens, Nate is at the center of it all. He pushes me out of my comfort zone. He creates these moments where I see how close I've become to all the women in this group. He always has my best interests at heart and goes the extra mile when he thinks I need something.

He's been doing it this whole time. While I was in my head, freaking out and doubting every step I took. When I was losing races and didn't think I could do this. He was there in the background, giving me encouragement and trying new things to just . . . get me out of all the self-doubt.

I've thought a lot about my life over the past couple of days. About where I want things to go, what's a priority for me, and what I would love my future to look like.

The only constant is Nate.

I'm in love with Nathan Murphy.

And my God, I'm so ecstatic about it I want to . . . to . . . to jump into the pool naked as I scream out that I love him. I want to go onto our building's rooftop and yell it to the entire city of Austin. I want to make him as much of a priority as he makes me.

So that's what I'm going to work on next. I have six races left, but I think I can still set time aside to take care of my man.

My man.

Is it weird for a thirty-year-old to kick her feet and giggle? I don't care; I'm going to do it anyway.

Nate Murphy loves me, and I love him. Now, to not mess it all up because I'm too in my head about things.

Chapter 41
Nate

Remi's writing in her journal, and I pay close attention to make sure she's not fucking up her wrists. I can't help but also observe her smile and just how damn happy she looks right now.

I'm still shaken up. The crash and her dehydration made me feel like I was about to lose the best thing that's ever happened to me. A brush with mortality, however dramatic that is, had me organizing this trip before Remi's full-on freakout. I needed it as much as she did, I think.

My phone vibrates in my pocket, pulling my attention from the woman I'm desperately in love with.

Beck:

Call me when you get a sec.

I hit the call button and wait for him to answer the phone.

"I didn't mean right now if you are . . . you know . . . busy." Beck clears his throat.

"For someone who literally spent four winter breaks fucking his woman like you were a rabbit, you sure are becoming a prude when I finally get a love life."

"So, there's a love life?" I can just imagine him smirking.

"Jesus, we're not talking about this now. We can grab dinner when we get back and gossip until your heart's content. What's up?" I redirect.

"Right, I wanted to fill you in on what we have so far and ask you a couple more questions. You got time for that?"

"Yep, go for it." If this helps bring resolution for Remi, I've got all the time in the world.

"So, the marshals fined Alejandro and gave him a grid penalty— twenty places—for the next race. It was clear as day that he intentionally jerked his wheel into Remi. Amaro is looking into things more, checking data from the rest of the year to see what all he's really done under their noses. I have the stuff you gave to Felix; do you have anything else? Times? Races?"

"Times, no. Races, yes. I thought I sent that over to Felix, but I'll do that when we're done talking."

"Great, that'll help us establish a pattern. Felix and Toni are looking into possibly filing charges against him. Well, Remi would technically file them."

I look over at Remi, who is finally out of the funk that Singapore put her in. "What if she doesn't want to do that?"

"Why wouldn't she?"

"Because if he gets reprimanded within the sport, maybe can't race again, that might be enough for her. She'd rather be the bigger person and show people what she's made of on the track than press charges and make it into a huge thing." She'd hate the attention, the speculation that would inevitably come with something like this. She wants people to recognize her from her own merit, not by getting someone arrested because she couldn't handle the heat. I'll never tell her that I think she should press charges because what he did was so out of line. And proving herself on the track doesn't mean she can't hold people accountable for their actions. But I know her too well, and I know this isn't what she would want.

"The stubborn-as-fuck women of Empress, I swear," Beck mumbles back before busting out in laughter.

"You've got that right."

"Is it a requirement? Like, in order to be this badass woman at Empress, you must also be a willful person who likes to take on too many things and have entirely too much pressure on your shoulders?"

Uh-oh, it sounds like Sydney's been pushing her limits too far.

"Uhhh . . ."

"Anyway." He clears his throat. "Send me everything you can think of. We're putting together a case to send to Amaro and the FIA. He shouldn't be in the sport at all if he's intentionally risking everyone's safety."

"On it."

"And Nate?"

"Yeah?"

"I'm glad to see you both happy. I know nothing is out in the open or whatever, but I see the change in you, and I see how you both look at each other."

"It's . . . complicated." I can't rightly tell him that we're lying low until season is up. I can't tell him I'm head-over-heels in love with this woman—not without Remi being fully on board. Even if he's my best friend.

"It always is man. It always is."

I chuckle at the ordeal he went through to be with Sydney, and even though Remi and I are complicated right now, I think how they got together takes the cake. Four years, he had to woo her. I would absolutely wait that long for Remi, but I would probably hate every second of it. Besides, it's not that we aren't together; we're just keeping it out of the public eye. It's a totally different situation.

"Talk to you soon." Beck interrupts my musings and hangs up without fanfare. Love that about him.

My laptop is in the bedroom, so I head there and try to get all the information I can remember, as well as notes from sessions that I have with Alejandro that document his behavior. It takes me longer than I want it to, and by the time I'm pressing send on the email, Remi is strolling into the room.

"Hi there, stranger," she says.

"Hey. You doing okay?"

"I'm doing wonderful. Are you working?" She gives me a hard look, but she's too adorable to pull it off right now. No, not adorable. That bikini is anything but adorable on her luscious body.

"Just sending Beck something he asked for."

"And does that something have to do with a certain asshole who crashed into me?" She walks close, pushing my laptop to the side and straddling my lap.

"I plead the Fifth."

"You aren't supposed to be working." She tsks, wrapping her arms around my neck.

"What are you going to do about it?" I brush my nose against her cheek, pressing a kiss there.

"Well, I think we should be enjoying this mini vacation, no?" Her hips grind against mine, making me groan.

"That was the plan," I mutter against her neck, nipping it and gripping her hips.

"Then show me."

I'm nothing if not attentive through and through to this woman.

Flipping us over quickly, I lift her up and move her toward the top of the bed.

"Oh!" She squeaks.

In this moment, I feel so many intense things for Remi it's overwhelming. I'm protective, needy, *greedy,* but most of all, I'm in love. And all I want to do right now is show her that. I don't want to just tell her; I want her to feel it with every move I make, every breath I take.

I want her to feel it deep in her bones that I'll spend the rest of my life being by her side and taking care of her when she lets me. Loving her through every bump and bruise, celebration and loss.

I lean back onto my knees and just look at her.

"I don't know where to start," I admit.

"I vote getting naked." Remi reaches behind her and unties her bikini top, tossing it to the side once it's fully off.

I stare, mesmerized.

"Anytime now, *Nathan.*" Her exaggerated use of my full name gets my ass in gear. My shirt and shorts are off in a nanosecond.

"Commando?"

"We're alone here. I figured you'd like easy access." I wink, trailing my fingertip up her calf to her thigh.

"Can I petition for you to always go commando?"

"You want everyone to see my boner at races?" I reach the crease at her hip, briefly touching her clit as I move to the other leg.

She moans. "Seeing me race gets you hot?"

"So fucking hot, Rem." I focus on the goosebumps that follow my fingers on her leg before I can't take it anymore.

I shove her legs open wide and lie flat on the bed between them.

"So wet for me already. Am I not giving you enough orgasms?" My knuckle grazes her opening, up to her clit ,teasing her.

"Not recently."

"Well, that's a damn shame," I murmur.

"Nate . . ." She moans as I gently circle her clit more.

"That's right. Beg me."

"Please . . . please. Put your mouth on me."

"Atta girl," I whisper before ducking down and licking her ass to clit. I waste no time sucking the little bud into my mouth, pulsing it as her hands move to my hair, gripping hard. One arm wraps around her thigh, pressing my hand right above the pretty pussy I'm currently eating, while the other slides one finger inside of her.

Her back arches off the bed. "Holy shit," she breathes out.

I just need to get her off once before I do anything else. Once, then I'll happily slow us down and show her what it feels like to be truly loved.

Two fingers crook inside of her, tapping on that spot that gets her going every single time. She's yanking at my hair so hard I'm sure she'll be pulling some out, but I don't give a shit. *Pull away.* I'll happily show it off as a point of pride that I know how to pleasure my woman.

When she pulses around my fingers, I press harder on her stomach and suck hard, licking her clit as I do. She goes off like a rocket. Panting, slapping the bed, while I make her ride it out.

Once she collapses back onto the bed, I slowly release her from my hold, licking my fingers as I crawl up her body.

"Hey," I say when we're face to face again. The need to touch her more is so strong that I cup the back of her neck, my thumb brushing over her cheek.

"Hi." She graces me with my favorite smile.

"You think you can handle more?"

"No . . . but yes." She lifts up and kisses me quickly.

I don't let her drop back down, the hand around her neck holding her up so I can really kiss her. My tongue glides along her bottom lip before I nip it. Her leg wraps around my back, pulling me closer to her, and I'm all too happy to oblige.

As our kiss deepens, I grind against her sensitive clit, my cock gliding up gathering all of her orgasm, before I shift my hips and somehow manage to notch at her entrance. I'll never be able to line up so perfectly again, but I'm running with it.

Our tongues intertwine, not battling for dominance but dancing to the song that's our love. I slide slowly inside of her.

Her gasp has me tightening my hold on her neck. Her reaction to that first thrust turns me on more than anything. My hips canter, curling around her body, as I bottom out.

"Oh God." Remi pulls back and moans.

My forehead presses against her as my mind begs me to hold on.

The hand not gripping her neck slides down her thigh to her ass, holding her as close to me as possible, before I slowly pull out, torturing us both.

"Fuck, Rem. I can't get over you. You're a goddess, a warrior, my love," I wax on, barely coherent of what I'm saying.

My pace stays slow, and I kiss every inch of skin I can reach while we're tangled together like this. Remi's moaning my name, with her arms wrapped around me. We're as close as two people can get, and yet it's not enough.

I don't think it'll ever be enough.

Every time I fill her, I pause and circle my hips, hitting her clit.

"I can't," she pants into my ear.

"You can, Rem. Just feel it." My eyes are clenched so tight as the tingle at the base of my spine intensifies.

"It's too much." She tosses her head back and forth in protest.

With my hands on either side of her head, I force her to focus on me. "Eyes, Remi. Eyes on me."

Her glazed-over eyes open.

Every dream I thought I had in my life, every hope, every wish, is nothing compared to this moment. I didn't think it was possible to have this with someone. To love someone so much it hurts. Or to have this need to be closer to them even though every ounce of your skin is touching theirs.

"Let go. I've got you," I choke out, trying so damn hard to hold back my emotions.

"Together." She lifts her hips. "I've got you too."

Then her lips meet mine, and it's all over.

My pace grows erratic as our moans get louder and, in the blink of an eye, we're both coming hard.

I collapse on top of her, trying to wrap my mind around what just happened.

After what feels like several long minutes, I roll over, pulling her against my side.

"What the hell was that?" she asks, still trying to catch her breath.

"Nirvana." I sigh.

We crash for a midday nap shortly after that. I'm content that she knows exactly how I feel about her.

Chapter 42
Remi

I missed the perfect opportunity to tell Nate I loved him in the Bahamas. I have no excuse except I overthought it and then we fell asleep. Falling back into old habits seems to be my default.

So, I've been working up to it, looking for the perfect moment to share my feelings. But it's been almost a week and a half. At this point, I just want to pull him aside, kiss him, and tell him how I feel.

But today is Practice 1 and Sprint Qualifiers in Austin.

I literally have no time to do anything except focus on racing.

Sprint weekends are hard because you have very little practice time. We get one practice, then it's straight to the sprint qualifiers, then the actual sprint race and race qualifiers, and then the main race on Sunday. A lot of points are up for grabs, and the first step in getting as many as possible is to do well in the sprint qualifiers.

Strong, callused hands run over my shoulders, massaging them. My shoulders drop an inch, and I lean back into Nate.

"You're too stressed."

I bark out a laugh. "How am I supposed to not be?"

"Well, I thought I gave you enough orgasms last night to solve this, but apparently not. You want to go to your office?" I can feel his smile against my head as he presses a kiss there.

"One-track mind, I swear." I spin in his arms and bury my head in his chest.

"Can't blame a man for trying. Seriously, though, how can I help?" His hand rubs up my back.

"I have no clue. I just want to get the sprint over with."

"Well, let's take it one step at a time. You ready for practice?"

"Yep."

"Good, because they just called you."

I look over at the table, where my phone sits, and see the message lighting up the screen.

He cups my face in his hands and kisses me before pulling back.

"You've got this. Focus on the track. You know Austin better than anyone, so show them how it's done."

And with that vote of confidence, I head out to the garage.

***

I killed it in practice. I don't say that lightly. I almost set a track record, and it felt so damn good that I'm no longer panicking about the sprint.

Which is good because it starts in about ten minutes.

Murph walks over to me and puts his head on my lap as Nate walks into the room.

"My woman is going to blow everyone out of the waaaaaatterrrrrrrrrr!" he singsongs in what I assume is a version of a song he just made up. It's . . . interesting, to say the least.

"Can we make a deal?" I ask.

"Always." He rubs his hands together.

"Never make up songs again."

"Seriously? I thought that was good!"

"Terrible, honestly. Look. Murph had to cover his ears." I point to the cuddle monster, whose head is almost completely engulfed by my T-shirt.

He scoffs. "You two are impossible."

"And on that note, I do need to get dressed." I stand up, to Murphy's utter disappointment.

"I really do have the best timing ever."

I bite my bottom lip to suppress my smile as I take my shirt off. "Just make sure you don't pop a boner letting everyone in the garage know what you're thinking about."

"Like they don't already know."

"So, you want them to think about me naked? Or us boning?"

We've been . . . less discreet around people we trust, which is a good chunk of the Empress crew, since the Austin race weekend started. I don't think everyone knows, but the ones who know us well are certainly suspicious about how close we truly are.

"Absolutely not."

I giggle at him being so appalled by the mere suggestion.

Once my race suit is on, I walk up to him and rise up on my tiptoes. I press a quick kiss to his lips.

"Wish me luck, stud."

"None needed, Ace. Go show those boys what a real winner looks like," he murmurs against my lips.

After sprint qualifiers, I'll tell him I love him.

I walk out without another word and proceed to do exactly what he told me to. I finish in pole position, feeling damn good about the upcoming weekend. But I never get around to telling Nate I love him.

***

It's finally time for the actual race. I won the sprint race, which gave me another eight points, and I'm in pole position for the Grand Prix.

Life is fucking good.

Except for the fact that Nate's been suspiciously quiet. I wonder if he's nervous or if something is happening with Alejandro that he's keeping to himself. All I know is that Alejandro's starting in the pit lane today because of the huge grid penalty he received in Singapore. But maybe there's news. I try to stay phone free for as long as possible before a race, so I'm not changing my routine now to find out the gossip. Nate will tell me after the race if it's important.

"Ahhh!" Daisy's scream could pierce an ear drum. She holds Evelin in her arms as Sydney and Toni follow behind her.

"Well hello, friends. To what do I owe this special visit?"

"It's our home race! We had to all come and support our girl," Sydney says like I should know this already.

"I'm super glad you all are here," I say, and for once, I mean it. The kinship we've found, however fucked up our schedules are, has been just as illuminating as my relationship with Nate.

I reach out for Evelin, who immediately reaches for me, so Daisy hands her over.

"We need to get you a little race suit, missy," I say against Evelin's cheek, inhaling that euphoric baby scent that still lingers in her hair.

"Beck's getting one made," Sydney adds.

"He is?" Daisy's voice takes on that tone that means she's tearing up.

"Don't cry." Toni winces.

Evelin starts babbling, telling me a very in-depth story of complete nonsense, and I love every single second of it.

"Are we going to that Italian place after the race?" Sydney asks.

"Hell yes, we are." I've been craving that pasta for weeks, but it's not on my current diet plan. After the race, though, Nate can't deny me. I know how to pick my battles.

I glance at the clock on the wall and realize it's time to do our formation lap before the anthem and the usual theatrics.

"Well, thanks for stopping by with my favorite tiny human. I'll catch you guys after the race." Giving Ev one last kiss before I let go, I hand her back to Daisy.

"Kick ass, lady. You've got this," Toni says, bumping my shoulder.

Sydney gives me a hug. "Show those fuckers who the real boss on the track is," she murmurs in my ear, making me laugh.

"Yes, ma'am."

I leave without waiting to get reprimanded for calling her ma'am, zipping up my race suit and attaching the Velcro at the top. I meet Cruz by the back shelf, where my helmet is.

"Ready?"

"Absolutely. I feel like I was born ready for this."

This race.

This sport.

This life.

I'm so fucking ready for it all.

"Then let's show the boys."

I laugh, knowing Sydney must have given everyone the same damn pep talk.

Looking around, I scan the crew for Nate but don't see him. I'm about to put my helmet on and climb into my car when he steps through the door, Murph following close behind him.

"I don't have a ton of time, but glad I caught you before I had to jump in the car."

"Sorry, got held up with Beck. You feel good?"

"I feel great."

"Good. Keep that feeling, and you'll be just fine." He's careful to not directly touch me since there are cameras everywhere.

"Thank you . . . for literally everything." God, I want to kiss him so badly. I wish he hadn't lost track of time with Beck so he could have seen me off in the backroom. I'm already running behind, though, and Cruz is looking at me and pointing to his watch.

"Go get 'em, Ace," Nate says softly, looking at my lips with longing that we both can't do anything about right now.

"See you after the race." I nod, shoving my helmet over my head.

He buckles it underneath and taps it twice for good luck.

Let the race begin.

***

This race feels like none I've driven before. I don't mean the track itself or the car; no, it's a combination of everything lining up perfectly in order for it to all feel *right* for once. This is how it used to feel at the academy—the ease, the way everything felt like it came so easily. I finally feel that way again, and it feels so fucking good.

I couldn't wipe the smile off my face even if I wanted to.

"Pace is stellar. We're looking at plan A, pitstop at Lap 19, then we'll reassess once you're in those," Jason says in my earpiece.

"Copy. Pit in ten laps."

And then I fly.

There's a sense of freedom, of feeling like this is exactly what I should be doing with my life. You know when there are people who are in professions, and you're just so damn impressed that they found exactly what they were supposed to do? That's how I feel right now. It's empowering in a way I didn't know I needed. I'll take Nate's praise all day. I'll take my team's words of encouragement, but they truly mean nothing until I really believe them.

I don't think I've ever believed in myself more.

There's a man who loves me for exactly who I am. I'm surrounded by a team that believes in me. An actual friend group that has my back.

If this is how you're supposed to feel in life, sign me the fuck up.

I lose track of everything except the track. My lines are ideal, and when Jason pipes up in my ear again, I realize I'm almost halfway done with the race.

"Box, Box. Box, Box."

"Copy."

Even my pitstop is quick. Cruz pumps his fist as I drive away, and my smile grows even bigger, if that's possible.

"Great stop, fastest of the season for us by a mile."

"All thanks to the team," I respond as I pass Sawyer to retake the lead.

The entire race, Jason keeps me appraised of where Sawyer is, letting me know when my lead increases or decreases. Overall, for the fans, it's a boring race. I lead the entire thing, and Sawyer never really gets a chance to battle me for it.

But for me?

This race is everything. It's my home race; it's the first time I feel like I didn't make a huge mistake taking this job. It's the first time in a very long time that I feel comfortable in my own skin.

Tears prick at the corners of my eyes as I cross the finish line.

Toni's cheers echo in my head.

"Damn good job today, Remi. So proud of you and the entire team."

"Thanks," I squeak out before clearing my throat. "Great team effort. Seriously, I couldn't do it without everyone. Thank you."

It's a release bigger than a good cry, bigger than the best orgasms I've had—well, maybe not, since Nate's been in my life, but it is damn close.

Once I'm parked in the winner's spot, I jump out of my car and weigh in as quickly as I can. My helmet comes off next. Then, I sprint off to the side where my entire team is waiting for me.

A quick glance down the line, and I find Nate standing in the corner. I head toward him immediately, jumping into his arms as best as I can with the barrier in our way.

"Good job, Ace. I'm so damn proud of you." He has to almost yell in my ear to be heard over the crowd.

I pull back, peppering his face with kisses to his utter shock, before palming his face in my hands. Media be damned. Being out in public be damned.

"I love you. I should have said it so long ago, but I love you. I love you so much, and I wouldn't be here today without you."

Chapter 43
Nate

She loves me.

I think I'm in shock that she actually said it. I don't reply because words won't come to me. All I can do is kiss the living hell out of her before she's dragged away by the team and event organizers for the podium.

Toni clears her throat, bumping my shoulder, pulling us apart.

"Glad that's all worked out, but it's time to hug the team quickly before the cooldown room."

I reluctantly let Remi go, winking to let her know we'll talk more later, then watch her in her element. The change she's gone through this year is pure inspiration. It makes me want to be better, *do* better in everything I touch.

Before the race, she caught on that I wasn't my normal preppy self. I couldn't sleep last night, too much on my mind, so I cracked open her journal just to read her words as a comfort while she slept soundly next to me.

Her last entry was a real shock. She confessed her love, yes, but it was more than that. It was the fact that she seemed so confident and happy with her life as it currently is. That I even had a little piece in that was incredible. It also made me panic. What if I fail this great gift she's given me? What if I'm nothing more than the party boy everyone knows me as?

So, I went to Beck at the expense of being there for Remi all morning before the race.

I regret it now, but I needed someone to let me vent and steer me in the right direction. Sometimes, hearing a voice of reason makes everything clearer. Hell, most of the time, I'm that voice of reason. But there's no one more logical than Beck.

Did it help or hinder that Luka and Felix were in Sydney's office when I went to talk to Beck? Who's to say. I got a lot of unsolicited advice in the process, so it remains to be seen.

Toni claps me on the back as we walk toward the podium, meeting the rest of our friends there. "Cat's out of the bag now. No one will care that she raced the race of her life or that she won. They're going to be talking about that kiss."

"Yeah . . . I didn't know she was going to do that, or I would have stopped her." I rub my hand across the back of my neck.

"You would have?"

"I mean, yeah, I always want her to get the credit she deserves. I never want to take away from her talent or achievements."

"You also can't make decisions for her. She knew what she was doing," Toni says as Sydney walks up next to her.

"It's about damn time, you two." She smiles.

"Yeah, I didn't quite expect such a public display, though." Luka smirks.

"Like I fucking planned it." I scoff.

"Hey, these Empress women run at their own pace. We're just here to follow along and make sure they're taken care of," Beck says while looking at Sydney.

"I booked that Italian place you were wanting to take Remi after the race. I figure since there's so many of us, a private room—since they have one—would be a nicer option," Felix adds in.

"Thanks, I really appreciate you doing that," I tell him.

"He's a planner." Toni smiles.

"It comes in handy sometimes," he tells her.

I clear my throat. "Thank you. All of you. For being there for Rem, for supporting me."

"Aww, he's getting all sappy," Beck says. I jab him into his ribs with my finger. "Ow, fuck."

"Serves you right."

"Now, now, children. Let's all play nice while our little rising star takes the podium." Felix gestures to the stage, where everyone is getting set up.

Daisy leans in close. "Proud of you both. You make a damn good team."

Do my eyes start to tear up, or is it the fall allergies in Austin? Who can say. What I can acknowledge is that Remi looks fucking incredible standing dead center on the podium. I know it'll be one of many. I rub the top of my knee, right over the spot where the Murph tattoo I got from her first win is. If she wouldn't kill me, I'd tattoo something for every single one of her wins.

Once the ceremony is over, I head over to the garage as everyone breaks up. I wait, admittedly not so patiently, for my woman to make her way back.

Shockingly, it only takes a few more minutes, which leads me to believe Sydney or Daisy ran interference, God bless them.

Remi walks cautiously toward me, and I wait her out. When she's close enough to grab, I pull her to me, cupping her jaw and kissing her with everything I have.

It's both slow and intense. I pull away before either of us are ready, but I have important things to say.

"I love you. So damn much. And I'm so proud of you. You are everything I needed in my life and never even realized."

She shuts me up with a quick kiss.

"I'm so in love with you. I have no clue what will happen next, with the media and attention this will absolutely be getting. But I know I want to weather it all with you by my side. And . . . and I know I'll mess up, but if you could just . . . bear with me when I do, I'd really appreciate it." Her watery chuckle betrays her true worry.

"As long as you can stick with me when I mess up, we're good, Rem. So fucking good."

We kiss—maybe a little too much for where we currently are—when a couple of throats clear behind us.

"Hey, lovebirds, we've got a reservation to go to," Beck calls out.

"We'll meet you there," I say without taking my eyes off Remi.

"Don't be too late," Sydney adds with a laugh.

I end up grabbing Remi's hand and dragging her across the walkway, avoiding the throngs of people and making my way to her little office.

"What—"

I spin her so her back's against the door. In one quick flip of my wrist, I pull the Velcro at the top of her racing suit apart and slide the zipper down.

"Nate . . . I'm disgusting right now."

"Don't care," I grunt. Shoving the suit off of her shoulders, I let it fall to her waist. I hook my thumbs in her open suit and catch her underwear as well, and push them down even farther, making just enough space for what I need.

My hand slides down her stomach, my forehead pressed against hers. "Say it again."

"I love you." She smiles.

My fingertips reach her pussy, the middle one slipping between her lips before drawing back up to her clit.

"Do I get this every time I win?" she breathes out.

"You can get this anytime you tell me you love me." I circle her clit, steady and strong.

"It's dangerous to give me"—she gasps when I press harder—"that kind of power."

"I will beg you to take advantage of me, Rem." I slide my middle finger down, pushing inside her, as my thumb moves to take its place on her clit. "Anytime, day or night."

Her hips start to match my pace. I can't help myself; I grind against her leg to get some relief even though this is about her. I'll go to dinner with blue balls; hell, I'll go to bed with them. I don't matter tonight. The whole night will be a celebration of Remi—who she is, what she's accomplished, and every single little detail I can point out—so she sees herself how I see her.

"Oh my God." She moans as I tap that firm spot inside her that drives her wild.

"Better get there quick, Rem. Everyone's waiting for us." I kiss down her neck.

She's trying desperately to stay quiet, biting her lip to mute her moans. I never thought I'd be okay with silencing her pleasure in any way, but knowing that she's struggling and we're in a potentially compromising place is more of a turn-on than I was expecting.

"More. Add one more." She gasps.

I add another finger without breaking my rhythm, and that stretch is all she needs. Her head tips back on a loud moan, and I buck my hips into her leg as she comes. I keep my hand where it is, helping her ride through the waves, when I feel her fingers slip into my shorts and grip my dick.

"Oh fuck."

Three hard pumps. That's all it takes, and I'm joining her in orgasmic bliss. I should be ashamed, but I'm the furthest thing from it. She hasn't moved, her head still thrown back, a dreamy, slightly sinister smile on her face and eyes closed. I bury my head against her chest, peppering it with kisses, as I try to catch my breath.

"Dammit, woman, that was supposed to be about you," I murmur.

Her hand comes up around the back of my neck. "Exactly. I wanted to see how quickly I could get you off after you were so worked up."

"Siren," I growl, making her giggle.

"Not apologizing."

When we've calmed down enough, I pull my hand out of her underwear, resting it on her waist, and stand straight.

"We're really doing this? All public and shit?"

"Yes, caveman, we're really doing this, all public and shit."

My lips find her again; I'm unable to stop myself.

"We've got to get changed," I say softly once I pull away.

"On it." She takes a deep breath, focusing herself on the task at hand. She goes to walk around me, but I stop her.

"In case I didn't say it in between all the declarations of love . . . Way to kick ass today. It was a helluva win."

"Why thank you." She does a little courtesy. "Couldn't let the assholes win." She does break free of my hold then. "Speaking of, do we know anything new?"

"I'll be honest," I say, stripping out of my clothes and following Remi to the cabinet. "Most of my blood is still in my lower half, so I can't remember."

"At least you're honest. I'm sure we'll talk about it at dinner."

I press a kiss to her shoulder once she's completely naked and wrap my arm around her waist to pull her back to my front.

"I love you, and whatever happens with the assholes, I'll be here with you to figure it out, okay?"

"Okay," she whispers. "I love you too. But we really do need to get dressed."

It may take us another ten minutes to finally get dressed, but I'd say it's worth it.

***

The clapping starts as soon as Remi enters the rented-out space, and I step to the side. She tries to shush them as a lovely shade of pink tinges her neck and cheeks—a shade I thought only happened when I got her off.

"Oh, now she's humble." Toni chuckles.

"Hey! Being in the car is completely different. This is, like, spotlight energy. In the car, I know there's attention, but I don't actively see it." Remi shakes her head.

"She's right." Beck looks at Toni.

"Sit, sit. We ordered all the things," Sydney says.

Evelin blubbers on happily, leaning forward on Luka's lap to reach Remi as she walks closer. The moment she takes her in her arms, I see a vision I *never* thought I'd want in my life. Sure, in an obscure way, I think a family would be cool. I'm not totally inept with kids, but this? Seeing my entire reason for being in this world holding a baby and cuddling her?

Suddenly, I'm thinking about career trajectory and when would be a logical time to start working on a mini-Remi.

A hand claps my back, and I turn to find Felix next to me.

"I know that look. Good luck waiting." He chuckles.

"Even if I knew what you were talking about, Remi's career comes first."

"You know, I wasn't sure about you when Toni said she wanted to bring you on. Beck had high praise, but I've seen the articles, the pictures, and I didn't think you would be a good fit, especially with Remi. I was wrong. You're the best kind of man, particularly *for* Remi."

"Thanks, I think." It's actually high praise coming from him. I'm unsure how to really take all the support.

A couple of waiters come in with drinks and appetizers, so I take my seat next to Remi.

Leaning in close to her ear, I whisper, "You look really good holding a baby, Ace. Makes me want to knock you up."

She looks at me with a sparkle in her eye. "Patience. I've still got a lot of ass-kicking to do."

"What I'm hearing is it's not off the table." I arch an eyebrow and tip my drink to my mouth to hide my smile.

"Practice certainly isn't."

I damn near spit my drink out but choke on it instead. Remi laughs as she pounds on my back.

"You're an evil woman."

"Can you guys stop with whatever weird foreplay that is?" Luka asks, holding out his hands to take Ev back.

"We do have more information about the . . . accident," Sydney cuts in.

"Oh?" Remi looks up, clearly interested.

"So, Amaro is cutting ties with Alejandro. Today was his last race with them. The FIA has also banned him from participating in F1 or any lower levels for the next decade."

"Holy shit," Remi says, eyes wide in shock. Personally, I think it should be harsher, but at least he's out of Formula 1.

"Amaro was set to drop him the second it was being investigated, but they needed time to sign someone else. So, it's official, or will be shortly," Toni adds.

"Amaro also lost their sponsorship with Lifenote Tech, so they are also out around sixty million dollars," Felix says, scratching his beard.

"Jesus, what a loss for Amaro," Beck says, grabbing some food. "Why didn't you call out Alejandro earlier?" He turns to me.

"No hard proof. I can't exactly go around making accusations of cheating when I have nothing to back it up. Who would believe me over an F1 driver?"

"That's why you quit last season," Sydney says, putting the pieces together.

"Sorry about that." I shrug.

"What about Sawyer?" Remi interrupts.

"Sawyer is"—Toni sighs—"getting dropped at the end of the season. It's not public knowledge, but he's been very difficult about the entire investigation and refuses to work *with* us. He has said things that support the idea he was in on the whole thing. He's also said some very off-the-charts shit about you, which I will never stand for."

"But he's winning the Driver's Championship this season." Remi glances at me, confused.

"And that's a great high to leave us on. I would rather have good people on our team than anyone with questionable morals. He'll land somewhere . . . maybe. Depends on if anyone is okay with him having a hand in cheating and causing another driver to crash, allegedly. It's not our problem anymore," Toni says with confidence.

"Umm . . . Wow. Okay. Do we have another driver signed yet? I mean, it's fine if you can't tell me," Remi adds quickly.

"We're signing our reserve, Bruno Holl. He knows our system and tested well last week. We'll be putting him in the car for two practices in the upcoming races to get him used to the car," Sydney says.

"You guys really don't run like any other team." I chuckle. The relief of Sawyer not being on the team once the season's done is a weight off my shoulders I didn't realize I was carrying.

"Thanks!" Daisy says cheerfully, shoving an arancini into her mouth the minute the waiter puts it in front of her.

Conversation gets quiet as more food arrives, all of us digging in and stuffing our faces.

The ladies talk about their favorite dishes while the guys talk about soccer, or football to Luka and Felix.

I sit back with my hand around Remi's chair, in complete awe of what my life looks like now.

All thanks to a one-night stand in Japan a year and a half ago.

Chapter 44
Remi

Abu Dhabi. The last race of the season.

I've stayed pretty consistent over the last five races, winning two and placing second or third in the others.

Sawyer's been a moody bitch, but I'm riding such a high that it doesn't bother me.

I never thought there'd be a day where I was this happy. Working hard, giving back when I can? Absolutely. But truly happy? I didn't think I would be one of the lucky ones.

"What's running through that pretty little head of yours?" Nate asks as he and Murph walk into my office just off the pitlane.

"Oh, you know, make-up and dresses and what shoes to buy next."

"Ha, you know the last time you 'bought' anything new was Toni handing you more Empress gear." He leans down and plants one hell of a kiss on my lips.

Sighing, I lean back in my chair. "Just thinking about how this is the end of my first Formula 1 season. How it was . . . very wild. I'm glad it's coming to an end, but I'm also sad to see it go. Does that make sense?"

"Makes a lot of sense." He sits on the ground in front of me, hands resting on my legs. "It's been not only a learning experience, but you also got dealt the shit hand with everything that happened in Singapore. It's been a lot. But it's also been really damn good." His hand skims along my calf.

"It's been so good," I whisper.

"Are you still thinking about what you want to do over winter vacation?"

"Kind of. Is it bad that I just want to stay home and have a quiet month? Well, as quiet as I'm able to, I suppose."

"Not at all. We can make one of our apartments our central hub. Do movie nights, eat all the takeout we can manage," he says, "unless you need a break from me. That's okay too."

I lean forward, kissing him again. "I don't need a break from you. At all."

"Good, because Murph and I have some plans already."

I bark out a laugh. "I just told you I wanted to lie low; how do you already have plans?"

"Contingencies, Rem. I've got plans on plans on plans."

"You are highly prepared. What happened to the carefree Nate I met in Japan? The fly-by-the-seat-of-his-pants Nate?"

"He fell in love and wants to do everything to make his woman happy every single day."

"Damn, getting sappy before I have to race . . ." I sniff, holding back tears.

"You'll still kill it, Ace."

Murphy nudges his head in between us to get some love too. *This is my family.* The ones who abandoned me, who judged me and never supported me, were never really my family. This one, though? The one I've built with Nate, Murph, and all of our friends? It's one I never want to lose. It's a priority for me to nurture these relationships. For a long time, I would make friends on a face level. Remembering information about people is easy, but letting them into my life? Letting them see my flaws? Never.

But Nate's seen them all. Every breakdown, every doubt and hesitation. Every good day and bad.

He's still here. Still telling me he loves me every chance he gets. It's hard to get out of the habit of keeping people at arm's length, but here I am. Proof that it's possible when you let the right people into your life.

"Okay. It's race day. Suit up, hot stuff." Nate rocks back on his heels before standing up, holding his hand out to help me up.

"Orgasms if I win, right?"

"So many you won't be able to celebrate the end of the season with the team." His grin makes me wish I had more time.

"That feels like a challenge," I say as I strip out of my leggings and Empress shirt.

"You can't say that while you're getting naked. I'm just a simple man, Rem." Nate sighs, tipping his head to the ceiling, with his hands on his hips.

I can't help it; I laugh as I grab my pants and shirt that go under my race suit.

"It's really not that funny."

"Oh, I beg to differ. Torturing you is always a good time." I quickly get geared up, turning around to grab my race suit, but Nate's beat me to it.

He holds it out for me to step into, and once it's over my hips, we're standing very close together with his hands lingering.

"One last sappy thing."

I gulp, knowing whatever he's going to say is going to make me emotional. I nod anyway.

"I am so fucking proud of you. You've worked harder than anyone I know. You've dealt with adversity, with so many people doubting you because you're a woman, and yet you never were malicious. Never treated anyone without respect. Little girls everywhere have a role model who's not only insanely talented but who's one of the best people I know. They have someone to look up to, someone who shows them it's possible to be kind while also being so damn fierce. You inspire me every single day, and I just hope that I add a little bit of good to your life."

I surge up on my toes and kiss him, hard. He has no idea what he's given me. This found family of mine is all because of him. He pushed me outside of my comfort zone when I needed him to, but he was always right by my side when things got hard. I wouldn't be here, racing, let alone driving *well* without him. I wouldn't have my phone blowing up with group texts from the girls without him. And I sure as hell wouldn't be getting the number of orgasms I am on a regular basis, but I won't tell him that. No need for his head to get any larger; it wouldn't fit through the door.

A tear trickles down my cheek, and his thumb brushes it away as he pulls back.

"I am . . . so thankful Empress brought you on. I wasn't expecting you. Hell, I pushed you away with everything I had. But letting you in was my greatest accomplishment this year. I love you." I press one more kiss to his lips before breaking away. "I really will be late if we keep up the love fest." I sigh.

"I'd happily pay the fine." Nate's eyes are dreamy, nothing but love shining in them.

"Yeah, well, I'd rather you use that to buy me all the pasta over the next two months."

"Jesus, woman, you're going to eat ten grand worth of pasta?" His eyebrows shoot up.

"You limited me during the season. Be prepared to compensate." I shrug with a smile on my face.

"Might as well see if they need a business partner. Might be worth the discount," he grumbles.

"You're the one who got it for me the first time. You only have yourself to blame."

"Well, I'm not finding you new places to eat that I think you would enjoy ever again."

"Lies." I roll my eyes, shoving my arms into my suit. "You like seeing me happy, so I bet you already booked reservations for tonight at a place I will love."

"That was before this conversation. I can always cancel."

"You won't," I say, zipping up my race suit.

"But I could. Just because you have me wrapped around your little finger doesn't mean I won't—"

"Won't what?" I taunt with a smile.

"I don't fucking know." He throws his hands up. "Edge the shit out of you? Make you do super intense workouts on break?"

I chuckle. "Do I have you flustered, *Nathan?*" I run my hands up his chest to his shoulders. "Because those don't sound all that miserable. Especially the edging."

"Is death by arousal a thing? Especially when it will turn into blue balls as I watch you race?" He looks pained, but I kind of love it.

"How close are you?"

"Embarrassingly close."

I check my watch and calculate how much time I have. Ten minutes before I need to be in the garage. Completely doable.

I drop to my knees and unbutton his pants. He dressed up today, and for once, I'm annoyed I don't have easy access even though he looks fucking gorgeous. The zipper follows shortly, before I drag his boxer briefs over his straining erection.

"Rem . . ." Nate moves to cup my cheek and pull me away, but that's not happening.

"Call it a preview for tonight. Plus, I wouldn't want my man to get blue balls watching me race. Let me take the edge off, show you how much I love you." I smile up at him with an arched eyebrow.

"You're trying to see how fast you can get me off, aren't you?" He's grinning. Our competitive nature plays a part in our sexual escapades more than I'm willing to admit.

"Absolutely. Record is four minutes."

"Game on." I look up at him from my position, grabbing the base of his cock and slowly stroking it. "Set the timer," I breathe, getting turned on.

He doesn't set the timer; instead, he leans down, cups my face in both of his hands, and kisses me. His forehead touches mine as we breathe each other in.

"I am so lucky that you're mine."

"Ditto. Now, let me suck your cock so I can go win the last race of the season."

He bursts out laughing, letting me go and gesturing toward his dick. His pants have fallen below his knees, and I see something that wasn't there before.

"What?" I drag my fingers over the fresh ink. "What did you do, Nate?" I murmur.

"It's just a little something." His voice is soft, strained.

But it's not *just* a little something. It's in the same American traditional feel as his lighthouse, just above the outline of Murph's head. An ace of spades that looks more in the style of a decorative fleur-de-lis with a string of pearls entwined around it.

"I—" I have no words.

"You're my ace." He shrugs, like getting a tattoo for someone is just another item marketed off of a checklist.

"The pearls?"

"Margret. In Greek, it apparently means 'pearl'."

"You got a tattoo for me?" I whisper.

"I did." His soft eyes do nothing to quell the emotion rising up in me. "And I got it on my slutty little thigh, so you really will have a hard time focusing when I wear shorts."

A shock of laughter bursts from me.

"I was wondering why you were all dressed up today."

"You weren't supposed to see it until tonight."

"Well, I'm glad I saw it now." I press a kiss to the inside of his thigh, where a fresh tattoo is healing. Then, dragging my lips along his length, I look up at him. "Start the timer, love."

His wicked smirk doesn't fade as he clicks a button on his watch, and I waste no time, doing everything I know that gets him off the fastest.

When I tug at his balls, he's a goner. While Nate may be a tad embarrassed at how quickly I can get him off sometimes, it's wildly good for my ego. It tells me he can't resist me. It tells me that I turn him on so much he can barely contain himself. Sometimes, a woman needs to know she can bring her man to his knees every once in a while.

I lick him clean, carefully tucking him back into his underwear and pants while he tries to catch his breath.

"Two minutes and fifty-six seconds. I give myself a D. I give you an A++ because, holy shit, you just sucked my entire life force through my dick." He pants. "Pitiful."

I stand back up, wrapping my arms around his neck, trying to hold back my laughter.

"Or a sign that I'm really fucking good at blow jobs."

"You are definitely that. Sometimes I think you could blow on it, like a breeze, and I would go off."

"The highest of compliments." I peck his cheek.

"You're a real fucking gem, Ace. An international treasure."

"Luckily, you're the only one who gets this side of me."

"Lucky indeed." He kisses me once more. "Now get out there and win, so I can give you payback later. I'm thinking how many orgasms in thirty minutes."

"Hmmm, maybe three?" I tilt my head.

"Not if I use the vibrator you always bring with you." The gleam in his eye should scare me, but honestly, if we have to extend our stay a little longer because he literally fucks me unconscious, I will not be complaining.

"Well damn, guess I better win."

He pats my ass before squeezing it one last time. "Go. Seriously. I'm about to drag you to the couch." He groans.

I giggle as I step back from his hold. "Love you! See you after the race."

"I love you too, Rem. So damn much."

***

I win.

The last race of the season, and I win. It easily locks in the Constructor's Championship for Empress, and I'm beyond proud to have had a hand in it.

The first person I jump to is Nate, of course. He whispers words of praise, of support, of pride in my ear before releasing me to the rest of our friends.

It's a chaotic mess. Daisy's crying, jumping up and down while holding Ev. Luka looks panicked as he tries to get her to calm down. Beck and Sydney are embraced, clapping at me like I just won it all. Toni is teary eyed, but she doesn't let them fall. Seeing her emotion directed at me makes me feel ten feet tall. The woman is hard as nails, and yes, she's always treated me like a sister. But she still holds me to a standard that she knows I'm capable of and doesn't let me get away with the negative side of things. Felix claps in his own aristocratic way, tilting his head in my direction as an acknowledgment when I lock eyes with him. Cruz is off to the side, but he's cheering and screaming at the top of his lungs. He starts a "Re-mi" chant, and the entire group joins in.

This is what life is about. Not the attention or the prizes. No, it's about the connections. The village that you create for yourself. The people who are your ride-or-die.

Nate grabs my hand over the barrier and squeezes it. He pulls me in close so I can hear him.

"It's all because of you, Rem. Every single person here is so damn happy just to be in your orbit. Never forget this moment."

I never will.

It's the culmination of so many chance things happening in my life.

A one-night stand that I couldn't stop thinking about.

The job of my dreams.

A trainer who was never supposed to change my entire world.

The love of my life showing me that I can have it all.

And it's all just the beginning. I have so many plans, and I can't wait to do them all with Nate and Murph by my side.

Epilogue
Remi

Two years later . . .

My hands are shaking as I climb out the car. It all feels so surreal.

Stepping onto the top of the halo, I raise my hands up, shaking my fists in glory.

I just won the Driver's Championship.

It rattles around in my mind, yet I can't grasp it.

I almost slip off the halo, quickly jumping down before I really make a fool out of myself and weigh in. I have a man to hug. And kiss. And ravish if I can get away with it.

The second I step off of the scale, it all hits me at once.

I drop to my knees, and the emotion washes over me. Tears flow freely as I put my head, still in my helmet, onto the ground.

Frantic hands grab my shoulders, lifting me up and popping open my visor. Nate has tears streaming down his face with a smile so big I didn't think was possible.

"You fucking did it!"

I nod, speechless.

He must see the freakout written all over my face because he calms down and grabs the sides of my helmets.

"Hey. You're okay. You're good. I know this is overwhelming."

I hiccup a laugh.

"Take a breath."

I do as instructed. He's never let me down before.

"Now *feel* whatever you're feeling. Absorb everything. You're the best driver in Formula 1, and I don't want you to shy away from that."

"I did it," I say shakily.

"You won." He nods, smiling.

"I'm the Driver's Champion," I say more confidently.

"Say it again."

"I'm the Driver's Champion."

"Louder."

"I'm the Driver's Champion!" I yell, laughing at how absurd that is but also so fucking proud of myself.

None of this journey was easy. I'd like to say things were easier after the Alejandro scandal, but they were just harder in other ways. There were a lot of doubts still surrounding my ability as a woman, a lot of bullshit media conferences. There were countless rumors about Nate and me that I'm ashamed to admit got to me more than once.

It was hard, but it was worth it to get to this point.

I pop up off the ground, Nate holding out his hand to help me. With a running start, I jump onto the crowd of employees from Empress. None of this would be possible without every single one of them.

I hug Toni, Sydney, Daisy, Beck, Luka, Cruz, and Felix all individually. Every single one of them tells me how proud they are of me and how they never doubted me.

I desperately swipe at my face, willing the tears to stop. The pictures will all be shit if my face is beet red, and I'd like to frame at least one good one at some point.

Once I'm finally free of the group, I'm ushered to the cooldown room. I wish I could just sit with Nate, but it's just not possible.

As the other drivers congratulate me and talk about all the drama of the race, I zone out.

I've been thinking a lot about my future this season. Where I see myself in a year, five years. Hell, ten. A plan finally came together last week.

I want to finally marry Nate. It's no secret this is where we're headed, but I've pushed off getting engaged because I wanted to focus on racing. I know exactly where the ring is. He proposes to me almost weekly. On those nights where it feels like we can't get close enough. When the sheer intensity of loving each other becomes overwhelming. Nate always jokes that, one time, he'll give me so many orgasms that he'll ask and I'll say yes without thinking. It doesn't bother him that I haven't said yes yet. I never turn him down; I just say "not yet". He knows me better than I know myself. He never pressures me; it's more that he wants me to know that, whenever I'm ready, he'll marry me the next day. It's a form of reassurance I've grown to love so much.

But it's time.

I feel secure in most things. Driving has gone well, and even if I mysteriously drop off next season, I'll still have today. My name will go down in history books as the first woman to ever win a Driver's Championship, and that means something.

So, tonight, I'm saying yes. Even if he doesn't ask, which I suspect he won't. Even if he wants to have a longer engagement. None of it matters. All that matters is shouting to the world that I've locked down Nathan Jude Murphy. And our two dogs. Yes, I eventually lost the bet, and a few months after our first season together, we adopted Reese, who is the smartest little border collie mix and the perfect sister for Murphy. Now, we do a lot of packing naked because rushing to leave places isn't on our priority list anymore.

The rest of the evening is spent at the podium ceremony—I won't get my Driver's Championship trophy until the big gala in Paris in a few weeks—and taking a million pictures with the team. Talking to every single member on my team is a priority to me. I want them all to know that this win is as much theirs as it is mine.

All the while, Nate is never far. Murph and Reese run amuck in the garage, but they're both well loved by the team, so we don't have to watch them tirelessly.

By the end of it, the sun has long set, and everyone is starting to break down the pitlane garage.

"Time to go, Ace." Nate whistles for the dogs to join us, leashing them and heading out to the shuttle van that will take us back to the hotel.

I'm exhausted, but it's the good kind. The kind that tells me this day will be one I'll never forget—and it's about to get a whole lot better, if that's even possible.

Nate

I pat my pocket, checking for about the hundredth time that the ring is still there.

Today was the culmination of so much hard work, so much time and sacrifice for Remi, but she did it. It was close, hard fought, but those are the best kind of victories.

Now, I'm hoping we get one more win.

I've been asking her to marry me, mostly so she knows I'm not going anywhere, for the better part of two years. I knew it wouldn't happen until she felt like she had accomplished what she really wanted to in her career. That wasn't necessarily winning the entire damn thing, but about midway through the season, I knew she was going to pull it off.

So, I set a plan in motion.

I wasn't sure if it would come down to the last race, but it was a good bet, and I'm glad I had the forethought.

Our room is decked out with decorations, thanks to Sydney being the hard-ass on staff. Nobody ever tells that woman no, so she's a good ally.

As we ride the elevator, Remi tucked underneath my arm, we're both quiet. It's been a long day, and none of it has been silent.

When the doors ping open, my hands start to sweat. I'm not nervous. I don't think she'll say no, but I do wonder if maybe I should have waited until she got some rest under her belt.

My gulp is audible as I open the door, Reese and Murph running in immediately. Remi walks in, not really *looking* at anything, which gives me time to look around.

Champagne and a whole selection of snacks line the dining table. Flameless candles are on every surface, giving the room a romantic glow. It's not super flashy, but it's exactly how Remi would want it.

She finally looks up and gasps. "What in the world?"

She turns around, letting me grab her hand and walk her to the bedroom. In here, the candles are still everywhere, but they are interspersed with rose petals too.

"Nate . . ."

I step in front of her, holding both of her hands in mine.

"I've asked you about a hundred times. I would have gone down to the courthouse or planned a huge-ass wedding, inviting every single person we knew at any time over the last two years. But I knew getting to a place in your career where you felt like you had finally 'made it' was important to you. Remi, you are . . . God, I don't even have words. I didn't think to write anything down because I thought it would all just come to me." She lets out a watery chuckle. "You are everything to me. You are my lighthouse, my best friend, my lover. You are the embodiment of everything good in my life, and I cannot wait for you to be my wife. I love you so much, Rem. Will you marry me?"

She slaps me on my shoulder, and my hands go up too late to block her.

"Ow, what the hell?"

"I had plans!" she tells me, a tear running down her cheek.

"What plans?"

"I was going to ask you tonight, and then you had to just go and do the most romantic thing on the face of the planet, which is so like you, and . . . and . . . and I love you so much. Yes, a million times yes. Tonight, tomorrow, every single day after, and even in death—I am yours, and you are mine." She jumps, circling her arms around my neck as I catch her under her ass.

"You were going to ask me?" I ask, completely bypassing the detour, kissing her before moving to her cheek and down her jaw.

"I was. But like always, you know me better than I know myself. I even got a ring." She sighs, content in my arms.

"You are the most perfect woman."

"Because I was going to ask you to marry me?" She kisses me where she can reach, which ends up being my temple.

"No, because we both planned a proposal on the same night."

"Yours is much prettier than mine."

"I've been planning it for a while." I shrug.

"You did good." She smiles. "And it's a good thing I planned a flight out to the Bahamas tomorrow . . . for our wedding." Her lips roll inward; she's holding her breath as I take in her words.

"For real?"

"If you want to."

"Oh, I want to." I walk us over to the bed, gently lay her down, and kneel over her. "Is the crew in on this? Or just us?"

"I invited the family." Her use of the term to describe our friend group never fails to make me smile.

"Sydney's a good little secret keeper." I smile, sliding my hands into her leggings, stripping her out of them.

"She knew about this?" she asks, trying to pull my shirt over my head.

"Oh yeah, set up most of it, actually."

"What a little hoe. I asked her if she thought proposing would be a good idea, and she had a full-on conversation like she didn't know you were already going to do this." Her feet hook into my shorts and boxer briefs, sliding them down my legs.

Once she's done, I strip her out of her shirt and sports bra. "She's been in on my plan for a couple of months."

"Months?!" she asks, outraged.

"Rem, I really wanted to do it right," I say as I kiss down her neck.

She doesn't retort, which is unlike her. Banter is our preferred form of foreplay, after all. And then her shoulders start shaking, making me realize she's crying.

"Oh shit, did I fuck up? I just needed help with the room. I already had the ring. I've had it since after Singapore your first year." I panic. "The ring!" I realize belatedly. It's still in my damn pocket.

"Singapore?" I can barely make out what she's saying through her tears, but she locks her legs around me so I can't go get her ring.

"Umm, yes?"

"Oh my God, I'm so dumb. Why did I make us wait?"

I cup her head in my hands and make her focus on me. "Rem. You're overwhelmed. Today has been a lot, and it wasn't my intention to add to it." I realize this all might be too much, but I can't take it back now.

"I'm just so happy," she says, her tears starting to dry up. "How is it possible to be this happy? How is this my life? Our life?"

"Just . . . feel it all. You deserve all of this and more. I intend to help you make all your dreams come true."

"Impossible. They already have." She smiles up at me.

"So we're getting married tomorrow?" My hand slides down her thigh, over hip, to my favorite spot between her legs.

"Technically, no. The flight is long as fuck, so it'll be on Wednesday. Jet lag and all that." She whimpers when I circle her clit.

"Wednesday sounds amazing." I dip my fingers into her pussy and lean down to kiss her sweet lips.

She breaks off with a moan as I notch my cock at her entrance. "You ready to be stuck with me forever?" she asks.

"Abso-fucking-lutely," I say before thrusting hard, stealing both of our breaths.

We get no sleep that night. We're up all night, talking in between orgasms. Talking about every single hope and dream we have, no matter how small. In the morning, just before we leave for our flight, I finally put the ring I've had for two years on her finger.

And three days later, I marry the love of my life, with our small little inner circle and our dogs in attendance.

Life is damn good for the Bouchard-Murphys.